SUBMITTING TO CERBERUS

NAOMI LUCAS

To Scott Goodsell for inspiring me to write a book about Cerberus.

BLURB

Cyane was delivered as a newborn to an orphanage with nothing but a cryptic note from her parents to come to Sicily for an obscure celebration on her twenty-fourth birthday.

Years later, desperate to get to the festival on time to finally confront her parents, she's tricked and dragged under the Ionian sea. Confused, fighting for her life, and near death she's pulled from the water by a man. An ancient Greek warrior with frighteningly animalistic eyes.

Cerberus, son of the dragon Typhon, hundred-headed hound to Hades, Gatekeeper to the Underworld, watcher of all the souls in Styx, and first shifter, senses an unauthorized mortal in Hades's domain. And when that mortal tries to escape, he does what he's always done best stops them.

What he doesn't expect is a beautiful human woman cowering beneath his blade. When she begs for his help to leave Hades's realm, his loyalties are tested unlike never before.

THE ARRIVAL

'*DEAR CYANE, come to Thesmophoria on your twenty-fourth year. We await you in Syracuse, Sicily. Your father.*'

She'd read it a million times. *Don't. Don't take it out.* Her fingers twitched. The note never changed, no matter how desperate she was for more information.

Cyane pulled her backpack towards her, found the zipper along the side, and tugged it up. She dipped her hand into the opening and rummaged around for her phone.

The midnight darkness of the hostel room fled as the phone screen turned on.

She shut her eyes against the light and resisted the urge to pull the damned note from her pocket and hold it between her fingers.

Tomorrow.

Tomorrow she'd make her way to Sicily to attend the ancient celebration of Thesmophoria, a festival honoring the goddesses Demeter and Persephone. Why her *father* wanted her to attend was beyond her, but it was the only lead she had to her parents.

They'd left her as a newborn and then vanished. The note

was her only evidence that they even existed. If she went to meet them in Syracuse, and they weren't there…

Cyane pushed the thoughts away.

She opened her eyes, hid the lit phone under her blanket, and scrolled through her photos. Brussels and her first day of the adventure, Berlin, Prague, Budapest where she'd started her trek southward to Skopje, and then, finally, Greece.

It was the adventure of her life, and she'd finally reached the Port of Piraeus that afternoon, where she'd booked a hostel in southern Athens.

Tomorrow. Her ride would leave the port at six in the morning.

Cyane's eyes hooded as she stared at her pictures.

The phone dropped from her hand to lie softly next to her cheek as she drifted to sleep.

THE NEXT MORNING, trekking hurriedly through the industrial slums of the city, the cranes and machinery flanking her sides—a testament to how times had changed since she studied this place in history class—she made it to the port right as the sun's hidden-behind-clouds first light streaked across the sea. Gray wisps and distant haze filled her eyes, blanketing the ships in weak, morning shadows.

Another cloudy day, another cloudy morning. Cyane sighed.

She paused to read the sign, slowly translating the Greek letters, and raced to the passenger terminal, trying to reach the docks before the yacht set sail. The smell of sea brine and ship exhaust filled her nose.

I'll only be twenty-four once.

Which was incredibly worrisome if she couldn't make it to Sicily in time.

She tried not to think about it as she turned the corner of

the final building. Her jaw dropped. The waters were lit up in a perfect, Midas glow, with ships all around, and in the backdrop, the hills of Athens were haloed in it.

Piraeus was one of the largest ports along the Mediterranean, with a history fueled by Ottoman occupation and naval history. It was once a military harbor for Athens and had housed their incredible fleet. She could almost imagine the hundreds of millions of people who'd walked, worked, sailed, and gaped at the sight right where she was standing. Like ghosts in her head.

Her skin prickled.

A short time later, with a flyer and a map in her hand, she found the yacht group. Luxurious boats and yachts lined the private dock as she strode down it. The *Hermes's Mirth* rocked gently toward the end to the wave of other boats passing by.

Made it! Cyane grinned. The tension in her back eased.

She found a spot to rest her backpack nearby and shucked it off, stretching her back and arms. A cool breeze drifted across her bare arms and legs. The heat of summer lingered against the force of fall, and she wore shorts and a simple, loose tank top.

The New York tag large across her chest was more a beacon than even her accent. If she'd worn the same clothes as the locals, she would've blended right in. But she didn't want to fully blend in, she didn't want people to assume she knew more than she should.

Most had been kind enough, and—in broken English—helped orient her with her map. Some had even warned her of being a lone, female backpacker. Cyane knew her predicament more than anyone else. She kept a small horn and a knuckle keychain in her pocket at all times to startle any attackers; she never took unnecessary risks.

So, as she finally relaxed and returned her attention to the private yacht swaying in the early dawn, she knew something was wrong.

Why was it so quiet?

It wasn't supposed to be quiet. There were supposed to be people here working, preparing for the trip and their next set of wealthy guests. There was supposed to be *life*. There weren't even fishermen preparing their gear.

"Hello?" she called out, eyeing the abandoned boat. "*Kalimera?*"

No one answered her.

"Good morning?" she yelled a little louder this time, her stomach sinking when there was still no reply.

She was far enough down the dock that there were only a few people about, some looked her way as she glanced about. When she caught their eyes in question, they snapped their gazes away from hers.

"Dammit," she muttered under her breath.

Cyane returned to her backpack and sat down, digging her phone back out. She didn't have the number for *Hermes's Mirth's* captain, but she had the information he'd given her scribbled out on one of his flyers. She double-checked the name, the yacht with the picture, and glowered, looking around again. The other captains, and crew workers nearby, had gone back to what they were doing.

Signal was shoddy, but she was able to load the booking site of the ship. She tried the number which went straight to voicemail. The nerves in her belly grew with each passing minute.

Of course, this would happen. Cyane tilted her head towards the sky, sighing.

If no one arrived soon to prepare and board the yacht, she didn't know what she was going to do…let alone *how* she was going to get to Syracuse in time for Thesmophoria.

Cyane's heart pounded. She didn't want to miss the

festival or the chance to meet her family. The thought alone made her want to scream, as if all of her careful planning, frugal spending, and furious discipline was being stomped into the dirt. It hadn't been easy saving up the money for this trip—or finding work along the way. And even with what she had saved, she was forced to backpack and stay at the cheapest hostels.

Be prepared, be diligent, keep your expectations high...but not too high.

I have to be there.

She didn't know why, but her life depended on it.

A thread had woven around her heart, constricting it more every year. The festival honored the Greek goddesses Demeter and Persephone. It made no sense to her why the note wanted her to be at the celebration. But it'd become more than a note, it'd become her compulsion.

Maybe it was because she'd never had a mother growing up, and once she'd discovered her first mythology book, the idea that she might have had a godly matriarch such as Demeter made Cyane's childlike fancies magical. In her young imagination, she'd had a mother like the great Demeter waiting to meet her, and Cyane was just waiting to be found, embraced in loving arms. A hold that was unending and unbreakable.

Those sad musings returned hot and harrowing, tightening the invisible band around her heart.

Cyane inhaled deeply, calming her nerves. She glanced at the other people nearby and licked her drying lips. Rising to her feet, she approached the person closest to her, a middle-aged man checking a knot.

"Excuse me? *Signomi?*" she asked as he turned his head. She turned to point to the *Hermes's Mirth.* "Do you know where I can find its captain? I'm supposed to meet him."

The man looked at the yacht then back at her, crinkling

his eyes. He shook his head, made a dismissive noise with his throat, and went back to his work. Cyane stood there, biting her lower lip, before approaching the next closest person. Another man, younger by a few years, scanned her from head-to-toe, waved his hand once, and shooed her away like an unwanted cat before she could say anything more than a hello.

Dejected, she returned to her backpack and pulled it on. There was no help for her here. The only ounce of happiness on the dock was the blatant name of the yacht she was supposed to board. Mirth was the last emotion she felt. After trepidation, excitement, nervousness...*Fuuuck.*

Cyane pulled her phone from her pocket again. She was smart, she was capable. It was time to figure out a backup plan. If she only—

"Are you okay, miss?"

She peeked up to see a fit, elderly man walking towards her from the end of the dock. The golden-dawn glow haloed his already sun-bleached clothing. Even so, his jacket was black, albeit faded, and his skin was olive-toned, lined, and taut.

She lowered her phone. "Not quite. I was supposed to meet with the captain of *Hermes's Mirth* for a job."

He stopped a short distance from her. "A job? On *Hermes's Mirth*? That would be something."

She cocked a brow. "Oh? Why?"

"Haven't seen new flesh on the ship in ages, not unless it was a booking. Hermes's boat is a family business," he said.

Cyane's stomach twisted. *But I'd talked to the captain himself...*

"Oh, don't look so put-out," the man said. "Perhaps I can help you."

Put-out wasn't quite what she was feeling, but it was damn-near close enough.

"I'm not sure you can." Cyane slid her phone back into her pocket. "The job was supposed to be my fee for transport to Port Messina in Sicily. I need to get there for a festival."

The man scratched his chin. "Thesmophoria?"

"Yes! How'd you know?"

"The women's festival is celebrated here as well. Why not celebrate in Athens?"

She'd thought that herself many times. Why Sicily? Cyane shrugged. "Truthfully? I don't want to stay in Greece that long." She laughed. "Don't get me wrong, I love it here, I feel at home here, but there's something about Syracuse that has always intrigued me. I don't know why, exactly, but I'm hoping that I'll figure it out when I'm there." She wasn't going to mention the note. She never had before, finding it far too personal to share with anyone.

It was like a gateway to the past, and every time she thought to bring it up, something stopped her. It wasn't meant for anyone but her.

The man smiled and nodded. "I think I understand. Well, come this way." He turned his back on her and walked to the end of the dock, heading towards a sailboat.

Her brow furrowed. The pack on her back grew heavy, and an unusually chilly breeze blew across her skin. Her mind fumbled. Did he want her to follow him so they could continue talking? Or was he trying to help her?

What if—a burst of hope, of wariness, seized her—he was offering her transit?

Cyane pushed back the strands of hair that blew across her face and glanced around one final time at the others on the dock, the ships, the quiet *Hermes's Mirth* swaying, and finally to the water itself. It reflected the gray of the clouds again now that the sun had gone to hide behind the clouds, uninterested in the people who sought eagerly to enjoy it.

"Well? We don't have all day!" he called over his shoulder.

He waved at her with one hand while he threw the rope anchoring his boat with his other. She approached him, reminding herself that she could walk away at any time.

By the time she reached his side, the boat was drifting away from the dock. He held the final tie in his hand.

"I'm confused. What are we doing?" she asked.

"Sailing to Port Messina, what else? Unless you've decided to stay?"

Cyane sized up the sailboat and the old man. The boat was in good, clean condition, and the man was lean but nearly-gaunt despite the defined muscles that his skin clung to. If she went with him, there would only be the two of them, which wasn't ideal.

But his eyes flashed something bright, blue, and intelligent. There were no weapons, so signs of entrapment, and as she hesitated to consider his gracious offer, he pulled a card from his pocket and handed it to her.

Haros C.
Private sailboat captain.
Charter boat.
Sail the Mediterranean in style.

She flipped the card over to find the other side blank. "You sail all the way to Sicily?" she asked.

"Water is the same as it is around the islands, as it is in the rivers, lakes, and even oceans. Sailed them all at one time or another. Once you know the ways of the wind and the water it's all the same."

Cyane handed him back the card. "Is it safe?"

The wrinkles lining his face seemed to deepen as she waited for his answer. "Yes."

She mentally checked the small horn resting in her

pocket, even though instinct told her she wouldn't need to protect herself against this Haros.

He continued as she mulled over the decision. "Make up your mind! It takes time to sail across the Ionian Sea, and I'm an impatient man."

"How much does it cost?"

"Do you have some of those American coins on you?"

"Coins?" Cyane reached behind her to pull out her wallet. "I guess my accent gives me away?"

"It does."

She fished out some nickels and pennies. "I have some cash but credit works bet—"

He snatched the coins from her palm and pocketed them before she could finish. "I'm an avid collector. Come now, lest you've changed your mind. The clouds are gathering."

Stunned, and yet filled with growing excitement, she stood with her hand still cupped in front of her, devoid of her money. She lowered it slowly as she watched Haros toss the last rope into the boat. He jumped over after it.

It was now or never.

Her palms dampened with sweat.

Now or never.

He reached out his hand to help her over the threshold. The step across was growing wider by the second. Cyane swallowed and leaped.

Haros pulled her in with a healthy jerk. The momentum pushed the sailboat away from the dock several feet. She released his leathery hand and turned back to see her decision finalized—the gap was too far to jump back across.

"Thank you," she said, breathless. The whip of sails rising and wind-beating-tarp filled her ears. She licked her lips and settled herself down at the end of the sailboat, away from where Haros worked. She pulled off her pack. "How long will the trip be?" she asked as they slowly sailed through the harbor. Athens, new and old, cruised by her in a blur, blending industrial and crumbling stone into one.

"Not long."

She waited for him to say more, but as he moved from one tie to the next, she realized he wasn't going to. As the harbor left them behind, the silence continued. Captain Haros wasn't a talker. Which was fine with her.

Taking out her phone again, she turned her attention to the views around her and took some pictures, the effort giving her peace with this unconventional transit. But that didn't last long. The Grecian shore grew smaller in the distance, and the only thing left to photograph was gray, choppy water. The wind whipped the sails and pulled hair from her tie, lashing the strands across her cheeks and eyes.

They picked up speed.

Water sprayed her face, drawing her eyes to the sea. Ships, small and big, spotted the water. A man on a fishing skiff waved to her, and she waved back. A wave brought on by a nearby barge rocked the sailboat, making her grip the edge of her seat. Cyane put her phone and wallet in her backpack and tied it into a place where it wouldn't get wet. Another wave crashed against the side, knocking her back and wetting her face.

She wiped the water from her eyes, blinking out the sudden salt invading them, and laughed. "I guess we're in for a wet ride."

"Yes."

His voice was suddenly hollow, old, and everywhere at once.

Cyane looked at Haros, and her smile faded.

The wind stopped. The sounds of the world dimmed. The sails of the boat were *gone*, and now only a haggard old man with an oar in the crook of his arm stood across from her.

"Captain Haros?"

Flashing red eyes shot to hers—no longer blue. A white hand emerged from the sea to grab at his leg. Haros lashed at it with his oar and it fell away.

Startled, she drew back. *That wasn't a hand I saw. It couldn't be.* All other ships had vanished. She searched for the man on the fishing skiff, but he too was gone. She looked past Haros to the coast, but it too had disappeared. Her fingers tensed, and dread shot through her chest. She swallowed thickly. "What's happening?"

She never got an answer. The sea opened up beneath them.

The boat gave way like smoke. Vertigo hit, and she lost orientation. Frigid, eternally cold waves consumed everything, forcing her to understand that death was assured.

The last thing she saw, as cold fingers grasped her ankle and dragged her down to hellish depths, was the black surface of the sea growing small far above and the glitter of coins falling ever farther under the waves with her.

She screamed, but water filled her mouth, her throat. In one breath, everything she knew vanished.

CERBERUS FINDS A MORTAL

CERBERUS STOOD IN THE SHADOWS, eyeing the gods and immortals flitting across the dance floor, clinging to one another. No one danced yet—it wasn't time for that—but their clothes flowed like silk and oil, not caught up in breezes or wind, but in time itself.

He ran his hand over the neck of the hound beside him.

As if on cue, Tantalus, carrying a jug, approached Cerberus's side and offered him a cup of nectar. Cerberus waved him away, and Tantalus moved on to the next guest.

The celebration would continue for seven days more until Persephone, his queen, returned to the Underworld and retook her place at Hades's side.

Cerberus scanned the ballroom for his lord but didn't find Hades amongst the growing crowd. He gave his hound one last pat and stepped back into the deeper shadows.

There he patrolled the party without being seen.

His canine companions prowled alongside him, always keeping a watchful eye on the individuals near the gates. No being, neither god, immortal, or undying could leave Tartarus without his knowledge and consent. Although, some could come and go as they pleased with contracts already in place. Though most of those who preferred the dark rarely left. But during the weeks before Queen Persephone's reappearance, the undying often came and went.

He hated this time of year.

He wouldn't be celebrating. He never celebrated with the others. His job was unending, eternal. He knew if he let his guard down, even for a moment, the gods and undying supplicants would know—they eyed him back with uncanny, devious intent.

Lord Hades had much in his kingdom that they desired. The souls of the dead only ended up in one place, regardless of their affiliation in life, and even gods detested losing their toys when they were not yet done with them.

Across the room, Hades appeared in a muted flourish, ignored by all but Cerberus, and sat on his throne. Cerberus stepped from the shadows again in solidarity for his lord. They shared a knowing nod. His lord was atop a slate and obsidian dais, seated on a thin, elongated throne that sharpened like needles at the top. Pieces of it glistened beneath the candlelight glow. Hades, in his dark majesty, leaned forward with his elbows on his knees, a cup appearing out of darkness to hang from the tips of his fingers.

The throne beside him sat empty—except for the dead and withered flowers strewn on and around it.

Despite their difference in station, they were one and the same, having been by each other's sides for eons.

A woman dressed in black veils walked his way, drawing his attention. "Oh sweet Cerberus, must you hide from me?"

He bowed his head and did not meet the goddess's eyes. "I do not hide to spite you, Melinoe."

She smiled, beautiful and grim. Her hair, white as winter frost, faded in and out of her body as it swayed without a breeze. "My lord father has worked you hard. Spite or not, will you dance with me this year?"

Cerberus scanned the crowd above her head. "I do not dance, Princess." And if he did, it would never be with her. Especially one as forbidden and horrid as *her*. Melinoe was one of the few that plagued his life, his eternal duties, day in and day out.

She plagued everyone. His mind warped painfully just knowing she looked at him.

He glanced her way. Sadness filled her eyes, but they didn't affect him. Disgust, like always, crept over his flesh.

"Not even if I owe you a favor in return?" She faced the room of immortals. "No one will dance with me, and I have asked. *Asked*. A goddess born of a lord." Melinoe turned back to him.. "You are my father's servant. You cannot refuse me, Cerberus." She reached out to take his hand, but he drew it away.

"I'm on guard."

"Will you not even look at me?" she asked softly.

He refused. Instead, he caught the eyes of Hades from across the room.

Cerberus left Melinoe without answering her. He crept along the perimeter of the ballroom as he made his way toward the dais. The sound of the goddess's cry followed him until he heard her run from the room. The immortals snickered in her wake. The fact that he never laughed like the others was the reason Melinoe thought he was her friend.

He had no friends. He didn't want them.

He finished his circuit and approached Hades, who sipped nectar with hooded eyes. Cerberus moved to stand at his left side, not deigning to bow.

"The last night before the celebration begins," Hades mumbled, lowering his drink. "Have you encountered any mischief?"

Cerberus's lip twitched. "All is well."

"What a shame. I see Melinoe pursues you still."

"She will not be a distraction."

Hades laughed low. "Very well. With what I have planned, such a boring distraction will not be worth it."

Planned?

Hades rarely voiced his plans, and when he did, it was never in the company of others. Cerberus flicked his eyes towards his lord—the only indication that Cerberus was thrown off—before returning to watch the party.

Asking for further information under the scheming gaze of the undying was out of the question. It was already questionable and dangerous when they were alone. Despite being Hades's confidant, his lord shared very little. Even with Cerberus.

"Yes…my Lord," Cerberus fumed.

Hades ignored his slight. "What do you think of the party this year?"

Cerberus sighed. "Lavish, successful, like every year."

"Always so frugal on compliments, Cerberus. Will you not enjoy yourself for me?"

"Who will feast on those trying to leave if I'm preoccupied?"

"I remade you in human image, and you squander the gift." Hades laughed. "You're no longer beholden to that monstrous form. Go, converse with a"—Hades scanned the ballroom—"a lusty Cocytus nymph, or better yet, one of the Erinyes. Make use of the gift you've received, or I shall become offended."

Cerberus straightened. "It's my duty to protect your realm. I find no pleasure in becoming a spectacle, not even for you."

Hades swept his gaze over his guests before landing on Cerberus. "You deny an order from the lord of the realm?"

"Was it an order?" Cerberus countered. "Or a request of me to alleviate your boredom?"

They glared at each other. Hades's jaw ticked. Cerberus usually stood at his lord's left, which was his place since Hades had taken a queen. The fact that Cerberus stood over him now was not lost on either one of them.

Hades threw back his head and barked out a laugh. "Well done. My boredom has fled." He returned his attention back to the undying crowd, where some now eyed him and Cerberus with curiosity. "I'll get my way with you eventually." A threat. "Now go, for we will speak when Styx's waters glow with daylight. I have a feeling my guest of honor is about to arrive."

Guest of honor? Cerberus narrowed his eyes and began composing clever words for his departure, but he never had the chance to use them.

A prickle slithered across his flesh, an internal alarm telling him that something dared move back towards the gates of the Underworld without permission. Cerberus vanished from Hades's side.

He appeared on the shore of the river Styx, where the rocky, underground gates of Tartarus welcomed its visitors. His xiphos materialized in one hand, and his shield appeared strapped to his other arm.

The river Styx swirled and misted beneath the gates where it bridged the gap between the mortal realm and Hades's castle. In the far distance, the water turned into a black and red ocean that encompassed the entirety of the realm. Hades's castle rose up from the waters of the dead before it, malformed and warped, overlooking the gate, while also overlooking the ocean.

The peaks of the castle didn't blend into the rocky cavern above, but sharpened into wicked points, much like his lord's throne. The castle itself was a weapon, awaiting the day the mortal realm fell from above to catch it in its sharpened embrace. The stones always glistened, as if they continuously bled, waiting for such a day to come.

Everything here hungered, even him. Even the castle.

Those who resided in the castle were trapped inside unless they had another means of escape. The river goddess Styx, also forever ravenous, rested in eternal slumber. To bathe in her was to be cursed and eternally dirtied. No one, not even another god, would risk such a fate. Although, sometimes, Styx would delight in those who bathed in her and would reward them instead.

But those who dared to enter the waters seeking such a rare blessing—or were thrown in—often found themselves cleansed of all their memories, consumed with unending pain and tears, or enveloped in fire. The black of her waters reflected Tartarus itself, while the red was her blood—and the blood of all the mortals who'd ever died.

The only ones who were unaffected were those who were already dead and waiting for judgment.

Water splashed, and Cerberus's vision sharpened. One such soul swam even now. They fought the current that led towards the castle and the Erinyes, away from the gods who would judge their fate.

His nostrils flared.

Desire gripped Cerberus's belly, his throat, as he watched the white creature swim upward from the depths. All other concerns fled from his mind.

Harpies yelped from the tops of the gate and descended to circle the trespasser. The swimmer reached the surface with an unearthly scream. A chorus of high-pitched shrieks assaulted the air in response, the screams coming from all around. The cries echoed out into the distance.

Feast. Delicious. His teeth ached as his stomach hollowed out for the incoming meal, being devoured was a suitable punishment for any being who dared defy the laws of nature.

Cerberus lowered his sword a hairsbreadth as the bobbing head fought to stay above the surface.

Something was off.

He licked his lips anyway.

The soul wasn't swimming back towards the gates, but upward. It wasn't entirely unusual—any direction was better than the unknown.

He couldn't place the source of this uncertainty, but he had done this job for millennia, and his instincts were well-honed. He sheathed his sword and his shield vanished as he moved to the water's edge.

His canine companions barked and ran along the shores on either side.

The white creature thrashed above the surface for a second. "Help! Hel—"

They disappeared back under the black waters.

Cerberus stared, waiting for the dead mortal to give up its deceit and swim towards the gates that led back topside.

That was it, the oddness. A soul couldn't normally shift the waters of Styx. Regardless, this one was, but it was neither swimming with the current nor pushing against it. It struggled, flapping, crying out for help... *Drowning?* The waters of Styx splashed once more as a hand shot out, grasping to stay above the waterline.

He edged closer to the water's edge. The prickling sense that something was trying to leave Tartarus began to fade.

His confusion fled as his curiosity piqued. Charon's boat was nowhere in sight. Nothing was out of place. Where had this creature come from?

Cerberus cursed under his breath as the soul finally dropped below the water's surface and did not return. The water's surface rippled and calmed. He continued to stare at those ripples, ripples that shouldn't be there at all. The dead didn't have substance but this creature, whatever it was, did.

This isn't right.

He swept out his arm and a small skiff appeared, he jumped into the vessel and took up an oar, plowing through the dark waters. The figure was beside him, below, its hair drifting around them, wide eyes pleading, and hand still grasping for the surface.

A woman? Even below the surface, her sex was unmistakable.

Without thinking, he dropped to his knees and reached his arm into Styx and grabbed her wrist.

He yanked her out of the water with one sure tug, gathered her in his arms, and laid her out on the skiff. The boat rocked as he flicked Styx's water off his arm and peered down at the intruder.

He would have to cleanse himself later, but he wasn't worried. Styx had been a constant companion to him for millennia, and he'd touched her waters before without repercussions.

The female lay before him, drenched, her body garbed in clothes he didn't recognize. Her white shirt was plastered against her flesh, and her pants had been tailored short to reveal her thighs. They left little to his imagination. She was not dressed as he expected a female would be, and nor was she nude like newly dead mortals, who were stripped of their worldly possessions upon death.

Her hair rested in wet tangles across her shoulders and chest, framing a mortally beautiful, but unmoving face. The waters of Styx clung to her, gathering in droplets across her exposed skin. Cerberus reached out to lay his hand on the woman's cheek, debating whether or not to throw her back into the water or even eat her essence right then and there, as his right.

She jerked up with a sputtering cough.

Spittle hit his face, startling him back, she shifted onto her palms, hacking out swallowed water. He pressed his hand upon her shoulder as her eyes opened wide to stare wildly at his.

A hush settled over them, and the female's skin warmed under his hand. It wasn't right. The dead were not warm. They didn't have substance like this woman. Was she really dead? Or was she one of the undying guests playing a trick? An incredibly dangerous trick at that. The warmth under his fingers grew.

She pivoted from him and heaved over, coughing out more of the dark water.

He drew his hand from her shoulder, only for his fingers to get trapped in her hair. He pulled the strands away curiously and moved closer to sniff them. A rare smell flooded his nose.

Mortal. Alive? Intruder.

INTRUDER!

His lips twisted into a sneer. He leaned over her, preparing to eat her up, his jaw gaping large, hard, and heavy, stretching his man-suit painfully.

He was a man now, torn from his original form, given a new one, but free to devour all at his lord's request. But when he was overcome with raw emotion, he could resume his original bestial self.

Cerberus seized upon her with darkening eyes.

Yes.

He would devour her gladly. He reached for the blade at his side with his jaw extended.

JUDGEMENT

Fear for her life filled Cyane's veins, throat, and belly—literally. No matter how hard she coughed, the stranglehold of death only grew more painful.

Her surroundings were dark. She was on a boat and out of the sea, but that was the limit of her awareness. Frantic, she pulled in shallow stabs of air through her nose. Desperate, she expelled the salty water from her body.

Something warm gripped her shoulder, but the sensation didn't last. She barely noticed it. Nothing mattered until she could inhale fully and alleviate the growing, agonizing pressure in her chest. She pulled her legs towards her, curling up onto her side. Despite the pain, she couldn't stop gasping. Her eyes, one second wide and searching for help, would wrench closed the next moment.

Pressure filled her head. A shudder wracked her. She gasped again, and—finally—her lungs opened up, and she took in an excruciating breath of air. Tears filled her eyes as she exalted in the simple sensation of air flowing through her. Each breath was a knife-stab in and out of her throat, but she didn't care because she was breathing.

The hand of her savior returned to her shoulder and gripped it hard, forcing her from her fetal position to look up.

It wasn't Haros who saved her.

Dark eyes and even darker shadows met her, revealing the outline of a man, but her gaze didn't linger, moving to the glinting short-sword poised between them.

Cyane jerked back, her eyes widening as the point of the sword pressed against her chest.

"You've committed a great crime coming here. Who are you?" The shadowy man's deep, rumbling voice suited his dark mien.

He was her savior no more.

She leaned away as the tip pushed a shallow dent in her skin, but her back was already against the floor of the boat, leaving her trapped. The ache in her throat returned when she opened her mouth to speak. All that emerged was gasping, hacking coughs.

He made an animalistic noise and withdrew his blade.

His strong arms banded around her, drawing her off the floor of the boat and against his chest. He slid his hands over her back and forced her head between her knees, pulling her wet hair away from her face. More tears filled her eyes as his palm hit the center of her back.

Water and saliva dribbled from her chin. She closed her eyes against the sight.

With each ragged inhale, sense returned, and her mind cleared. *Where am I?* It was too dark to be Athens. She opened her eyes. Dark water, dark cavern walls, and an equally dark castle filled her eyes.

Oh god, where am I?

The man's hand slammed into her back again, and she gasped.

Cyane gripped the side of the boat with shaking fingers.

"Stop," she croaked. "I can breathe now." She rested her brow on her hand and shuddered.

She shook and steadied herself, all the while knowing there was a strange man with a sword directly behind her, waiting for an explanation.

Not that she knew how to explain.

The castle loomed directly over her, its foreboding silhouette filling her vision. She'd never seen anything like it. And she knew if a castle such as this existed, with a hundred black, pointed spires stabbing skyward, she'd have learned about it by now.

The spires ended far above.

Her empty stomach dipped with nausea.

There was no sky.

She rose from where she huddled and strained her neck. There was nothing but blackness with jagged edges—it made no sense. It reminded her of the top of a cavern...but it couldn't be. The sky, if that was the word for it, was so far above her that it should be where the clouds were.

She sat there, gapping, but the man's voice snapped her out of her shock.

"Face me," he ordered.

The boat rocked as the man stood. Cyane shivered again and pulled her gaze away from the sky—or cave ceiling, she had no idea. She turned slowly—her eyes flicking again across the strange landscape one last time—before she released her death-like grip on the boat with one hand.

Her eyes fell on the man as he raised the sword in his right hand and pointed it toward her chest.

This time, she didn't squirm away from his blade.

He wore dark pants with plated metal armor over his shins and knees. The pants disappeared behind a muscled cuirass decorated with the glint of sculpted abs, sculpted pecs. Thick, leather strips hung from the bottom of the cuirass, shielding his groin and thighs. The leather strips were covered in clean but dull ornamentation of howling canines.

Her eyes squinted upon the well-crafted ancient Greek warrior armor. It was in excellent condition compared to anything she'd seen in a museum, and she found it as misplaced and unwelcome as everything else was. Armor covered every inch of him, including a dark, leather-like material down his arms. For a split-second, she wanted to laugh.

An equally unpolished black and silver helmet rested on his head, its points as sharp as the terrifying castle at her back. Only the glow of his pupils deep within the helmet's inner shadows indicated he looked at her.

"I'm facing you," she choked out to break the silence.

CERBERUS TIGHTENED his grip upon his sword. He studied the female before him. Her lips quivered, and her chest rose and fell with each shuddering breath. Even her shallow words gave her away.

She's not one of Charon's dead.

Questions beat at his mind. Not even Hercules himself had spent that much time in the water of Styx.

"Do you have any last words?" he asked. Though he didn't care for any answers she might give him. He had surprised himself already by helping her cough the last of the water out. He would follow through by giving her the dignity of words.

Her eyes widened. "L-last words?"

He raised his sword from her chest to poise at her neck. "All those who trespass or defy the laws of the Underworld are punished. Your soul will never return to the mortal realm, nor will it reach Elysium or Asphodel Meadows. Your crime will be judged by me. Here. Now."

She stared at him wordlessly. He swallowed and continued.

"I do not know how you came to be before the entrance to Hades's castle without loss of life or help, but it matters not. The crime has been committed. The law has been broken. I will devour your soul, but first, your flesh will be rent open by my sword's edge." The boat rocked beneath his feet. Styx's current was slowly pulling them towards the castle.

The woman trembled, and her eyes flicked from his face to the weapon in his hand. To his abrupt shock, she pivoted back around to look at the castle.

His hold on his xiphos wavered.

She was not reacting as any mortal—or even immortal—should be in the face of imminent annihilation.

With each passing moment, her breaths steadied further when they should be quickening. *If she has nothing to say, so be it.* Cerberus raised his weapon to lob off her head.

She turned back around. "I don't understand... Where are we? Is this some sort of horrible joke?"

Sudden fury filled Cerberus, hot and hard. The mortal's audacity drew molten rage through his veins. Had she listened to anything he'd said? Didn't she have respect for where she was?

He growled, his sword vanishing, as he snatched her neck in his grip. He dug his fingers into her flesh.

His body grew cold as the shadows coalesced within him, making him larger, and returning awareness of his prior monstrous form. Cerberus drew on it. He wanted to see her fear before he killed her.

Fear was powerful. It was delicious. And a mortal's fear... his tongue lashed the roof of his mouth.

Finally, as his mouth grew and malformed into a canine snarl behind his helmet, she released a scream of terror. Her hands came up to beat at his chest and clawed at his wrist in the effort to tear his hand off of her. The skies rang with the cackles of harpies as they watched from above.

Warmth surged into him where he touched the woman, where she fought him in defense. A warmth unlike he'd ever known in all his years in Tartarus. At first, he assumed this human must be an agent of Helios, or worse, Apollo, to bring such heat here, but then he tossed the thought away. The sun gods had never been known to scheme against Hades. They wanted nothing to do with the dark places of the world.

Cerberus's grip loosened when her nails dug deep into the cloth covering his forearms, ripping it.

"Let go of me!" she shrieked.

Blood welled beneath, startling him long enough for the woman to kick hard at his chest, pushing him backward. The momentum forced him down, and he barely caught the side of the boat, stopping himself from falling overboard.

He heard a splash, and his fury returned. He rose to see his devious intruder swimming madly away.

He surged to the side of the boat to catch her limb. He touched her flesh but missed her ankle by a hairsbreadth. The currents swept her up as she tried for the shoreline. But it carried her towards the castle instead.

His hands tightened into fists as the female disappeared under the dark archway that led directly to the Judges of the Dead.

A pair of oars materialized in his hand, and he began his hunt.

Cyane struggled against the current but quickly gave up. There was no point in fighting it. The water had a mind of its own. It wasn't like the ocean's current but the will of a living being.

She kept her head above the water, kicked her legs frantically, and tried to get as far from the man on the boat as fast as she could.

Please. Please, please, please. The word pounded in her head with every stroke.

The foreboding castle loomed ahead of her. She thought she was headed for the gate, but with a final surge, the water pushed her towards a dark cavern that opened at the rocky castle base. Cyane grasped for the sidewall just as the opening swallowed her up.

The current was faster here, desperate, hungry, and far more powerful. Her fingers dragged across the wall without finding purchase, and the faint light from outside shrunk as she slipped farther into the darkness beneath the castle. She was about to give up hope when she caught the edge of a stone. She gripped it with her life. Several of her nails snapped as the current tried to drag her away. Sharp pain surged up her fingers but quickly vanished in the numbing cold of the water. The current rushed around her like eager, grasping hands.

"Take my hand!" the Greek soldier from before roared, his boat quickly slipping past. His fingers grazed over her shoulder as he reached for her. He was gone, disappearing into the darkness beyond before she could make a choice.

The last thing she saw before he completely disappeared was the sheen of his eyes from the shadows of his helmet.

Cyane whimpered and closed her eyes. *I don't know what to do.* Her fingers ached, everything ached, and the adrenaline that kept her going was diminishing, leaving fatigue behind. She didn't know how long she could hold on.

All I wanted to do was to meet my parents. Tears streamed down her cheeks. The pain in her fingers returned with the strain of her clutching.

Something grabbed her leg and tugged her off the wall.

With a frightened wail, she kicked off the thing holding her.

The current shot her forward, deeper into endless darkness. Despite the water's speed, her head remained above the surface. It was as though the water itself was trying to keep her alive. But to what end?

Blindly, she called out for help, to find the man and his boat, to find anyone who could help her. No one answered. When she reached for the wall again, there was nothing but slick, wet rock.

Death awaited her. She was sure of it now. She'd escaped it twice, but a third time wasn't always a charm.

The water froze her to the bone. And just when she thought she'd lost hope, as the endless blackness threatened to drive her past the point of insanity, a light appeared in the distance.

Cyane stared at it, transfixed.

It grew bigger with each passing second. Relief flooded her. Even if death awaited her, at least hell wouldn't be an endless journey in which crushing anxiety drove her mad.

The tunnel opened up into a cavern with stalactites hanging from the ceiling. She gazed at them mutely as the current delivered her into a shallow pool in the middle of the cavern. Three old men stood near the bank awaiting her. Suddenly she was beside the shore, floating unmoving as if the current had never existed at all. Her feet found the bottom, then her knees as the water grew shallow.

She crawled weakly onto the edge of the bank and fell upon the dry ground with a cry.

"Leave, Cerberus, she is in our domain now, not yours," one of the older men said.

Cyane huddled into herself, fighting off the deep cold penetrating her flesh. *Cerberus?*

Nothing makes sense.

She frowned and forced herself up on trembling arms. The Greek warrior stood rigidly a short distance away, staring at her. A silvery haze and pulsating shadows enveloped him.

An uncertain truth settled in. Her frown deepened. He couldn't be a dream, could he? He appeared poised to rush to her, but something held him back. Cyane tore her eyes away from him.

The three elderly men in Grecian robes surrounded her. She wiped the water from her eyes as she fell onto her back.

A low growl of a dog vibrated through the space as the closest of the old men knelt beside her. "My name is Aeacus, and I find you unfit to take my hand and join the western dead in the afterlife."

Cyane blinked, and the man was gone. One of the two remaining men took the first's place beside her.

"My name is Rhadamanthys, and I find you unfit to take my hand and join the eastern dead in the afterlife."

This time, Cyane held her eyes open. Rhadamanthys stepped back and vanished like vapor. She pushed herself up on her elbows to search for him, but he too was now gone.

The third man settled into the same spot the previous two had.

"I don't understand," she said, her voice cracking as he smiled kindly down at her. "What's happening?"

"Cyane, you have made your way to the Judges of the Dead. Not an easy feat for one still alive. My name is Minos, and I find you unfit to join either Aeacus or Rhadamanthys in deliverance to the afterlife." He offered her his hand. "Take my hand."

"I'm still alive?" she blubbered. "Why? If I'm still alive?"

"Would you prefer to stay in this vestibule with three old men forever?"

He eased his hand closer.

Cyane stared at it, at Minos. She was in Hell, Hades, Tartarus. Or she was so drugged that she was envisioning all of this. She rose up further until she was in a sitting position. She turned her face back to the Greek warrior who was still furiously tense in a statuesque pose.

The old men called him Cerberus.

Isn't Cerberus a three-headed monster?

But two men vanished into thin air.

She shook her head. It didn't matter. She was alive—with her head still firmly attached. She looked back at Minos and took his hand. He helped her to her feet.

"If I'm not dead..." The words tasted weird leaving her mouth. "What happens now?"

"I will take you above where others, those better fit, can decide your fate."

"And him?" Cyane nodded in the direction of the Greek warrior. "He said I committed a crime."

Minos hummed with mirth and slowly led her away from the pool, towards a stairway that materialized from the dark. His arm went around her shoulders, lessening her shivers.

"You have, in his eyes, but now you are here. You have escaped his domain, and so he cannot do anything more to you...unless you try to leave."

All she wanted to do *was* leave. "I need to get to Sicily."

"First you need to rest and remove Styx's blood from your flesh. Only the dead are immune to her power."

Cyane glanced down at her drenched clothes and discovered black and red rivulets sluicing down her arms and legs.

What am I thinking? This is all insanity. But she couldn't deny the shock that the black and red water filled her with. She touched her fingers to her forearm and wiped the water away, her belly sinking into an abyss. A scream lodged in her throat.

Minos hummed again, stealing her scream, cleansing the growing terror from her mind.

He drew her up the stairs, and Cyane let him. But after a few more steps, she glanced back to find the cavern and the pool far, far away.

Her feet stilled.

This really can't be happening.

Her eyes settled on the Greek warrior who was a dozen or so steps below her.

He's still here? Why was he following her?

For some reason, she felt attached to him now. *He saved my life and pulled me from the water.* With everything else churning her brain, even considering that the warrior had also tried to kill her, she wanted to confront him again and demand answers.

He'd seen how she'd arrived. Maybe he'd know how to leave?

Cyane removed herself out from Minos's arm and fully turned around, taking several steps down the stairs towards the warrior. He tensed as she moved closer, but as she lowered her foot down onto another step, Minos's arm snaked around her chest and stopped her. His humming continued.

She struggled out of his grip. "I want to talk to him."

"Talk to a monster such as him?" Minos's arm tightened, his lips suddenly upon her ear. "A true beast of old?"

An uncomfortable shiver coursed down her spine. "He's just a man. He saved my life."

"And now you feel indebted to him?"

Her brow furrowed. "No. I—"

"You're a young, youthful creature, swimming in waters that are not your own. Look at him closely. See him for what he truly is."

She tried again to break free from Minos's hold; her strength was no match against his. His continued humming soothed but also addled her mind. She didn't like it. At all. But her body gave in to it, betraying her. Her struggles ceased.

Cyane stared fixedly at the warrior below her who did not intervene to help her.

The stairway pulsated, inhaling, as if alive. There was nothing but her and the warrior.

"Won't you help me?" she asked him without hearing her words in the air between them. *Help me.* Her thoughts echoed fervently, dreamily, in the back of her mind.

He didn't respond, didn't move. He acted as if her request hadn't been made at all. The only indication that he was even there, more than a statue, was his glittering red eyes with specks of silver that she could now see. They resembled faraway stars.

Except they moved.

The longer she gazed at them, the bigger they became. Air whipped past her ears, but there was no wind. She gasped in a breath. The stars grew and grew until they blotted out all else.

Somewhere, far off now, she heard Minos's humming.

Then she saw them. His eyes. All of them.

There were more eyes looking back at her, more than she could count, each forming heads that danced and slithered in and out of her vision. So many serpents with forked tongues that licked the air. Dozens of canine jowls with white teeth that had black tips. Tips like the top of the castle.

It wasn't real, it couldn't be real!

The warrior that had tugged her from the depths was still there, but he was only a hazy outline.

And as she continued to stare, she realized those horrid head-like shapes came from the man himself, formed from the shadows that clung to him, gathering directly behind him. Hundreds of mouths snapped shut then slowly parted. Stringy saliva strung like spider webs across their open gapes.

"Look away," they said in the warrior's voice, a hundred times over. Thousands of razor-sharp teeth warped outward in her direction. Their black tips glistening.

Cyane's mouth dried up.

Her throat constricted.

He was no man at all!

She screamed until nothing existed but the shrill sounds tearing from her throat.

HADES

CERBERUS STALKED the periphery of the ballroom with the mortal's screams still ringing in his ears. His canine companions did the same. Their shadowy forms and quiet steps meant they were better at concealing themselves from the crowd than he'd ever been. They were his eyes, his ears, himself. Once attached to him, but no more.

He missed their company sometimes.

They searched the faces of the undying, listened to their conversations, and reported back to him with their findings.

One of the servants offered him a cup of nectar. He shook his head.

With a breach in Tartarus, everyone was suspect until they weren't. It wasn't wholly unusual for a god to try mischief, but to bring in a mortal woman just to throw her to Styx's waters?

Bait. Cerberus never joined the celebrations, and now he remembered why. She'd been bait.

After she'd succumbed to hysteria—which had taken an impressive amount of time—he and Minos delivered the mortal woman to restrictive chambers for questioning.

Cyane, as Minos called her, had fallen into a deep sleep when he lay down next to her and hummed the torment from her mind.

Cerberus knew what he looked like. His lips twitched. Horrifying ugliness ran thick through his bloodline, but it wasn't until Hades gave him a human male's form that true self-awareness came to him. He wasn't ashamed of his once unique appearance, often finding that he missed it, longed for it, if only because it kept others away from him so he could serve without distraction. But he also found the value of being formed into a human male. His new body and all that came with it had a different type of horror and power he enjoyed utilizing.

He'd initially meant to destroy this mortal Cyane, like he'd done so to the thousands of souls over centuries who'd tried to escape their fate. He wanted to blame the fact that she'd been crazy enough to jump back into Styx, but it was more complex than that. He now wasn't sure if the mortal had even known it was Styx she'd jumped into. It wasn't just crazy.

It was beyond that...

When Cerberus had ridden through the tunnel, he'd questioned his tactics, his hesitance, and confronted his failure.

But by the time she'd turned up, still alive, his curiosity had been ravenous.

He was eager for her to awaken so he could question her. But that would have to wait.

Cerberus scanned the crowd again in search of Hades. He still sat upon his throne, conversing with another undying. Cerberus made his way towards them.

Several of the guests nodded in greeting to him as he passed by, but they did not meet his eyes. They rarely did.

He stepped onto the dais and positioned himself at Hades's left side.

The god, Hermes, laughed at one of his lord's jokes. "There is no one happier than the Lord of the Underworld this time of year!"

Hades smiled. "And no one more upset than our great Lady Demeter."

"She is beautiful when she mourns."

"Perhaps next year you will finally convince the goddess to join us in our dark revelry."

"And subject our queen to her mother's pecking even more? She may never forgive you!" Hermes placed his hands on his stomach and bowed over in laughter. "Would you risk an empty bed for another year? Another hundred?"

Hades's form darkened ever so imperceptibly. "You assume my bed is empty, Hermes?"

"Assume?" Hermes's laughter continued. "I have seduced my fair share of women. Not one has ever wanted their mother in on their seduction."

"No. I suppose you're right. Demeter would only find a way to sully my intention. What do you think, Cerberus?"

Hades and Hermes both turned to face him. The two gods shared a grin at his expense. Although their grins had entirely different meanings.

"Our Queen Persephone would not like her mother here," Cerberus said.

Hermes's grin widened. "Oh keep going, hound, tell us why?"

"Our queen is not one who would want her greatest ally to see her in the shadows."

"Ah, so you know our queen well?"

Cerberus straightened and looked at Hades, who nodded for him to continue. He turned back to Hermes. "I know my lord well. He jests in bringing the Goddess of Agriculture here."

Hermes turned back to Hades. "Is that so? Does Hades, the great God of the Dead, jest?"

"Persephone is not the humble maiden she makes herself out to be. Demeter is best left with her naivety in the sunlight. Same with your own, Hermes." Hades abruptly rose from his throne. "Cerberus join me. Hermes, we will speak again later." He dismissed the god with a flick of the hand, and Cerberus fell into step behind Hades as they walked through the crowd. The undying guests stopped their musings to watch.

When they were finally alone in Hades's study a short time later—the room was carved completely out of stone, save for a terrace that overlooked the gateway and subsequent gate towers in and out of the Underworld—Cerberus moved to the terrace and gazed at the spot where he pulled Cyane from the waters below. He heard Hades settle himself in a chair by the fire on his left.

"Hermes is not far off in his assumption," Hades mused.

Cerberus tore his eyes from Styx. "Do you think he spies?"

"Your paranoia is so much fun, but no. He's never been one to spy. In fact, he's been helpful in my plans for this event. But I wonder...if others have come to the same assumptions as our dear traveler."

"I wouldn't know."

"You do hear a great many things as my guardian, do you not?"

Many things, and then some. Cerberus sat down in the empty high-backed chair across from Hades. "Hecate wants fresh flesh, Melinoe schemes for companionship." Hades laughed at that. "The Erinyes still have not stopped arguing, and Hermes, well, I have nothing more than failed seductions to report on his part, not assumptions."

Hades glowered. "You do know what I speak of, do you not? That my bed is empty and has been as such for countless millennia. That Persephone refuses me even to this day?"

Cerberus knew. He knew much of what happened in the Underworld, but Hades was lord, and Cerberus's choice to not bring up such personal, quaint matters was his alone. What care did he have that Hades slept alone, when the gates of the Underworld were always open, needing Cerberus's watchful eye?

But he settled into his seat anyway. Then, unsettled, poured himself a cup of nectar he would only think about drinking. He resettled and sighed. "What would you have me do about it?"

"Do about it? You could stop being such a servant and implore me for one."

Cerberus swirled his cup and dully said, "Let me help you, my lord."

"Bah!"

"We've had an intruder, a mortal—"

Hades tempered his outburst. "Ah yes, the reason you vanished from my side? A mortal you say?"

"She arrived suddenly—"

"A woman?"

"Yes," Cerberus gritted.

"Very good!" Hades clapped his hands. "Where is she now?"

Cerberus considered taking off his helmet and shooting back his nectar. "Asleep, recovering in the Lethe wing. The mortal arrived here by no normal means—"

A sly smile twisted Hades's lips, stopping him from finishing the story.

"What?" Cerberus asked.

"My plan is coming to fruition. A god has the right to enjoy the success of his endeavors. I assume the woman is in good health, that you did not devour her soul? I would *not* like that."

Cerberus narrowed his eyes. He was loyal to Hades, above all else in this realm and all others. Not even his father, the great dragon Typhon who remained trapped far below in the bowels of Tartarus, could claim such loyalty from him.

"This plan…" Cerberus hesitated, he was not trained to ask questions. At least not ones that questioned Hades's motivations.

"Is the woman in good health or not?"

"She glimpsed my true form."

Hades burst out in laughter again. "No wonder she sleeps in Lethe's wing. Forgetfulness is a wonderful gift we give humans. I see, I see. Perhaps my bed will not remain empty for much longer."

Cerberus's eyes flared. "You're not concerned about how she got here?"

"I know how she got here. Hermes and Charon brought her here."

Hermes. Cerberus's demeanor shriveled as his lips briefly pulled back into a snarl. "And dumped her in the middle of Styx? To die an agonizing death from either me or the ancient Titaness?" No mortal or undying deserved such a fate. He recalled his own fierce fury at seeing the mortal break the laws of gods, but that fury was nothing compared to knowing that he'd been tricked.

"They did what?" Hades's anger materialized—the stone under their seats cracked. "They will answer to me. Styx is not to be disrupted, she serves us well and cannot be replaced. But she will not harm our mortal. I'll make sure Styx is compensated for the trespass."

"And me?"

"Perhaps you should've enjoyed yourself tonight instead of offending me."

Cerberus's fingers twitched around his cup. "And the woman? A mortal has not dwelled here in many years. This place is not for them. Especially not your bed."

"That is not for you to decide."

"Allowing a mortal woman into your bed, mere days before our beloved Queen arrives, will not excite Persephone into sharing it with you," he fumed.

Hades's terrible smile returned. "Implore me."

Cerberus's own anger festered, slowly. He stood, and lowered himself down on one knee before his lord, and bowed his head. "You are right, as always. What will you have me do?"

Hades placed his hand atop Cerberus's helmet. "Your job. The celebration is rife with schemers, beggars, and lesser immortals seeking power any way they can. Watch the gates vigilantly, let no one leave until the celebration is over."

"Yes, my lord." It was an easy request. One he was always willing to do. He wanted to say more; the other gods would not like being told what to do.

"And as for our special guest, when she has fully recovered, deliver her to me."

"Of course."

"Very good. You may return to your duty."

Cerberus rose and made his way to the door, at once eager to stay with Hades, but just as impatient to find out more about the woman, and how such a being found the attention of the Lord of the Underworld.

Hades's voice trailed after Cerberus when he stepped out into the hallway. "And Cerberus, do try and enjoy the party this year, lest I find my gifts wasted on you. I really hate being offended. Don't make me regret my actions."

Cerberus swore and continued walking.

THE DAYS OF MELINOE

Cyane woke with a start.

A scream tore from her throat. There was a monster! Demons. They existed! Terror swept through her. Sharp teeth, large jaws, and thousands of eyes clashed as one in her head.

"Shhh, shhhhh, it's okay. It was all just a bad dream." A beautiful woman crawled into the bed next to her, undeterred by Cyane's screams. "You're awake now."

Tears filled Cyane's eyes, and she clutched onto the woman pressed against her side. Fingers brushed through her hair, and warmth flushed her skin. She curled herself into the stranger and cried.

"Shhh." The woman wrapped an arm around Cyane and held her tightly. "Nightmares are no fun, no fun at all."

"It wasn't a nightmare, it was real."

"Then why are you in a warm bed, well away from all who would hurt you?"

Good question. Cyane pushed her face into the blankets piled around her. An image of the beast flashed in her head.

The woman petted her hair and shoulders as she struggled to make sense of it all.

The terror faded, fast and hard, almost as quickly as it had hit her. Memories resurfaced, and as the fear continued to dissolve, so did the unexplainably impossible images in her head.

Where am I?

Who's holding me?

Somewhere in the back of her addled head, Cyane knew she should be just as scared waking in an unknown bed, with an unknown person, but after all that had happened...

She was content to have a reprieve, a moment to think.

Her tears dried up, and she relaxed. The stranger readjusted so Cyane could rest her head in the woman's lap. The cooing and soft whispers she sang did more for Cyane than a healthy dose of Xanax ever could.

Fingertips softly scraped her skull, gently pulling out the tangles of her hair. Internal warmth flooded her chest. Cyane's breathing evened out.

She took the opportunity to study her surroundings.

Cyane lay on a soft, plush bed in the middle of a room that could've been part of a cave. It resembled much of what she'd seen so far: black and gray jagged walls with pillars of gleaming, wet obsidian-like rocks throughout. Candles flickered weak golden light, giving the room a homey yet obscured look and casting deep shadows in the farther recesses of the room, making it appear larger than it really was.

A hearth was along the same wall as the bed; no fire burned within. Perfectly designed furniture, seemingly made from the rocks of the cavern themselves, were positioned throughout. They were ornate in a way of smooth designs, which was the only detail that differentiated them from the cave itself. The furniture and bedding were covered in swaths of deep purple and black linens.

A smaller room lay across the way, much like the room she was in. Although a deep stone basin rested in the middle of it with what looked like steam rising into the air. She could smell something floral and clean, reminding her of bath oils and Epson salts.

Countless stalactites hung across the ceiling. And like the castle, they looked ready to pierce all that lay beneath them.

Maybe this really is a nightmare. . .

She turned over to look up at the woman holding her. It was like the mother's hold Cyane often longed for.

But the woman that held her looked anything but maternal.

Cyane swallowed weakly as the stranger met her eyes. Whoever this person was...was the most beautiful, ethereally enchanting creature Cyane had ever laid eyes on.

Hair as white and silken as fresh snow, and looking just as soft, was clipped behind her ears with dark jewels. She wore black veils over her head, her shoulders, and dress, but where they didn't cover her, the woman's skin was just as pale as her hair, if not more so. As Cyane gazed at the figure who held her, she thought she saw the woman's body become translucent, her white locks falling through what should've been flesh and blood and bone.

Then there were her nails...

They were long enough to be claws and slightly curled as if overgrown.

Cyane shuddered. Now that she'd seen her, the woman's touch felt like ghostly fingers crawling up under Cyane's flesh, tip-tapping all the way to her head, where they settled in her mind like writhing maggots.

Between the woman and the room, she knew she was somewhere that shouldn't exist. Her stomach constricted, the room and everything in it wasn't...humanized. Everything was all too unreal...strange.

"Are you feeling better?" the woman asked.

No! No, I'm far from okay. So far from okay that I don't know what I feel anymore.

"Yes," she said. "Thank...you." Cyane shifted, and the discomfort brewing inside her vanished. A sigh escaped her. She stared at the stranger, waiting for the woman's hair to slip into her body again. Had it been her imagination? She needed that validation. "Who are you?" she asked.

"Melinoe, daughter of Hades and Persephone, a true power in this realm."

Cyane's brow furrowed.

Validation.

The woman straightened regally. "It would serve you well to align yourself with me."

Cyane sat upright herself. Something in the way the woman said *align* felt like compellment. "What? What do you mean align?"

Melinoe smiled. "You are a mortal, are you not? Everyone in the castle is talking about it. A mortal has not stayed among us in the dark in many years, at least not since I was born. If you were to show reverence to me, as a mortal should to all the gods and goddesses, I would favor you." Melinoe sucked in a breath. "I would favor you above all others."

Cyane clutched her head.

"Are you okay?" Melinoe asked. "Would you like a drink?"

She searched her memory for information on Melinoe but couldn't remember anything about the goddess. If Cyane truly was in the Underworld, and a fever dream hadn't taken over her mind, she needed to start paying attention to the details. She needed to get herself out of here.

She jerked. *The note!*

Relief hit when she reached into her short's pocket and pulled out the scrap of paper—which had miraculously survived the water. It was still with her. She inhaled. That's all that mattered. Cyane unfolded it and read the same simple sentence for the billionth time. She sagged and pressed it to her chest, but then her gaze shifted back to Melinoe.

"I need to get to Sicily," she said. "To meet my father—er—parents." She regretted giving away that much information from the moment the words left her lips.

"Sicily? There's no place here named as such." The supposed-goddess eyed her with curiosity. "I could ask my lord father, Hades."

"Hades?" Cyane said incredulously. She slipped the note back into her pocket. "No, Sicily wouldn't be here—" *I'm going mad.* "It's up there." She pointed up like a moron. "I need to get back to the...the world above."

Cyane scanned the cave-like room for cameras.

Please god, let there be cameras.

"Oh. I see," Melinoe said. "Sicily is a mortal place. Well, if you need to leave then you should speak to my Cerberus. He's in charge of who goes."

Cerberus. Cerberus? Cyane wanted to scream again at the sound of his name. She forced the images his name invoked from her mind.

Cerberus was the guardian of passage here. But the being she'd encountered wasn't a three-headed dog, he was a man dressed in Greek armor. She preferred that to the other more monstrous image stalking the periphery of her thoughts.

"The Greek warrior," Cyane muttered.

"Not quite. Cerberus is the offspring of dreaded Typhon and Echidna, like his brothers Hydra and Chimera. He was never a Greek, nor a warrior, but a creature from the old world, and only survived the passing of time through Hades, who gifted him a mortal body to escape Hercules at the end of the hero's labors."

Cyane threw her feet over the bed. "Yes, that's interesting." She really didn't want to think of creatures or this 'old world.' Not anymore than she needed to in order to escape. "But can you tell me how I can speak to him and have him help me leave this place? He tried to kill me after he saved my life… Is there anyone else I can ask?"

"Well, there is my father, but Cerberus will attend such a matter, as it is his duty. I'm certain you will speak with both in time."

Cyane closed her eyes and scrunched her face.

Thoughts of boulders being rolled up hills, eagles pecking her organs out, and endless torments come to mind. Only yesterday, she was stressed about finding cheap, safe hostels to sleep in at night.

At least she hoped it was *only* yesterday.

She looked at Melinoe warily. "What would you suggest I do?"

Melinoe clapped her hands and jumped off the bed. "We shall get you ready for the party!" The woman spun with excitement.

"Party?"

"Yes." Melinoe twirled back to her, veils swirling in an arch. "A party to celebrate the return of the Queen of the Underworld, my mother Persephone. Both my father and Cerberus will be in attendance. But you can't look like…like *that*." Melinoe grabbed Cyane's hands, eyeing her clothes as if they were a neighbor's bag of garbage left outside their door.

"A party to celebrate Persephone?" *Like Thesmophoria?* Could the same festival be happening here?

"Oh yes. We celebrate Her return every year. For a fortnight before Her descent. Immortals, gods alike, all come to join the Lord of the Underworld as he receives his bride.

Each day there is a new festivity, a new gift given by those most loyal or seeking favor from Lord Hades or Queen Persephone herself."

Not quite the same.

A fortnight before Persephone's descent. If that were true, she still had time to get to Sicily.

"Has the party begun?" Cyane asked.

"Yes, for several days now. The first day is the arrival, when all the immortals who wish to attend gather, then for the seven days following, there are feasts. During the final six days, we have festivities. A Day of Dancing, a Day of Gifts, a Day of Battles, a Day of Deals, a Day of Deviance, and then finally, the Day of Descent."

"And today is...?"

Melinoe smiled. "The final day of the feast. But first, your clothes."

Relief rushed through Cyane. She still had a week.

Cyane hopped off the bed, her bare feet landing on cold stone. "What's wrong with my clothes?"

She peered down at herself. Her clothes were still intact. She was no longer wet, and her hair was dry, but her shoes were missing. Besides several bruises and scrapes, and a couple of broken nails, she was fine. Someone had left her clothes on but had taken off her shoes and made her comfortable. She also felt clean, as if she'd been washed, or cleansed of the waters of before. It concerned her that she couldn't remember.

She didn't know if she liked the thought of someone touching her while she'd been unconscious, but as she looked back up at Melinoe, Cyane prayed it'd been the goddess who'd done so. Then the memory of Melinoe's ghostly fingers under her skin returned, and Cyane shuddered.

No. I don't like her touching me either.

"Where are my shoes?" she asked. She didn't bother

inquiring about her backpack or phone. Somehow she didn't think they'd survived. If they had, she didn't think anyone would help her retrieve them.

"Your clothes do little to emphasize your beauty, and it's much easier to get what you want when you properly use beauty as a weapon." Melinoe led her to the alcove where a large bath awaited.

Cyane didn't want to follow her, but the strange feeling of reverence, or something otherworldly, compelled her to.

"As for shoes," Melinoe said, amused, "you weren't wearing any when I found you."

Cyane frowned.

Without preamble, the goddess grabbed Cyane's shirt and tore it from her body as though it were tissue paper. Cyane yelped and tried to cover herself, but Melinoe laughed and plucked the rest of Cyane's clothes off of her body, tearing them with outstretched fingers.

Naked and shielding herself, Cyane scurried away, saving the note from her pocket and putting it aside. The goddess snatched her hand, spun her, and pushed her into the bath with a splash. Her strength was shocking.

Cyane emerged from the steaming water with a gasp, flailing her arms wide.

"You can't do that!" she shrieked. "I have rights!" She moved to the side of the tub to hold on.

But Melinoe was already on the other side of the room, laying out a long, cream gown on the bed. "This will make you look like one of us."

Cyane stared at it, at Melinoe, then wrenched her eyes shut and turned back around. She didn't want to go to the party, let alone get dressed up. Fear was very close to taking over her again. Fear that all of this was real. She didn't know if that was better or worse than insanity.

She slipped into the warm, soothing water, and drew her

knees to her chest. She appreciated the bath despite her lack of privacy, though it did little to ease her. The last time she'd been submerged, it...it hadn't been in proper water. She knew that now. At least she hoped she knew that.

I'll have to speak to Cerberus again if I want to leave...

Cyane shivered.

Fear could easily become terror.

METAMORPHOSIS

CYANE RUBBED the chiton dress between her fingers. The material was like feathers and warm air had a love-child, and the dress was the result of that union. Melinoe's excitement increased with each passing moment, making Cyane's head ache further.

The goddess stepped back to reveal a mirror on the cave wall. Had it just appeared? The spinning behind Cyane's eyes increased.

"You're ready," Melinoe announced.

Cyane didn't feel ready, though she turned to the mirror anyway.

The dress was as lovely as it felt, and it flowed like waves around her legs. A gold and purple sash wrapped around her waist, emphasizing her curves. A similar ribbon held up her hair in a loosely braided knot atop her head. The ends of her braids curled around the back of her neck where her hair dripped, still wet.

I look like a Greek goddess...

She blushed and fanned out the skirt. The dress's neckline hung low on her chest—which was comparably larger than the average woman's—and she couldn't help but compare herself to Melinoe in the mirror.

Her curves and height were outlandish next to the petite goddess. It wasn't like she was super busty, overweight, or overly tall. She wouldn't even consider herself outside of the norm. But next to Melinoe, Cyane was all those things and more... *lacking in every way.* Or having too much. Whatever she was, she felt outrageous and unpretty beside Melinoe.

Cyane turned from the mirror and pushed the thoughts away.

I need to get away. From her, from this. The longer she spent with Melinoe, the worse her head spun, and...shapes began to flutter at the edges of her vision.

Unreal shapes. From the corner of her eye, she'd glimpsed odd shifts of light, flickering humanoid outlines, and wraiths of sobbing women, but each time she tried to catch them head-on, they vanished into the shadows.

A screaming man appeared beside her.

Cyane wrenched her eyes shut—holding in a shriek— begging for it to end. More sobbing women appeared behind her closed eyelids. Cyane snapped her eyes back open and shoved her father's note into the neckline of her dress, securing it as best she could in the folds. *I'm okay. I'll be okay.*

"Let's get this over with," she gulped, turning towards the door. "I have someplace to be."

Melinoe, in a titter, agreed and led her from the room.

They soon entered a series of dark, dimly lit hallways, traversing them through numerous twists and turns. Cyane wasn't surprised that the decor was the same as everything else she'd seen—cave-like and ominous, with candles perched on carved-out slates everywhere. Beads of wax dripped from all, but the wax never seemed to reach the floor.

She pitied the person who had to light all of them.

Melinoe talked up a storm ahead of her, but Cyane barely heard any of it. She knew she should listen, knew she should find out everything she could about these people and this place. But she...couldn't. The same reverent cloud in her mind that urged her to supplicate herself to the goddess also carried with it an undercurrent of wrongness.

Melinoe wasn't *her* goddess. They *weren't* aligned. And so, she fought the compulsion.

God, what is wrong with me? She'd been kidnapped—or saved, threatened, saved again, and now... She didn't know what was going on. All she knew for sure was that one moment, she'd been with Captain Haros on his sailboat, and the next, she was deep underwater with white hands tugging her down, drowning and struggling to resurface.

Somewhere during that time, she'd left a moody morning on the Ionian Sea, to enter a giant cave, to have a man dressed in armor pulling her from the depths.

Either, she really was in Tartarus (what the hell?) or she'd been drugged up with some shit that would sell for a fortune on the streets and was now part of a live-action-roleplay-group—one who was too committed to realize she wasn't acting.

Music filled her ears, lilting tunes played on flutes and strings, echoing softly off the walls around her.

"We're almost there, sweet Cyane," Melinoe said over her shoulder. "You must dance with me."

The music built with each step and was soon accompanied by laughter and voices. Up ahead, the hall opened into a decadent foyer with even more candles than Cyane had ever seen in her whole life, creating endless sparks as far as the eye could see above her. Sheer purple and black linens draped precariously throughout, magically avoiding the flames. Some of the flames seemed to bleed together in her mind to create streaks of fire up and down the walls.

This didn't make sense. It wasn't right. Pressure built behind her eyes. She rubbed her brow, trying not to panic.

People lingered around, talking, whispering, and laughing in small groups. Cyane and Melinoe didn't remain near them as the goddess pulled her onward, through the foyer, towards the entryway to the ballroom. A hush settled over the strangers. Cyane sensed their attention like arrows to her back.

Her mouth parted in awe.

A dark ballroom filled with the beautiful and the grotesque stretched before her. Sweeping ceilings soared so high overhead that the darkness clinging to them was as deep and endless as the night sky. Sparkles and whirls of color danced far off in the dark providing the sensation of sickly, twinkling stars.

The walls were formed from the same gray stone, except each stone seemed to vary in design. If she looked out of the corner of her eye, she could see patterns emerging, which disappeared when she gazed at them deliberately.

The room compelled her eyes forward, across the floor, towards the dais on the other end of the room. The throne atop it echoed the castle that housed it, but she couldn't focus on any one aspect as everything seemed to be swallowed up by the imposing figure seated upon it.

Hades. His name filled her head with wonder and terror. His darkness eclipsed everything else.

"Cyane? You're gaping," Melinoe teased. "Come. Do not make them wish to eat you alive. Most would love to do just that." She gripped Cyane's hand tighter and pulled her into this doom with a giggle.

Cerberus caught sight of Melinoe entering the ballroom a moment before his eyes landed on Cyane. Melinoe tugged the girl after her into a dance, forcing each step by dragging the mortal woman behind her. Their movements were strained with awkward confusion.

His nostrils flared.

Anger rushed through him as he watched the women dance. The mortal tripped and stumbled but never quite fell, being caught up by Melinoe's embrace again and again.

He stepped out from the shadows and made his way towards them. The swirl of dresses had nothing to do with it.

He'd hoped to keep Cyane separated from the others, but it hadn't occurred to him to hide her from Melinoe. He'd planned to keep Cyane locked up until he got the answers he wanted from her. The goddess's nose for fresh meat was akin to his. She would do anything for a scrap of attention.

It didn't matter that Hades was the reason the mortal was here. That question was answered. What mattered was *why* Hades would go to such shocking and surprising lengths to capture a mortal woman when his lord had never been known to do such a thing before.

At least never with a *mortal*, and never with one so lacking in the attributes Hades coveted in women.

Cerberus couldn't fathom his lord's intent, and that infuriated him. *The rare times when he's unpredictable, he abducts and rapes his brother's daughter.*

No, he didn't like it when Hades acted outside himself.

"A mortal woman? Here?" One of the nearby undying said, pulling Cerberus's thoughts away from Hades.

"Who is she?" another asked.

Good question. Who in all the damned souls was she? The dance between the women came to an end.

"Is she part of the entertainment?" a god said, voicing Cerberus's thoughts.

Cerberus walked slowly around the undying, ignoring their questions, keeping his attention on Cyane. Tantalus approached her first and offered a cup of nectar, which she refused after a lingering look. Melinoe tried to engage with the gods around them, but like always, was ignored. Hermes bowed deeply, his winged shoes arching him off the floor, startling the weak female creature that currently took up all of Cerberus's thoughts.

As he drew nearer, he noticed her eyes were wide with fear, her skin ashen, and her hands moved nervously at her sides.

She gives herself away so easily.

Her gaze fell first to Hermes's winged sandals, flicked to Hades across the room, and returned to the winged god before her.

So painfully easily.

Cerberus could glimpse her mind breaking with each subsequent reaction.

It allowed him to travel the ballroom in peace. Every immortal was focused on her, sizing her up, reading her like he did, determining if she was a threat or just meat. Deliciously weak meat in an alluring form.

The mortal didn't notice when he reached her side. *Her* gaze was now only for Hermes. Cerberus's jaw clenched.

"Beautiful Cyane, it's delightful to meet you." Hermes bowed his head, the god's attention flickering towards Cerberus before returning to Cyane. "I swear we've met before, long ago." Hermes's smile deepened with frustrating warmth and admiration upon the intriguing mortal. His eyes strayed to her breasts and lingered there. "I'm certain we've met."

Cerberus's jaw clamped further. *Distasteful.* Regardless, Hermes's charm was infectious, especially to women.

Cerberus wasn't about to let another god fuck and break the mortal his lord had his sights on.

"I wish to speak with you," Cerberus interrupted with a scowl, facing Cyane.

A CHILLING, familiar male voice broke Cyane out of her transfixion.

Cerberus.

Hermes's flying and his winged shoes faded from her mind. Each microsecond as her eyes slowly moved towards Cerberus was dread incarnate.

"You do?" she said lamely, still breathless from the dance. He wasn't the amalgamation or creature of teeth, snake heads, and rabid snouts that her imagination filled the blanks in with. He was back to being a Greek warrior, helmet and all.

Thank god.

Heh. Her temple still pounded.

She didn't think she could take another shock so soon. Or ever.

Cerberus cocked his head to the side as if her question was nothing more than confusion on her part.

Melinoe squealed with excitement, saving Cyane. She found it hard enough with one god-like man staring holes through her flesh, let alone two. And she could feel them looking at her—it wasn't a sixth sense, it was physical and disorientating. Her flesh crawled from it.

Cyane collected herself as Melinoe stole the gods' attention. Dancing with Melinoe had been spellbinding and torturous. She'd been a ragdoll in the smaller woman's arms, unable to stop, unable to shy away for fear of seeing screaming phantoms descending upon her, eager to rend her flesh and pull her into the dark.

She was beginning to fear what would happen to her if she offended Melinoe. If she offended *anyone* here, even if it was by accident.

They were fairly alone in this central area of the ballroom. Others had moved away when she wasn't paying attention, although some of their whispers still reached her ears. They eyed her, gathering around the edges like her fear and confusion was the most delicious entertainment to be had.

Cyane shivered and rubbed her arms and met Cerberus's eyes where he towered over Melinoe.

"Sweet Cerberus," Melinoe cooed softly. "Our delightful guest wishes to leave."

"Is that so?" he said. "It appears we seek each other then."

"Yes." Cyane swallowed.

Melinoe smiled. "Do you think you can help her? She needs to get to some place called Sicily."

"Leave us, Melinoe," he snapped.

"What? Why?"

"Our conversation will be private."

"You left her alone, so she is with me now. Me!"

Cerberus stiffened and slowly turned toward Melinoe.

The air caught in Cyane's lungs.

"With you?" he said, his tone darkening.

Cyane didn't know why, but his shining eyes made her skin heat. *I can't even see his face... Maybe that's for the best.* Melinoe was almost too sickeningly beautiful to look at, Hades to torturously dark, and Hermes...

What would Cerberus look like without his helmet? She already feared him the most. Would her fear turn to horror? Terror? Inescapable dread?

"Yes," Melinoe said, breaking Cyane's thoughts.

"You claim her?"

"Yes."

"She is a guest of Lord Hades."

A wave of relief rushed through Cyane. *Guest.* She was a guest. Guests could leave.

"Do you still wish to publicly claim her, Melinoe?" he asked again, slower this time.

Melinoe winced and glanced at the dark figure sitting atop his throne.

Cyane sensed the tension between them rise. *Claim?* No one was going to claim her, not until she made it to Sicily dammit. It wasn't like she ever sold her soul to the devil or played with a ouija board or...or...

She butted in despite the trepidation closing in on her every breath. "I want to talk to you too, Cerberus." Her voice held relatively strong. Stronger than she felt.

He faced her, spotlighting her with all his strained anger. If he happened to glance down at her hands, he'd find them shaking uncontrollably.

"I want to leave," she said.

He didn't immediately respond, but instead looked across the room to where that dark figure sat on his throne. She didn't need to ask who had the most power here. Melinoe and Cerberus had done it for her.

But if she had to make a choice, to implore the supposed God of the Underworld or his supposed monstrous hound for help...well...

Her heart raced at the thought.

When she was at the Orphanage of Claudette Skies, the headmistress was much like Hades. A figure to fear, to never approach. Claudette didn't like children even though her profession served to help them. If this place was anything like the orphanage, she was better off not getting herself involved—or noticed. Being noticed really wasn't that fun. It was easier being an onlooker rather than a participant.

Cerberus turned back to her. His eyes in the slit of his helmet gave her a narrow view of him. There was pale skin and the hint of dark brows. The longer he stared without saying something, the smaller she became, the more her hands trembled. One could suffocate under the weight of his stare.

"Please," she whispered.

His brow furrowed, his irises sparked, and she wondered why she caused such a reaction in him.

"Follow me," he said, startling her.

Was it that easy?

Cerberus didn't wait for her as he strode towards the foyer outside the ballroom. Melinoe mewed sadly at her side. Cyane stepped forward to follow him.

Hermes flew down in front of her. "So you wish to leave so soon? After only one misplaced dance? What a shame." He smiled wide, and giggles erupted within the room. "If you'd but stay and celebrate, I would show you what it's like to twirl in the air." He stepped closer, filling her vision.

"No, thank you."

His smile grew, if that were at all possible. He also wore a helmet, but it didn't cover his face like Cerberus's, and Hermes's helmet had wings sprouting from the sides, like his sandals. They flapped softly as if they were alive.

Cyane frowned. *Some creature's wings were plucked to make those.* Something in her told her that that creature still lived. Wingless. Broken. Eternally.

She tore her eyes from his winged adornments to the man himself.

Hermes was as beautiful as Melinoe. His hair was short and curly, his eyes were a pale blue, and he didn't have a shirt on. A lean, softly golden, and shallowly sculpted chest nearly blinded her.

She tried to move around him, but he stopped her, stepping in front of her.

"No, thank you?" He mimicked her words. "Well, I don't believe I've ever been rebuffed with such etiquette." Hermes laughed.

Melinoe wrapped her arms around Cyane. "She is a sweet and interesting creature, isn't she?"

Hermes glanced from her to Melinoe, his charming face twisting with disgust, but when he looked back at Cyane, his beauty returned.

Cyane pulled away, but the goddess tightened her grip.

Hermes leaned in far too close to Cyane's face. "She *is* quite sweet."

She leaned back as far as she could. The sickly smell of a thousand different flowers, pungent and overwhelming, filled her nose.

"Sweet enough for me to steal a kiss. If I can't have a dance."

Cyane swallowed, unsure how to talk her way out of this.

Suddenly, Hermes was torn back, and Melinoe's grip vanished. Cerberus appeared in front of Cyane, grasping her wrist and tugging her away from the god and goddess. She staggered behind him, tripping on her skirts until they reached a corridor much less lively than the one she'd traversed earlier.

The music died in the distance, and it was like being released from a terrible, heady bubble.

Shaking hard now, Cyane jerked her hand free from Cerberus's hold. She drew her arms to her chest and fell upon the nearest wall, shaking. "What's happening to me? Who are you really, and what do you want from me? I can't...I can't take this anymore!"

She slid down the wall and pressed her hands to her face, squeezing her eyes shut to stem the tears threatening to spill. Everything that had happened in the last day rushed through her, forcing a whimper from her throat.

***

CERBERUS GLARED at the girl who was damn-near hyperventilating against the wall, pounding her palms against her forehead.

His lips twisted.

What does Hades see in this woman?

Looking at her now, his lord's motivations eluded him. More so than before, if that were at all possible.

And if she was anything like the wretched mortals that no longer believed in them… Disgust filled him. The mortal obviously didn't believe in them. Which made her less than nothing, only worthy of the blood sea beyond Hades's castle. But as Cerberus watched her, waiting for her antics to cease, his curiosity piqued. A little. This Cyane… She was a mortal who had infiltrated the Underworld, who was a blight to his duties, who represented his first true failure.

She took in a slow, deep breath.

Her breathing is evening out. She's calming.

It was an improvement over last time but not enough to assure Cerberus he was any good with mortal females or any females at that. Even Minos had noticed his inexperience, calling him out when he had carried her over his shoulder, upside down, and then under his arm. Minos had scowled and instructed Cerberus to cradle her. But even now, Cerberus contemplated throwing her over his shoulder and tossing her at Hades's feet.

Her breathing relaxed even more, and she lifted her face from her hands.

He knelt before her.

"To answer your questions, nothing is happening to you. Nothing that you haven't brought upon yourself. You may not want to believe it—I have seen enough dead float through Styx to understand that being here can be a shock —but you are in the Underworld. The sooner you accept this, like all who've come before you, the better it will be for you."

She sniffed but remained silent, and he took it as permission to continue.

"As to what I want." He stood. "I want you to get off the floor and tell me why Hades has brought you here."

He offered his hand, and as he took in Cyane's wide, brown eyes, he watched as she surprisingly raised her hand to take his.

Cerberus pulled her to her feet as warmth flooded his limb. He released her and curled his hand into a fist.

He didn't turn to see if she followed him as he continued down the hall. There was no need, the ever-watchful eyes of his dogs told him she was. Besides that, there was only silence between them.

Cyane's gaze was on his back, his armor, his xiphos sword. He, like most of the undying ones, had a great sense of when they were being watched. Prayers, sacrifices, and celebrations honoring them often had so much pull to one of his kind, even if many of the mortals had forgotten that.

So he knew without looking that Cyane's attention was on him. Like a soft touch or a tickle along the spine.

"Are you really Cerberus?" she asked suddenly, ending the silence he enjoyed. "The three-headed dog that guards the river Styx and is a companion to Hades?"

"I'm a three-headed dog now?" He hummed. "Yes,"

Her footsteps scurried up to his side. Cerberus slowed his gait to let her catch up.

The closer she was to him, the easier it would be to tear her secrets out.

"I hate to point this out," she hesitated as if she was afraid of offending him, "but you don't look like a three-headed dog."

"No. My lord gifted me the form of a man. I've been told it would be rude to ignore his generosity."

"The thing I saw earlier…"

He glanced down at her.

The female stood a foot shorter than him, with golden skin not unlike the gods that lived above. Now that he had the time to really look at her, he took in his fill.

She's staring at the floor anyway.

Her hair was a light brown, much like the sacred dirt on Olympus that he would never get the chance to stand upon. It was tied up by a ribbon with curls bunched around her neck, falling down a little and more like the way of maidens who'd just lost their innocence styled their hair. A new emotion bloomed within him, compelling him to thread his fingers into her hair and undo it, let her hair fall free around her shoulders, to return her stolen maidenhood. A scowl threatened to return to his lips.

"…every time I picture it in my mind, there are more teeth, more fiery eyes, and tongues lashing out at me than I can count," Cyane said, her words breaking through the fog in his mind. "I don't even think there were tongues before…"

His eyes snapped away from her when she looked up at him.

They turned down a dark path that led to a stairway, leading her deeper into the castle.

"Perhaps your mind is playing tricks on you. I heard your kind imagine all sorts of things in the dark," he said.

"It wasn't a three-headed dog. It was something…something else. Where are you taking me?"

"You wanted to leave, correct?"

"You're letting me leave?" she asked with a hopeful tone.

Cerberus came upon a large red door with his symbol carved into it—not the three-headed beast Cyane had questioned him about, but a hundred-headed one. He opened it to reveal a wide, open space with a large terrace that overlooked Hades's Castle and the river Styx before it.

Cyane fell silent beside him, staring across the way at the castle. Cerberus ushered her into the room and stood quietly in front of the door as he watched her slowly make her way towards the terrace to look out at Tartarus.

She gasped. "I thought… I thought we were inside Hades's castle."

"We were. Until you crossed through the door."

"How? How is any of this possible?"

"This realm, like every realm of the gods, is free from mortal reality. The shadows obscured the entirety of this place. All parts of Hades's castle are connected by the darkness, regardless of where they sit or lie here. This room is no different."

She turned to face him, and he couldn't help but pause to acknowledge the absurdity of the situation.

He'd had limited interaction with mortals who were still alive, and those previous exchanges had gone poorly. Each mortal who'd come before had tried to steal from Hades, at least the ones who dared enter his lord's domain while still alive.

The fact that he had one now, a female at that, standing in his haven, wasn't lost on him. No other being had ever infiltrated his private space before. The place where he watched over all the souls of Styx making their final journey.

Confused innocence faced him, and he narrowed his eyes.

"I suppose that makes as much sense as anything else." She glanced around the room. "And now?"

"Now you tell me what Hades sees in you."

Cyane shook her head. "I don't know what you're talking about."

"You deny it?" he asked harshly, making her eyes widen.

"I'm just trying to get to Sicily."

"You're a long way from Sicily, human."

She shuddered. "I've figured that part out."

He had taken a step towards her when a prickle coursed down his back.

Hades.

Damn him.

His lord sought him. Leaving the party, in the way that Cerberus had, could have repercussions. And since the scene had played out in front of all the gods in Tartarus to see…

Cyane's arms moved up to band around her middle. The motion pushed up her breasts and made her dress rise. His gaze flickered, fighting the urge to examine the shift in her clothes.

She was curvy like a naiad, a nymph—a creature of temptation. Of course, they no longer existed in the mortal realm, their mystical touch having diminished after centuries of breeding only with humans.

His mind wandered further, to the erotic nature of such alluring creatures, when the mortal before him cast her eyes downward, flooring him.

Subservience.

Something he understood well.

His groin twitched.

It was a rare trait in a god or goddess, one he hadn't seen since Queen Persephone was under the throes of Hades's desires. Even Zeus's closest followers weren't subservient to him, not truly. But this human mortal gave Cerberus a taste of it, of what it would be like if he were a lord, and she the worshiper.

His hand was halfway to her with the intention to lift her chin when the prickle of Hades's call slid across his back again. Cerberus snatched his hand away with a low growl.

He couldn't stay.

Nor could he get attached.

"Look at me," he ordered.

Cyane met his eyes, and a tiny thrill coursed through him. He didn't understand it. *I intimidate her.* Then her gaze hardened, and the spell of her subservience was broken.

"Stay here," he ordered, turning away from her before he got sucked in again. "We'll speak when I get back."

"What? Get back from where?"

He ignored her as he made his way towards the door and opened it.

"Cerberus," she called his name, and the damnable, confusing thrill returned. "You're going to let me leave though, right?"

Cyane grabbed his arm. The warmth of her hand seemed to bleed through his armor even though he knew that was impossible. The chill of the Underworld had long ago settled in his bones for good.

But where she touched him, he warmed up, just a little.

"Leave? No, Cyane, I'm not going to let you leave. Not yet."

He removed himself from her presence and firmly shut the door to his room.

GODLY REVELATIONS

WHY DOES he think Hades brought me here?

Cyane frowned. She didn't know how long she stayed in place, staring at the door after Cerberus left. One moment he'd been right in front of her, *something* growing between them, and in the next, he was gone.

She'd have another chance to persuade him. She was sure of it.

The headache returned behind her eyes, and she turned away from the door.

She believed. She freaking believed her circumstances. If the huge open window framing the castle and the waters from before wasn't enough, her recent experiences were.

I'm not dealing with men and women...

Dread and excitement gut-punched her.

Were the gods omniscient? Were they watching her now? Had one of them brought her here?

Why?

Maybe Hades really did bring me here. It's the only answer she'd received.

Part of her wanted to slam her fists against the door and scream at the top of her lungs, for help, for anyone, for fucking Cerberus to come back and give her more answers. She resisted the urge. Fatigue, frustration, and anger pulsed through her, all longing for an escape, but she'd never been a violent person. She never had the luxury, always fearing punishment should she speak out.

The nuns at the school made sure of that. Once, she'd snuck out of her room at night to see her friend only to be caught and punished for her transgression. Mistress Loraine had sheared off her hair, forcing her to go bald for a year by roughly shaving her scalp weekly. The other girls had avoided her after that, and she ended up alone behind stone and plaster walls. Even now, when Cyane stroked her fingers over her head, she felt the scars hidden beneath.

All her scars were hidden away.

Even if she screamed for help, it might not be Cerberus who answered her call... It never was who she wanted when she screamed for help at the school.

Cyane searched for a place to sit and wait—to hope that she wouldn't be left alone long—when it occurred to her how bizarre the room actually was.

Paintings decorated every wall, all in reds, blacks, and grays with the occasional startlement of white. They depicted battles, meetings, monsters, and conquests.

Cerberus was within every image, and it floored her that she recognized him regardless of his form. In some, he was the monstrous dog, but as she turned, figuring out the order, she recognized the man in the later images.

She recognized others as well. Hades, Charon—who looked suspiciously like Captain Haros—Hermes the psychopomp, and even Hercules with his lion's pelt. That image made her stomach drop; it depicted Hercules holding a chained Cerberus for all the crowds of humans to gawk at.

The very next image showed Hades bestowing Cerberus a man's form.

She hadn't come to Europe, to backpack through Greece, and not familiarized herself with *some* mythology. Everyone knew the myth of Hades and Persephone, Icarus and the sun, and Zeus and his lightning bolt. She knew them too, but only in broad strokes. She wasn't a scholar and didn't know the detailed hierarchy and its inner workings.

But it was the first portrayal of Persephone that finally convinced Cyane to approach the wall.

Her breath caught in her throat.

The pain in her head grew.

I recognize her!

She recognized the woman in the crudely painted image. Cyane stumbled back a step. She longed to linger on it, to let her fingers brush the image, but the pain behind her eyes expanded.

She scurried across the room to the lone chair facing Hades's Castle, sliding into it. She rubbed her temples until the worst of the pain abated, tried to read the images again, but the horrendous ache returned tenfold, nearly laying her low. She gave up after that, despite her desperate curiosity.

Time crept by, and with no sun or moon to indicate the time of day, she quickly grew restless and uncomfortable.

The god's punishments tend to last for eternity. What if eternity is just a frame of mind?

Her eyes hooded as she gazed out of the room to look at the waters below. Weariness crept upon her.

Countless pale wisps materialized the longer she watched the water. They followed a singular current that started from directly below her, where the water rushed under the gates to hell, and straight into a dark hole under the castle.

She'd made that journey not that long ago. Seeing it now,

sitting in a lone chair, in a quiet room, kept her circumstances solidified in her thoughts.

This place reminded her of the solitary prayer room at the orphanage. The one where the mistresses sent her if she had stepped out of line.

You're dealing with gods now, abandoned girl, you better fucking pray.

She closed her eyes.

"Tomorrow is the Day of Dancing." Hades swirled his nectar with disinterest. "However, my daughter decided to take the first dance with our human guest—on the wrong day. For which you did not stop. I'm annoyed, Cerberus, annoyed."

"Melinoe is not my problem," Cerberus scoffed. "Demand someone else to solve this problem."

Hades waved his hand weakly. "Eh."

"Is there anything else?" He wanted to get back to Cyane. He didn't understand why, but it worried him. He wanted to feel what he had before with her and study it. Cerberus didn't like not knowing what had happened to him.

"The whole lot of them know I have a special guest now. I don't want *her* to hear about it. Make sure no one but Charon comes or goes before Persephone arrives."

"And Hermes?"

"The messenger stays."

Cerberus didn't know how he felt about that. Hermes was one of the few beings who could leave the Underworld without Cerberus's permission. It was the winged god's role to rule crossings, and it wasn't for Cerberus to deny Hermes's mandate.

But he'd never befriended the god, and denying Hermes passage may bring Cerberus a moment of mild satisfaction.

Cerberus's lack of response brought Hades's eyes to him. "Does that bother you?" Hades sipped his drink.

"No. I was pondering my satisfaction in such a request from you."

"I knew you would alleviate my frustration." He lowered his cup. "You lied to me, Cerberus."

Cerberus's gaze hooded. He bowed his head. "Not intentionally."

"Cyane—"

It was strange hearing Cyane's name come from Hades. The names of mortals were below his lord's notice.

"—was well enough to steal the first dance with Melinoe. Her unfortunate descent must not have been so hard that she needed recovery since she was well enough to transgress. Why have you not brought her to me yet?"

Because something in him feared for the fragile mortal. Cerberus stamped the thought down. No, he feared for his queen's state of mind. He loved Persephone as one should love their queen. The longer he kept the mortal from Hades, the better it would be.

"I believe she is in shock." It wasn't quite a lie.

Hades studied Cerberus, his darkness swirling around the hound in a soft caress. Cerberus remained still and silent under his master's perusal.

Then Hades's sly smile returned. "Where is she now?"

"Put away in a place your daughter—or any other immortal—will never find her."

"Is that so?"

"Yes, my lord."

"Cerberus, my dear hound. Do I sense *concern* coming from you? For a *mortal*?"

Scoff. "No."

"Hah!" His lord leaned forward and rested his elbows on his knees. "Your responses are intriguing. Has our mortal guest stolen your attention? Are you afraid?"

"Afraid?" Cerberus's eyes narrowed. The fire within him rose. He was the son of the most feared titan of them all; fear was an emotion for his opponents. "Do you want me to bring her to you now?"

"Oh no. I will see her on the morrow when the dancing begins. Bring her then. If she is well enough to show her presence, she is well enough to dance her shock away."

"Very well, my lord."

Hades turned to the crackling fire in his hearth, and Cerberus took that as his cue to leave. He turned towards the door.

"Cerberus," Hades said, stopping him. "You should be afraid."

Cerberus placed his gloved hand on the knob and, closing his eyes, walked into the darkness.

A short time later, he stood over Cyane's sleeping, slumped over form in the chair overlooking Styx. Her hair had come loose in the back, and slightly curled tendrils had fallen over her face and spilled down her chest.

The light brown of her hair was nothing to sing about. The shapeliness of her body was the same as any fertility goddess. She had sunspots, an asymmetrical face, and she certainly didn't look solely Greek. A mortal mutt.

Yet, there was something about her, something he couldn't quite place. Perhaps it was her imperfections that caused it, maybe it was something else. Cerberus shrugged it off.

It was strange, staring at her without her knowledge. He —like most undying—rarely slept. He took the opportunity her continued weakness gave him.

She *was* weak. He moved to stand in front of her. There was something about her weakness that returned the thrill to his senses. He didn't understand it, he never found much satisfaction in anything but keeping the wayward souls below in line, but there it was. Thrill.

What would he do if he'd been born as such a powerless creature? For all his eons of watching mortal souls, he never stopped to think about what it would be like to be a mortal.

If I were powerless, I'd find someone stronger and give myself over to them.

If I were a mortal, I'd find a god and give my life to them for protection.

He had a sudden need to brush back her fallen hair and awaken her, but reflections from his conversation with Hades burned in the back of his mind.

He'd done just that—given his loyalty to a god more powerful than himself. *He*, the son of the greatest Titan and grandson to primordial Tartarus himself, grandson to Gaea —the world. Even now, Cerberus could feel his father moving deep below, in Tartarus's gut, waiting for the day Zeus would be overthrown and Typhon's eternal chains would break away.

No, I'm not weak like her.

A soft whimper sounded in his ears, and something bumped his hand. Cerberus looked down at the hound seeking his attention. He knelt and idly scratched behind its ears as he watched Cyane. Several more of his pups came out from the shadows to await his attention.

Teeth, tongues, and long sharp snouts. Cyane's inability to describe his true form brought a rare smile to his lips. His hounds were as much a part of him as he was one of them.

One-by-one they settled around him and Cyane.

Her chest rose and fell in a steady rhythm. The red flush of her skin from earlier was gone.

Maybe I am afraid.

Cerberus looked out at Styx. Not one soul swam against the current. He watched the waves all the same while the mortal and his companions slept.

THE BEGINNING OF THE END

CYANE AWOKE, completely aware of where she was, what had happened, and this time, there were no nightmares to frighten her awake.

Something soft and cushy enveloped her. She realized that she wasn't lounging in a chair anymore, but was in a bed again, with blankets and soft pillows cushioning her body. She sat up with a yawn.

She was still in the same barren room with the singular chair across from her. Hades's castle rose up like a stunning monument to fill her eyes, as sharp and foreboding as ever.

"You're finally awake."

Her belly flipped.

Cerberus leaned against the wall, gazing out over the landscape.

"Creeper," she muttered under her breath.

He shrugged.

How could I have fallen asleep? Sudden anger and concern filled her. When did he get here? How long has he been in the room with me?

He'd moved her to a bed.

His bed.

It had to be. There hadn't been a bed before and now there was. She wanted to question where it'd come from, but she was pretty sure she already knew.

She frowned, fisted her hands, and checked her body. *Fine. I'm fine.* She'd never woken up in a strange man's bed before.

Cyane began to crawl out from under the covers when something moved under her hand. A big black dog slept next to her, curled into a ball. There was another sprawled out at her feet, and a third on the other side of her, all partially burrowed in the many blankets.

She spent the next few minutes extricating herself from the god-like man's bed without disturbing his potentially soul-eating, murderous hellhounds.

When she was free, she peeked up to discover Cerberus watching her.

"How long have I been asleep?" she asked.

His eyes ran up and down her body. Cyane crossed her arms.

"A while," he said. "Time is different here compared to what you know. The darkness makes things slower, quieter."

"Am I allowed to leave now?"

Cerberus pushed himself off the wall. "No."

Cyane's breath hitched. Hope fled. "What? Why?"

"Hades has shut the way until after the festivities."

It took a moment for his words to sink in. Somehow, deep down, she knew she was fucked, but she'd refused to acknowledge it. If she just kept her focus on her task, and on her quest to reach the destination in the note, she'd make it. She had to. Her determination had never failed her before.

But what if this time determination wasn't enough?

She slumped back down on the edge of the bed and palmed her face. "You lied to me."

"That's the second time I've been called a liar in a very short time."

Heavy steps made her drop her hands. The Greek warrior, helmet and all, towered over her.

Cyane shot to her feet. "You said if I wanted to leave, I should follow you."

"And you did leave—the ballroom. I saved you from Hermes's clutches. You do not belong where the gods walk. You're nothing but a mortal, a mere plaything to them."

"I thought you were going to lead me out of this place!"

"You thought wrong."

"You just said I don't belong here, Cerberus." She took a step closer to him. "I'm not supposed to be here, right? You saved me from drowning, then told me to say my final words, that I'd broken some law. Then I was woken up and dressed to attend a party, only to be led away shortly after I was forced there to begin with." Cyane wrang her hands, fuming. "I don't know what's happening, I'm confused, I'm scared. None of this makes sense… but somehow it makes all the sense in the world."

Cerberus cocked his head mockingly in answer.

"Why am I here?" she whispered.

She wasn't above begging, in fact, she'd get down on her knees right now and beseech him if it meant clearing some of the confusion in her head. This *warrior* considered killing her not long ago—and she knew she needed to remember that—but he was also the only one who felt right to her.

Maybe because he was the only one who agreed that she didn't belong.

He can be persuaded.

His gaze flared in the opening of his helmet, going from a dark brown to a deep, fiery red. They were like the last dying embers of a lava field before it cooled into basalt or the first spark of fire when a star formed. She'd never seen anything like his eyes in the world above. They had the power to mesmerize.

Things this terrifying and this beautiful didn't exist.

It was wrong that this man had such beautiful eyes.

And I can't even see the rest of his face.

Without realizing it, she reached up.

He grabbed her hand before she could touch him.

Cyane stilled as his hand tightened around hers. She thought he would be warm to match the ruby glow in his eyes, but he was frigid—so unlike the fire in his gaze that it froze her veins. The cold slid over her flesh before it slipped deep within, holding her soul hostage in an embrace she wasn't ready for.

It wasn't right. *This* wasn't right.

She tried to tug her hand free but it remained his hostage. A shiver wracked her body.

"Don't be scared," he said.

His words stopped the rapid chill taking her over.

His fingers loosened on hers, and she realized she didn't want him to let her go. Not yet. She gripped him, keeping them linked together when he went to pull away.

"Why am I here?" she asked again.

"Lord Hades brought you here."

It wasn't enough.

"But why?"

Cerberus removed his hand from hers. A deep crease formed between his brows, taking away the fire in his eyes and the cold of his touch. The moment was broken.

He strode away from her, and the giant dogs all stirred from the bed and jumped up to follow him. One came to her side and sniffed her dress.

Cyane hugged her one hand to her chest and then cupped it with the second. What'd she done to make him so angry so quickly?

"Fix your hair, straighten out your dress, and prepare yourself," Cerberus snapped. The dogs gathered around his feet. "Hades has requested your presence for the Day of Dancing."

"I don't want to join in on your festivities," she snapped back. "Why should I do anything *he* pleases when I have no idea why he brought me here in the first place?"

Cerberus turned back to her. "You dare to defy a god?"

"He's not my god."

Suddenly, Cerberus was in front of her with his hand around her neck. "Not your god? How quaint. I have a word of advice for you, mortal woman—think long and hard about the history of the pantheon, and think of those who denied the gods what was theirs. The ages have not been kind to them." He released her abruptly with a scowl in his voice. "You look like a drowned harpy. Put yourself together because whether you like it or not, you'll do as you're told or suffer consequences. And not me, nor any other being, will save you from it."

He stormed towards the looming, red door. Without opening it, he walked through like smoke and vanished.

Cyane stared after him, shaken.

His touch had made her feel safe, comfortable. For a moment, she'd imagined all of her questions would be answered and he would understand, but that feeling had disappeared as quickly as it'd come. Maybe it hadn't actually been there at all.

The monstrous dog beside her yawned deeply, drawing her eyes downward.

One of the other dogs came forward with a tennis shoe in its mouth.

She recognized it.

The dog dropped the shoe at her feet, and she picked it up, turning it in her hands.

Fine. She reached her hand into her dress and found her note. If she needed to play the part of a puppet to get out of here alive, then she damned well would. Memories of her childhood threatened to emerge again.

God gazes lovingly upon those who honor him.

The last thing Cyane wanted to do was smile, but she would do so anyway. She wasn't happy about it, but it didn't mean she couldn't play the part to protect herself.

As a child, waiting to be adopted, she'd hoped that maybe the people in the next room would be her real parents. That they regretted giving her up and had returned for her. That maybe God had looked lovingly down on her, and she wouldn't have to wait until she was an adult to meet them.

But, clearly, that hadn't gone according to plan either.

Cyane nervously stepped into the foyer that led to the ballroom. Beside her were Cerberus's hounds; two flanked her while the third led the way. They were her jailors, and she their captive. With precise nudges, a few terrifying growls, and several nips at her heels, they'd forced her to do what they pleased.

She'd hoped they'd leave her alone, forget about her.

Still, she'd come to prefer the large beasts with wide jaws and sharp teeth over the ethereal beings and their intimidating ways.

I like you guys more than your master. Her nostrils flared briefly.

She smoothed out her dress and brushed her fingers through her loose hair, encouraging it to fall around her shoulders. She had no idea if she looked like a harpy or not. There'd been no mirror in the room, nor anyone, to tell her otherwise.

Back in the gatehouse room, it'd taken both time and courage to step beyond, even as the dogs forced her towards the door.

She'd considered jumping out the window and into the water. She'd try to make her way out of this place without help, but Cerberus's warning came back to her, and the fear of defying a force like *Hades* stopped her.

No one, as far as she could recall, had ever escaped the Underworld without help. And the ballroom was maybe the place she might find someone to ask for it.

Music drifted into the corridor. The vibration surged up her feet and legs. She started, finding her jailors gone. She searched for them, but they were nowhere to be seen.

Fresh thoughts of running never fully materialized as the steady pounding drums loudened. The music entered her ears, her skull, her bones. Her body vibrated. A deliberate beat she couldn't place, nor had heard before, yet it resonated throughout her being, making her heartbeat wild and uncontrolled. She lifted up onto her toes and lowered back down.

The Day of Dancing.

Cyane moved to the entrance of the ballroom and peeked in. She fought desire, refusing to cavort into the room beyond, a little afraid of what the music was doing to her. It wasn't human music, which seemed more like noise now in her memories, but ancient and eldritch. *It's not meant for human ears.* A breath escaped her.

Her father's note burned the flesh of her chest, reminding her not to get caught up in the magic.

Hades sat at the far end of the ballroom upon his throne. A direct path was open from where she stood to where he peered with hooded eyes out over his guests. Cerberus was next to him on Hades's left, imposing and alert. Decked out in the same Greek armor she'd seen him in earlier.

She discerned Cerberus's eyes the moment they found

her. Like a red-hot laser to her flesh. The beat changed as they stared at each other.

They're ancient and eldritch, too.

The music began to accelerate.

War was on the horizon. Worlds were about to fall. The sun exploded from the sky above. She saw and experienced it all in the melody.

"Today marks the beginning of the end," Hades's voice boomed out, adding to the gravity of the ritualistic pounding.

With her gaze still on Cerberus, with the desire to see his face building like the tune, someone roughly ushered her to the dancefloor.

THE DAY OF DANCING

Hades settled back down on his throne. Tantalus refilled his cup.

Cerberus glowered behind the shield of his helmet.

He'd felt each time Cyane had considered leaving Tartarus, like her thoughts, her intentions to be free of this place, were strong enough to provoke him despite the distance between them. He rarely received these feelings, as he was barred from the wants and intentions of the powerful undying that came and went from this place.

Cyane was a mortal, he reminded himself, and that made her weak, incredibly so.

So why am I feeling her?

It was like when Hades called to him. Or when a rare soul tried to swim against the current. But despite the itch, Cyane never actually tried to leave. He sensed it all the same.

He was attuned to this weak mortal. *Perhaps it's because of her weakness?* Cerberus shook his head as if he could fling the annoying thoughts from his head.

Either way, he couldn't feel her now, not since the music began—a tune played by Hypnos and Pan—as she had no thought of fleeing. But, while freed from this sensation, he stalked her through his hound's eyes. All entrances and exits were guarded by them—by the parts of him that were now somewhat autonomous—just in case.

There was no escape. Not from him.

She was jerked into the embrace of an Arae, one of the many daemons that dwelled here, before being pushed into the arms of old Menoetes, who even from where Cerberus stood, smelled rank from cattle.

No other female would deign to dance with one such as Menoetes, and for good reason. The old undying not only reeked but was as large and lumbering as a giant, slobbering over the females with undisguised lust. Cyane was his first partner in eons. It mattered not how unwilling she was.

She was passed to Trophonios, who brought a smile to her face, then to Cocytus, who made tears fall from her eyes. Each man pressed Cyane up against them, taking in her naivety and her ignorance. They took advantage of her and her weakness.

She is meant for Hades. Cerberus scowled.

He gritted his teeth as something strange took hold of his mind and churned his gut.

Before he could stop it, he spoke out of turn. "Who is she to you?"

"A means to an end," Hades said.

"Why did you bring her here?"

Cyane was twirled by a different Arae to the lilt of Pan's flute. The Arae released her, and she fell to the floor with a gasp before being picked back up again.

Hades turned to him. Cerberus couldn't tear his eyes off the mortal woman to address his lord properly. He would never know how Hades eyed him then.

"Would it please you to know?" Hades asked.

"Yes," he responded, annoyed. His jaw ticked, and he

stretched out his fingers to loosen the tension building within him.

"She's here to serve."

Cerberus's eyes shot to Hades. It was the perfect answer, the worst answer, and the best answer.

For the first time in his long existence, he wanted to draw his sword, his many starving heads, all to strike his lord to the ground.

Hades would never tell him what he truly wanted to know.

Several thousand years ago, Cerberus had been little more than a monstrous animal, although sentient and powerful. Maybe he didn't know what it was like to be purely humanoid. His body had changed, grown substance, and given the form of an ideal man at Hades' hand.

It had been no small feat. His lord had extended himself on Cerberus's behalf, far beyond anyone ever before. Hades had only gone to such great lengths for two others: Persephone and his brother, Zeus, during the Titanomachy.

Cerberus was and always would be eternally loyal to Hades. No god, not above nor below, could boast of having a more loyal guardian than Hades.

He turned back toward the ballroom to find Cyane gone. He scanned the crowd searching for her. His other eyes— piercing through Erebus' twilight—roved as well.

"You've never had a consort, have you?" Hades asked.

Cerberus found Cyane before his hounds. She was half-hidden, perched against a wall, catching her breath.

"No, I've never taken a consort," Cerberus muttered.

"No, I suppose you haven't."

Cerberus cocked his head, and silence fell between them. He'd never considered taking a consort, had never had the inclination. The few with the power to tempt him, those female goddesses of desire and love, had never encountered him, or he they.

What would he do with a consort if he had one? Lay with her in a bed? He wasn't willing to shackle himself to a weakness if factions arose against his lord. How could he knowingly place anything above his loyalty to Hades?

Cerberus swept his eyes over the ballroom. There were lamiae, with their serpentine tails and naked torsos, wrapped themselves around the men below, seeding desire. He found nothing enticing about those who took the form of his mother.

The mormolykeiai weaved in and out of the crowd, taking on the bodies of the most beautiful human forms over the centuries and offering them up for perverse delight. Their cold eyes were as hard and deep as his own. He couldn't look at them without seeing himself.

And then everyone else, who had a name in the pantheon of his choices for consorts, were never appealing enough to bend his loyalty for, at least not long enough to form a bond.

He saw Hermes break away from the dance and float towards Cyane. Cerberus's eyes narrowed.

She'd moved away from the wall.

He took a step forward, slowly placing his hand on the hilt of his sword but stopped when Hades stood up. The music halted, and Hades spoke.

"Our Queen Persephone captivated me when she spun in the dappled sunlight above."

A soft laugh could be heard from the guests.

Hades smiled wickedly. "On this day we honor our queen with such a dance, as we have from the start. This festival echoes her story. As many of you have noticed, our gifts change like the seasons each year, and my gifts change as well."

Cerberus eyed the Lord of the Dead warily.

"Melinoe," Hades said.

Melinoe stepped out from the shadowed curtains behind them to kneel before her father. She wore a sheer chiton dress that hung from her slight curves, draping from her pointed nipples and hips. The goddesses' hair was woven into the fabric, becoming apart of the dress as well. The waves of soft linen floated like smoke down her legs.

"My daughter"—Hades didn't spare her a glimpse—"and Cerberus, my most loyal guardian, will now come together like my queen and I had, so many eons ago."

Cerberus stilled. The guests clapped. Exuberance followed by all but him. He slowly tore his gaze from Hades to settle on Melinoe, who rose up and looked at Cerberus with an adoration that sickened him.

Hades retook his seat.

Melinoe wasn't Cerberus's to deal with. Anger burned through him. She was a blight, a tarnish to Hades's power and his rule. She was everything Cerberus would never be: betrayal manifested in physical form.

Regardless, Melinoe waited for him to take her hand and lead her to the dancefloor.

The other guests cleared from the floor, drifting to the darker reaches of the room.

They waited for him. Cerberus glared at Hades and was met with a bored smile.

Furious, Cerberus stepped from the dais, near shaking with disgust.

"Sweet Cerberus, I'm thrilled," Melinoe whispered up at him with even more apparent devotion than before.

He bowed his head and took her hand. Melinoe's long nails grazed him. She froze his skin, even through his glove—a stark contrast to the mortal's heated touch.

Melinoe beamed up at him, delighted to have a willing dance partner for once (none of the others would dare), and his face went blank. From the corner of his eye, he saw Cyane hesitantly accept a cup of nectar from Hermes.

The music roared back to life, and Cerberus pulled the daughter of Hades close.

———

"Are you certain we haven't met before?" Hermes said.

Cyane watched through a blurry haze as Cerberus brought Melinoe close and sharply moved with the goddess to the slow-building drum of music. His armor, paired against Melinoe's revealing dress was in as sharp opposition as the beautiful music was to the terrible men who forced Cyane to dance with them against her will.

A snap and pull, a push and tug.

Melinoe laughed, and the sound of it twinkled through the room.

Envy filled Cyane. She didn't understand why. But she hadn't laughed that way when she'd been thrown into the dance. Instead, she had been passed off from one groping disturbing man to the next, knowing she had no one to rescue her as they contorted her body into unwanted shapes. They pressed up against her, took away her space with glee, and laughed when she struggled to pull away.

Men with wings, men with dripping horns, men that smelled like rotten death, and others that smelled of vinegar and roses. She still hadn't caught her breath from their brutality. Her skin crawled with molestation.

She'd hoped against hope, as her world had spun, that Cerberus would take her hand and guide her from the maelstrom. To tell her not to be afraid like he had before.

"What?" she said distractedly. Hermes had asked her something?

But why would Cerberus save her? Or even say such comforting words to her ever again? He wasn't beholden to her. What distinguished him from all the others in the room was that he didn't look at her like she was a piece of entertaining meat, and he'd been there when she was at her most vulnerable. When her last ember of resistance had finally been quenched by the unforgiving river, it had been his hand that had come out of nowhere and returned her to the surface.

The memory fueled her envy.

Melinoe pressed herself against Cerberus. Those around her barked out another wave of snickers. A flash of red light bled from the openings of Cerberus's helmet.

Did it mean anger? *Lust?* Did the fire in his eyes even have meaning? Or was it chaotic, like everything else?

Why do I care? Cyane frowned. But as she watched Melinoe, in blooming mirth, the goddess's beauty beyond earthly description, so joyous—living each moment in Cerberus's attention—Cyane didn't think she could ever compare. Not in a billion years.

A human's never won over a goddess in anything.

Something nudged her thigh, and she peered down to see one of the dogs from earlier. It sat regally next to her leg, its head level with her waist, and stared out over the dancefloor. She tentatively trailed her fingers over one of its pointed ears. The dog growled, and its nostrils flared. She yanked her hand away.

Maybe it doesn't like to be touched?

"I said, I swear I've met you before," Hermes said.

Cyane startled and finally turned her face toward him. He was studying her curiously.

His golden beauty and honed muscles were hard to look at, especially next to the shadows and formless darkness that seemed to drift over every surface. The miasma touched him too, but in an eerie, incomplete way, like rustling bushes blocking a distant fire.

"It's not possible," she said, fiddling with the cup of nectar he'd given her. She'd know if she'd met a god before. She was sure of it. Doubt began to creep forward. But would she? The things she had seen in the last day made her question reality. Sometimes sanity needed to be put on the backburner when there was something larger at stake.

"Perhaps it is not, but it does lend to why Lord Hades requested my help in bringing you here."

The dance, the music, Cerberus and his warrior's armor, and Melinoe's damselled allure fell from her mind.

"You?" Cyane said. "You know why I'm here?"

The corners of Hermes's lips lifted. "No. I don't know why, only that you are."

"But I was brought here for a reason? It wasn't a mistake?" She needed to hear directly, from someone, that she didn't just end up in hell by accident.

"A mistake? I'm hurt." Hermes laughed, turned, and raised his glass towards Hades before swallowing the rest of the contents down. "Gods don't make mistakes. Lord Hades came to me and offered me latitude for allowance of your crossing between the realms. It was a most unusual request."

Cyane's head spun. It was like Cerberus had said. Hades had brought her here purposefully. She hadn't wanted to believe it—hadn't wanted to believe *him*. But now, unsolicited, Hermes had confirmed it.

Hermes turned back to her and continued. "It's happened before. Mortals, half-mortals and the like, being brought to Olympus, Tartarus, even Poseidon's watery graveyard, but not in a very, very long time."

Cyane looked at Hades still sitting on his throne. The dark god forced a shiver down her back. The God of the Dead. The ruler of all this darkness. With just one sideways glance, she was prepared to lay down at his booted feet and genuflect, if only to protect her immortal soul—while at the same time, she wanted to run in the opposite direction.

No, she really didn't want to talk and ask him directly. *Call me a fucking coward.* But if what Hermes said was true, she knew she'd have to talk to him eventually.

Hades did not look back at her. The god's eyes were fixated on the dancing couple, the same god who had involved other gods in his endeavor to bring Cyane here.

There was nothing special about her. She tried to think back on her entire life for an occurrence, for anything that would put someone like *her* in a situation like this, but nothing came to mind. Nothing.

She'd grown up in an orphanage in America, although it hadn't been called an orphanage officially—they'd been phased out in states long before her birth. But within the walls of Claudette Skies School for Children, it was known as such. She'd always preferred to call a spade a spade.

Her name, Cyane, had been written within the note left with her as a baby, and that was what the nuns had called her, and they had raised her like an obedient but willful daughter. She'd always known that her parents were out there because of that note. She completed her elementary schooling, she'd been moved to a transitional center for children and the courts took an interest in her.

They placed her into the foster care system, where she was taken in by an older couple. They never adopted her, but she'd lived with them through high school. She studied and earned herself a scholarship, and with the help of governmental assistance, she was able to go to state college and secure her autonomy.

There are thousands, hundreds of thousands, of lost children who have suffered far stranger and more terrible circumstances than me.

I'm not a victim.

She hesitantly raised her cup to her mouth.

She'd never done anything growing up that would make anyone, let alone a god, take notice of her. Cyane knew she was fortunate that she could believe her real parents were out there, waiting for her when all the other kids she'd grown up with knew for certain their parents were dead, abusive, or had chosen drugs over them.

With the note, Cyane could believe that her parents had given her up for a reason.

I'll never know that reason if I don't get out of here...

Tears sprung in her eyes. She'd felt cursed, doomed to wonder *why* for her whole life, and now, when she was about to get answers, something thwarted her.

Fuck this place. Fuck these gods. They weren't hers.

She turned to Hermes. "If you helped bring me here, would you be able to help me get out?"

The dog growled at her side.

"I *am* the God of Crossings," he said.

Suddenly, the snide laughter of the crowd returned.

She snapped her eyes to the dancefloor.

Cerberus no longer held Melinoe in his arms. The goddess fruitlessly tried to get his attention back.

No, he was looking at Cyane, with his sword drawn and pointing straight at her.

The cup fell from her slack fingers.

He was the warrior that pulled her from the depths. He was also the monster who threatened to kill her. Now his sights were on her, as if he'd read her thoughts, heard her words.

The left hand of the God of the Dead. Her stomach fell to pits. The same foreboding aura that surrounded Hades shadowed Cerberus now, and she was afraid of him once more.

Cerberus took a step in her direction.

Run.

Hermes pulled her against his chest, his hands every-where at once. Cyane tore herself from his arms. The crowd's laughter grew in volume.

I'm not supposed to be here. Fear choked her.

Run.

But where would she run too?

Cerberus was now striding towards her. The other-worldly power spreading from him sucked the festivities dry. How had she ever thought that he was her savior? Savagery bled from his glowing red eyes.

Run!

Anxiety surged.

Someone pushed her hard toward the grand entryway, and she fled.

AN OATH TO STYX

THE GRAND FOYER was split like a star, each point a different path, while the central path led to the ballroom. She picked a direction at random and ran. The path went on, with only the rocky cavern walls and candles on either side of her.

No doors, no windows, nothing.

Then it occurred to her that there were no sounds of pursuit. She stopped. The only thing she could hear in the hall was her own labored breath.

How far had she even gone? Could she still be seen from the foyer?

She turned around to check—and there was Cerberus, soundlessly stalking her, with his sword drawn. As if they never left the ballroom at all.

Cyane's throat tightened, and she jerked back around with a yelp, sprinting, pushing her body to the extreme, down the corridor. She didn't want to die. Regret choked her. Why had she thought that running would help her? She could feel Cerberus's hot breath against the back of her head, could sense him behind her even without the sounds of pursuit. He was almost upon her.

As she ran, she couldn't stop imagining the hundred-headed monster with tongues that licked out through the darkness to taste her hot-headed mistake.

Cyane couldn't stand it anymore. She spun around, threw herself against the wall, and cried out, "Please don't hurt me!"

Her heart thundered. She didn't fully understand what she'd done wrong, only that she must've done something to anger Cerberus.

Cerberus towered over her. She shrunk away from him, pressing herself flat against the wall, but he caught her by the neck, wrapping his fingers around her throat, pinning her in place. He applied just enough pressure to hold her still without choking her. Jagged edges poked into her back. Her fingers twitched at her sides before she pushed at his chest to keep him at a distance.

"Hermes cannot help you," Cerberus warned, his voice exacting. "He is loyal to no one but his own hide."

He *had* heard her.

How?

The dog. Cyane's brow furrowed as realization hit.

Cerberus controlled them.

She swallowed against the tightness of his palm as he lifted her back to her feet. The heaviness of his presence made it hard to speak, and part of her wanted to start running again if only to get a moment to find those words. But then she remembered he was more than she would ever be. Powerful. Powerful in a way she could barely comprehend or even begin to understand. She'd never escape him.

She'd been envious of Melinoe, but now that Cyane was back with Cerberus, a monster of myth, she realized she must've had some misguided power herself. She'd stolen the attention of the monster.

She hated to admit that she'd wanted to be in Melinoe's place, especially after being thrown from one frighteningly forceful dance partner to another. The idea of being held by one such as Cerberus had seemed...safe.

Now that he stood before her, with his hand around her throat, she didn't understand why she felt that way at all. He was anything but safe. Nothing was safe here. This was the realm of the dead, and she feared she was about to join their ranks.

"You're watching me," she finally said. She would say anything to break the brutal silence and the wait. "W-why?"

Cerberus released her with a hiss. He sheathed his sword, and the darkness that seemed to be part of him flared, swallowing Cerberus and Cyane in pitch blackness before vanishing in the low light that came from Styx.

She started, and her hands came up to rub her throat. Her eyes flickered over her new surroundings, half expecting to be back in the ballroom where everyone could laugh at her while she was executed. It wasn't the ballroom though.

We're back in the gatehouse.

The endless hallway and its thousands of candles were gone. She dropped her hands to her chest and peered, disoriented, out over the dark waters around Hades's castle. She saw thousands of naked bodies swimming towards the castle right below the surface.

Cyane jerked away from the edge, holding back a scream.

Cerberus crowded her. "You dare ask me why? When you have shown up here unexpectedly, fought against the laws of nature, and contribute to a plot of one of the most powerful gods?" He leaned in close, stealing her air. "The last time Hades brought someone here against their will—"

"Persephone?" she whispered.

"—the world as we know it changed. First, the rape," Cerberus continued, his voice lowering. "Then came Demeter's agony and winter was born, a genocide of all life on Gaia, and finally, the prospect of war between Olympus and

Tartarus. Do you know what happens when gods war, little mortal?"

She could only imagine.

He leaned in even closer, and what Cyane could glimpse of his face filled her vision.

"The realms unravel," he whispered dark and low. "Do you feel it?"

At first, she didn't know what he meant, how could she separate one feeling from all the forces that entrapped her. He was so close, so intimidating, and unlike any man she'd encountered.

The ground trembled.

"What is that?" she breathed. Her feet parted for balance.

"Typhon, the God of Destruction, my father."

The trembles stopped.

"And he is not alone," Cerberus said.

Only something enormous could make the world shake like that. Not just a world, but the afterlife. What kind of primordial beast was below her feet? If it could make hell shake, would what it do to Earth?

The gravity of it frightened her.

At least she understood why he'd been watching her. She'd done nothing wrong and had been forced to this place against her will—but to him, she could be a catalyst, a bad omen.

Nah. She was none of that. *I'm going to get out of here, forget any of this ever happened, and find my parents. Happy thoughts, happy family. Happy trails to this nightmare.* Cyane held in an insane giggle. Those were just dreams. Not long ago, she'd been forced to dance, had envied the sight of Melinoe with Cerberus, and had cared about her appearance. All of it was done without actually considering what the effect of her presence had on everything around her.

She had nowhere else to look but at Cerberus and ingest what he was telling her.

"I never asked for any of this," she whispered once her shivers stopped. She wanted him to believe it, needed him to believe it. *I'm innocent.*

"Would you swear on it?"

For the first time since getting on the sailboat, a flicker of hope returned.

"I don't want to start a war," she said. "Yes."

His eyes narrowed, and she caught sight of the edge of his eyebrow.

So human. For having seen only Cerberus's eyes and his armored physique, it was beginning to alarm her that she didn't know what he truly looked like. She was beginning to suspect he was handsome, but what if he wasn't? What if he were ancient and diseased? A skeleton?

An illusion?

"A war will not happen. Not if I can help it," Cerberus said.

She didn't want war either. "What can I do to help?"

Cerberus drew back, and she took a much-needed breath of air from the space he'd provided. Cyane hadn't realized how hard it had become to breathe.

Silence fell between them. He'd stiffened as if her question was a surprise. *He thinks the worst of me.* He thought she didn't care, but that wasn't it at all. She cared. She cared too freaking much. She'd barely accepted this new reality—and that had been quite the feat alone—but Cerberus didn't seem to realize how different her world was to his.

Perhaps I've been too selfish.

His eyes roamed over her. Cyane curled her arms around her middle, hiding from his gaze, diverting her own.

The thrill was back.

It surged through him like stolen lightning the moment he'd sensed Cyane's desperation to leave in the ballroom, and it had thundered when he'd heard her ask Hermes for help.

Hermes was a trickster, a thief, and a lackey to some of Hades's most powerful opponents. The winged god's loyalties were easily swayed, and to think Cyane could've slipped from the realm in Hermes's arms made the primordial beast in Cerberus furious. If she'd escaped with him, war could've easily happened.

It's my job to do Hades's bidding.

But as he stared down at Cyane, hiding behind her arms, he wasn't sure if he had chased after her out of duty. He didn't have a name for the way she made him feel—the thrill was not always the same.

She wouldn't meet his eyes.

The damnable pounding inside him grew. *She wants to help.*

To *serve.*

Hades's words came back to him. *Serve.* Hades?

The same feeling he'd discerned as he'd seen her next to Hermes returned to him now.

"You wish to help?" Cerberus asked if only to hear her response.

"I don't want anyone to die on my behalf."

It wasn't the answer he wanted, but he took it all the same.

"Would you swear such a thing to Styx?" *Would she dare?*

"Like an oath?"

"Yes."

Cyane licked her lips, and his gaze was drawn to them. It was such a strange thing for him to want to watch.

"I will if you will," she said.

She dares.

He reached forward and grabbed her wrist, drawing her against his body as he called the darkness. The next moment, they stood on the rocky shores of Styx. Cyane pulled away from him with a shudder, and he grudgingly let her go.

He turned to the black and red waters. The gatehouse he resided in was up and to their left, and Hades's castle to the right in the center of the beginning of the ocean of blood. Harpies swarmed so high above that they could be mistaken for birds by the human.

Cerberus sensed her hesitation. An oath was no small thing, but an oath to prevent war was not such a hard one to make. He knelt at the water's edge. "Don't be scared."

She gingerly joined him on his right and lowered beside him. "What happens if an oath is broken?"

"Divine punishment."

"Will you let me leave when this is all done? Will you believe me if I make it?"

He nodded again but didn't believe she'd have the courage to go through with it. Cerberus had no fear swearing his own convictions to Styx, having made many oaths to the wet goddess over the countless years of his life. Styx was fond of him for protecting her shores and for his adherence to his oaths.

But would Cyane commit a vow that would last her mortal life?

Instead of answering, he bowed his head. "I vow on Styx to protect this realm." He lowered his face until it was right above the waters. He breathed in its sweet scent.

A red mist rose from the waters and enveloped him, touching him all over before it dissipated into the air.

It took less than a minute for the binding to take place. When he was done, he rose back up.

And in awe, she mimicked his position and bowed over the water.

"I vow on Styx, on you," she whispered to the water, "to do all in my power to…to do no harm to this place."

Cerberus watched in shock as she breathed in, and the red mist enveloped her. When it was gone she rose up as well. She tilted her head back, closed her eyes, and inhaled again. She'd not only listened to him.

She trusted him.

Stunned, his hands tensed at his sides, finding he had no idea what to do with them. He wanted to grab hold of her again but didn't dare. A god would never give an oath so easily. Gods were afraid of their own words. But this human had done what hundreds of divine beings would never do.

He'd always looked down upon humans. They'd always been beneath his notice—the live ones at least. What else would the mortal do if he asked it of her? If he demanded?

How far did her trust actually go?

Was this what Hades saw in her?

Is this what it's like to be worshipped?

"What happens now?" she asked, peering around nervously.

The thunder in his chest built to a crescendo. He stood slowly and reached his hand out. She took it, and he helped her rise.

THE DAY OF GIFTS

CYANE WOKE feeling like she'd slept for a hundred years. There was no more pain. She wasn't even hungry—not like she'd thought much about food in the last few days, and when she had, she realized she was neither hungry nor thirsty.

Which was fine since she knew what had happened to Persephone after she ate the pomegranate seeds. If she wasn't forced to eat in Tartarus, then she damn well wasn't going to.

She lifted up on her elbows to find Cerberus sitting in his chair, watching her.

She stilled before pulling the covers up to her chest and sitting up.

"You're back," she said a little too quickly. This was the second time she'd fallen asleep in the strange man's room and woken to find him watching her.

After she'd made her oath to Styx the day before, Cerberus had brought her back to the gatehouse before promptly leaving. And when he hadn't returned, the hours had melded together, and Cyane had succumbed to exhaustion. She hadn't wanted to sleep here again, but her choice in the matter had been taken away.

Something in Cerberus changed yesterday. Part of her still knew he was the same horrific creature that now plagued her dreams, but she'd ceased to see him as such.

I think I confuse him.

He confuses me.

"Today is the Day of Gifts. You're to meet with Hades," he said, scattering her thoughts.

Cyane jumped out of the bed and pulled one of the blankets atop it with her. "Okay." What more was she supposed to say to that? "You're still watching me. How long have you been sitting there?"

"Since you fell asleep."

Her face scrunched up. "I made the vow."

"You toss and turn when you sleep."

"And you don't?"

"I don't sleep."

"You have a bed."

"It's for you."

Her heart skipped a beat. She narrowed her eyes and drew her blanket tighter around her. Cerberus lifted his elbows off his knees and crossed one leg over the other, leaning back in his chair. It was such a human thing to do... *But humans slept.*

"It's not for me if it was already here," she said.

"It wasn't. You fell asleep on my chair on the terrace over Styx the first day. I put it there so you may sleep as the others do."

"In beds?"

"Yes."

She didn't remember whether she saw a bed or not when Cerberus first brought her here. But that seemed no stranger than anything else that had happened. She recalled the terrible headache, and how she'd first been transfixed by the art on his walls and then the overlook. It was possible. It hurt to recall the memories, and she guessed it was her mind protecting itself by denying that any of this was real.

"Okay," she said. Truthfully, what other response could she have? Maybe she could *okay* her way out of everything else. "Wait, I'm meeting Hades?" She questioned if she could *okay* her way through a meeting with the Lord of the Dead.

"Yes."

She tried not to let panic overcome her.

She was going to meet Hades. The god.

The same Hades who supposedly orchestrated her fall. The very being she should be demanding to meet so that she could go home.

But who in all the worlds, realms, or other such places that might yet exist, would *willingly* go before the devil?

Not fucking Cyane.

The thought alone alarmed her, even if the notion of 'devil' was skewed in her head.

Hades hadn't been a blue man with fire for hair like he'd been depicted in the Disney movie. Nor was he the devil from her religious studies, not a pitchfork was in sight. No, from what she glimpsed of the God of Death he was entirely different.

Black, curled hair fell down over his ears, tumbling wisps of shadow that danced around his body, making him appear as a mirage. The life in the room, for as much as it could be described that way, appeared muted, as if the raw power Hades exuded crushed everything around him into subservience. The air itself seemed to bend the knee. A dark smirk painted his lips as he lazily scanned the crowd, perched like a tiger surveying his domain. A note of fear coursed through her as if someone had thrummed a primal chord on her heartstrings. Dark eyes found her and paused before resuming their lazy perusal.

Cyane's mouth fell open.

Cerberus glanced around the room as if he had realized something, completely unaware of her growing panic. "What other things do mortals need?"

Cyane pursed her lips to blurt out *Space! Being as far away from the God of Death as possible!* But instead, she remained quiet, shaking the image of Hades from her head.

Cerberus spent more time with Hades than anyone else, even Persephone if the myths were to be believed.

He's not all bad.

He was disparity incarnate, which made it hard for her to pin down an opinion on him. Grave and intense, but calm and passive, frightening and strong but level-headed and controlled. He emanated boundless power.

In the short time they'd spent together, he hadn't molested her, hadn't offered her drugs, hadn't leered or mocked her. He hadn't threatened her just because she was a woman (at least maliciously) nor tried to bribe her. He'd been the exact opposite of the majority of men she'd encountered.

But how could such a man serve the evilest god in existence?

Despite her confusion, there was one truth she could illicit; she felt a little less crazy around him.

God, she really wanted to see what Cerberus looked like under his helmet.

"We need food and water," she said, a little too shrilly. "But I'm not hungry or thirsty, I assume it's this place."

Cerberus nodded.

Okay.

"We need clothes and toiletries, and light, real light. There's so little light here. Water for bathing and drinking, oh and probably freedom. Maybe a pistol? A six-pack of Coors Light?" Her nostrils flared. "You know, the basics?"

"Is that all?"

"Yeah, that's all. Freedom, shelter, sustenance, space, se—" Nope she wasn't going there.

"Don't move," he said, standing up.

"Why?"

The room went dark.

The flurry of her heart turned into a full-blown pound. This wasn't the type of darkness one normally encountered, this was the absolute absence of light itself. It was heavy. So heavy she bowed under its weight.

Then someone grabbed her arm, steadying her, and she nearly screamed. The light returned. Still muted, but it was back. Cerberus let go of her and stepped away, and a gasp escaped her lips.

The rocky cave-like room had been replaced with sleek obsidian walls, obsidian furniture, and dangerous luxury. There was a table laden with fruits, a large tub with steaming water, mirrors that hung on the wall, and large cushions scattered along the ground. One of Cerberus's hounds came out from the shadows, yawned, and settled on top of one of the cushions, while another loudly drank the bathwater.

All of it looked like it'd been pulled straight from the darkness itself. All except the golden light streaming from the dozen candles placed about.

The paintings along the walls that made her head hurt, the bed, the chair, and the large terrace were all that remained from before.

Cyane wandered the space, amazed, touching the surfaces as if they'd fade away without her contact. "Is this all for me?"

"Is it enough?"

"I…" She turned to face him. His burning eyes had never left her. His attention was doing things to her, worryingly things. She curled her fingers into the blanket still around her shoulders. "I've never had a room before."

"Never?"

Cyane licked her lips. "We shared rooms at Claudette's, the place where I grew up, and once I'd been placed into foster care, I shared a room with another foster kid in the same house I was in." College had been dorms, and now she was here. She shook her head. "But this isn't really mine, is it? It's yours?"

"I spend most of my time here watching the realm below. The vantage point is opportune."

"All alone?"

"I have my companions." Right then, hundreds of black dogs peered in from around the shadowed edges of the room before pulling back and disappearing.

Cyane's eyes widened. Where had all those dogs come from? How— She shook her head. She'd seen and experienced so many things she couldn't explain already, she should know not to question them by now.

"Who is Claudette?" Cerberus asked, curiously.

Cyane turned her face back to him. "A woman who ran a religious school for orphaned girls."

"Why were you there?"

She suddenly wished she hadn't said anything. What could she say really to that? "I don't know," she whispered honestly. "I wish I knew."

Silence fell between them, and she shuffled back and forth on her feet as Cerberus continued to stare at her. She hated talking about her life.

Cerberus knew who his parents were, much of the world had at least read about his myth once. He could scream his ancestry to the skies and be grounded by the knowledge he had.

Cyane didn't have that. She had no family. She could die

today and no one would attend her funeral. She'd had friends, but they'd all come and gone, as temporary as a breeze. Nobody had latched to her like family.

Sometimes, she imagined she was a puddle lying on uneven asphalt, and once the sun came out, she'd evaporate. There were no ponds, streams, lakes, or oceans to protect her from the world, to fall into and become apart of. No, she was alone.

She glanced at the lone chair.

"Thank you," she said eventually. "For the gift."

It wasn't actually hers. It wasn't actually like she needed nor wanted it. At least that's what she told herself. The room she wished for was always in a home in her head, a real home. This place wasn't home.

She hoped she wouldn't be here long enough to call it hers.

Ours. She blushed.

"You're welcome," he said.

He strode to her, stopping short of touching her. Cyane's instinct told her to back away, to put space between them, but she stood her ground. This was different, he wasn't coming at her with ferocity. Instead, he towered over her. She strained her neck to look up at him.

The only noise in the room was her thundering heart. *Please don't hear it.*

"You don't need to watch me anymore," she said a little breathlessly. "I won't run."

Cerberus tilted his head and reached up between them. His fingers caught a tangled strand of her hair. The light tug was enough to make her skin prickle with goosebumps.

"You swore an oath yesterday, bound yourself in the greatest way. Why?"

"It's not hard to swear an oath if it's true."

"Would you have done it if I hadn't asked?"

Her brow furrowed. "I'm not sure."

"Kneel for me."

The order came as a surprise. "What?" she asked.

He released her hair. "Kneel."

"W-why?"

"Because I ask for it."

Cyane fumbled, nearly tripping on the blanket when she realized what he was asking of her. This wasn't about proving to him that she wasn't there under false pretext, that she was innocent in any transgressions she might have made —her soul was on the line, was it not? No, this was something else.

But to kneel before him, after all that had happened, after what she was up against?

"Kneel," he ordered again.

The demand settled and took root inside her. It sprouted and grew, overtaking any fight she might have had.

It felt right.

So right that she wanted to scream and cry for all the women and men who'd fought against this. Those who fought for power themselves, so they could make the choice to subjugate or not.

Cyane unclenched her fingers and let the blanket go. It fell to her feet where it vanished into the floor.

This was about Cerberus and her. No one else. If only she could see his face...

She let her arms drop as she lowered to the ground slowly, her gaze following the sharp outlines of his armor. She settled on her knees. She bowed her head.

The floor was hard, and the wrinkled chiton dress bunched up around her. Cyane rested her hands on her knees and waited for direction. She stared fixedly.

Part of it reminded her of her childhood, of praying

against punishment, forced to kneel for hours. But also, this was nothing like that. Cerberus confused her, certainly, but—

Would he hurt her?

The room, the oath, the world itself fell away. The canines, the teeth, the bodies swimming below the water's surface, and even rationality she once held close...gone.

She'd never been powerful, never been anything more than small, and she'd never really cared. It wasn't power she was after—she never wanted it. She left that to the whims of others.

"Lord Hades will be pleased," he rasped, his voice so low she barely heard it.

Cyane's eyes snapped up.

He was gone.

And in his place was a white dress draped over a solitary chair.

Disturbed with herself, she licked her dry lips and stared at it.

THE GREATEST GIFT, STOLEN

CYANE MADE her way towards the ballroom much like the day before. She played with the edge of the note she tucked deep in the folds of her dress.

The white dress Cerberus gave her flowed around her legs like water, and like water, one could see her legs through it. It was extraordinarily sheer, showing off the shadows of her curves beneath. It was as lovely as it was uncomfortable to wear. In a public setting, at least.

Like a damned sacrifice...

But it was either wear what Cerberus had given her in hopes of pleasing Hades or continue to wear the wrinkled and ruined dress from before. In the end, she didn't have a choice. She wasn't about to go before Hades in rags.

On either side of her was one of Cerberus's hounds, herding her to their destination. They had appeared after she'd bathed and washed her hair. Their huge, black bodies were a hard contrast to the way she was dressed today. Saliva dripped from their maws, smoke rose with their breaths, and when they showed their teeth...serpentine tongues emerged.

Cyane shivered.

She thought of Cerberus and his hidden face. She'd knelt before him. Had shirked her pride and submitted. She realized with a little bit of horror, she would've done so much more if he had asked it of her.

I really am disturbed.

Like I'm some doll to play around with. It made her angry. It worried her.

Cyane sighed.

She'd secretly hoped Cerberus would return while she bathed...if only so she could gauge his reaction.

Heat blossomed on her cheeks. Curiosity threatened to drive her to tear off his helmet. She needed to see him. *My body responds to him.* She wasn't exactly in love with her reaction, but it happened nevertheless. The quivers, the annoying constrictions in her sex, the subtly growing need, and worse of all, the stupid flutters in her stomach.

If he tried to kiss her...

What would a kiss from a god be like? Would there be power behind it? Would it destroy her mind and make her a thrall to his desires?

Whether she was attracted to him or attracted to the fantasy of him she conjured, she was bothered either way.

She tried hard to push the thoughts from her mind. They didn't do her any good.

There's nothing about me that would make one such as him want me. Not with the beautiful, ethereal, godly women all around. Her heart fell a little.

I wouldn't survive anyway...

"There you are, sweet Cyane, I have searched the castle high and low for you!" Melinoe appeared out of the passageway's shadows in front of Cyane as if to solidify her thoughts on the subject.

One of the dogs at her side growled low.

The goddess pushed through the hounds and wrapped Cyane in a hug one-armed hug. "I missed my friend," Melinoe said.

Cyane went stiff. Melinoe was as beautiful as ever, making Cyane feel even lesser. Images of the goddess and Cerberus dancing rose in her mind like venom.

"You were looking for me?" Cyane asked, feeling played with.

Melinoe cupped Cyane's face and smiled. It felt like the goddess's fingers sank through her skin to stroke her brain. "I would always look for my friends. After my sweet Cerberus went after you with his sword, I thought the worst."

We're not friends! Cyane forced a smile to her lips. There was something fundamentally wrong about Melinoe. Like oil and water forced to combine.

Which didn't make any sense, since the goddess had been nothing but kind to her.

Melinoe released Cyane's cheeks and peered down at her dress. The goddess's smile widened. "Beautiful. You are beautiful, for a mortal."

There it was.

"Thank you."

Melinoe, in a deep black dress that pulled from the shadows, grabbed Cyane's hand and led her forward. The hounds flanked them both now, although Cyane noticed the bristle of fur upon their backs.

"Wherever you have been, you are here now, and just in time. The procession of gifts is about to begin. If we don't hurry, we'll be last."

'You're to meet with Hades,' Cerberus's words came back to her.

"Melinoe," Cyane said, tugging back on the goddess's hand. "I don't understand what's happening or what to expect. I don't have a gift to give. I don't want to offend."

"Mortals have everything they can give. I'm sure you'll think of something. Hades is most generous to those who have little but offer him what they have. You've chosen a dress of a vestal virgin. My lord father will be pleased with the sight of you alone."

Cyane flinched, disgusted. But she couldn't dwell on it. Melinoe was already pulling her again down the candlelit corridor.

"When I go before my lord father as a maiden virgin, he always looks upon me for a moment," Melinoe continued.

"But you're not dressed as one now."

"I want him to view me as a woman."

Um... "Why?"

Melinoe peered back at her with a twinkle in her eye. "There are two paths for a goddess—to follow the virgin queens of Artemis and Athena, or to join the flesh worshippers of Aphrodite."

"And Hades?"

"I want him to look upon me for more than a moment."

Cyane's internal flinching took a turn for the worse. But before she could ask more of Melinoe, the corridor opened up to its grand obsidian star-shaped foyer that led to the ballroom—the sound of lutes and whispers filled her ears.

Melinoe laughed and giggled, pulling Cyane into the center of the room, unaware that everyone else had fled their presence. The goddess peeked into the ballroom and clapped her hands. "Cyane! Isn't he handsome?"

Don't mean Hades...

"Who?" she asked.

She never got her answer as Melinoe darted into the dimly lit ballroom towards the dais. Atop it sat Hades, and beside him stood Cerberus.

Shivering despite herself, maybe because of the dress or maybe because of Melinoe's incestuous ways, Cyane took in the two dark men. They were one and the same when they were close. Hades with his dark curling shoulder-length hair, his shadowed eyes, and pale skin stood out in his equally pitch-black attire.

She hadn't bothered to study Hades before, hadn't wanted to for fear of being drawn into his devastating thrall. Evil gods of legend were often depicted as uncannily beautiful in stories, and it wasn't fair. She didn't want to find the devil beautiful—or handsome.

Although she didn't want to lay her eyes on a large, slobbering, slack-jawed beast as well. Her nightmares were already full.

But… Cyane chewed on her lip—now that she was doomed to meet Hades, part of her seized on the idea that she could familiarize herself with his appearance.

Something nudged her side. Cerberus's hounds were still with her. She ran her fingers across the nearest one's back. Petting it calmed her nerves.

Unlike Hades, Cerberus was cold and watchful. Just as frightening but in an unattainable, detached way. Even his armor looked cold.

Melinoe stopped in front of Hades and bowed deeply before him. Neither he nor Cerberus looked at the goddess.

Cyane tried to glimpse Hades's face, but guests kept weaving in front of her, obscuring her view. Some of the guests had gifts in their hands while others did not. Some danced like the day before, while others feasted vigorously, noisily along the sides of the hall where food was laid out, their hands and mouths covered in slop.

She discovered that no one else was dressed like her.

She gripped her skirt and turned away from the ballroom.

The lutes, now accompanied by steady pounding drums,

grew louder in her ears. The beat of it settled hungrily in her gut, making her sex ache unwillingly. The dress Cerberus laid out for her hadn't come with underwear. And she sensed wetness between her legs build.

I'm not turned on, she fumed angrily. She didn't feel turned on, but the slick was there regardless, as if forced out of her for the celebration.

If it didn't stop, anyone would be able to see it.

Cyane's stomach sank further. A loud creaking noise filled her ears. She shifted warily as she glanced behind her to see two, impossibly large black doors closing on her.

Forced to make a choice, Cyane fell back into the ballroom with a whimper.

The doors shut with a final groan.

Trapped.

CERBERUS'S GAZE zeroed in on Cyane. That delicious thrill the mortal had sparked in him when she bowed before him had refused to diminish, offering him not even a desperately needed moment of reprieve. It plagued him even now.

The mortal obeys me like I'm a god. A godhood he had a right to claim but had never desired. It made him want more, and that was a dangerous desire to harbor in Hades's court.

The undying bowed before Hades and Cerberus. Cerberus felt nothing for their subservience like he had with Cyane's. They offered his lord gifts of blood, gifts of jewels, the finest clothes, the ripest fruit, and Cerberus found he wanted none of that.

But with Cyane...

"Father," Melinoe breathed longingly.

Hades waved his hand, and the goddess vanished with a frightened cry.

Snickers rose from the guests around them. Cerberus was barely aware of it all as he breathed in Cyane's wet scent through his hounds that stayed poised at her sides. She smelled of lilies and purity. The dress he'd chosen emphasized her newness, not only to this realm, but as a young human. She bloomed life.

Like Persephone...

His thoughts darkened. He noticed the eyes of all the males who gazed upon her feverishly. Cyane was a tasty lamb amongst them. The only thing that kept them away was her status as a guest and his hounds' diligence. He didn't like the undyings' eyes on her.

Few knew that he breathed down the necks of all the undying in the room, held them tight within his hundred jaws, and could rend them into oblivion.

The dress he'd chosen for Cyane was for Hades and Hades alone.

Or was it? A streak of tension gripped Cerberus.

"You've outdone yourself," Hades said, his lord leaned forward to rest his elbows on his knees. "The mortal reminds me of the first time I saw Persephone. So sweet; so easy to pluck and possess."

Cerberus nodded stiffly.

Hades rubbed his lips with his finger. "I look forward to her gift most of all."

Something dark and ominous filled him at his lord's words. It circulated through him like curdled blood and sharpened his thoughts. Cyane shrunk away from the centaur, Chiron, and sought Cerberus's gaze from across the room.

So sweet, so easy to pluck and possess.

Yes. Yes. That's what she was.

This is what it's like to be a god.

He realized he wanted her gift too. Whatever she

intended to give to Hades, he wanted it. Cerberus's mood darkened further. He wanted her gift for himself alone.

The mortal hugged herself and skirted around the men and women engaging her.

"Lord Hades, Ruler of the Underworld, I humbly offer you my life," a lesser Arae, naked from the waist up, said as she bowed.

"Great Dark King of Tartarus, I bring with me the endless blood waters of my husband, Acheron, for another millennium of servitude," Gorgyra tilted her head and said as she placed a ceramic pot at Hades's feet. Acheron's serpentine nymph smiled and slipped away.

One after the other, those who celebrated with Lord Hades continued to offer him precious, pricey items and endowments. Menoetes offered him the best cattle stolen from above. Hermes offered a burned-out bolt from Zeus's own arsenal. Even Zeus himself had a gift sent from above of godly garments crafted by Hepheastus. Time passed far too slowly for Cerberus.

At one point a rain of dead flowers fell from the ceiling to bury them, brought on by Demeter's pain.

Cyane caught them in her hands in wonderment. Cerberus couldn't tear his eyes away from her, at least not for long. She was unlike any of the other creatures that resided in this place. His eyes dipped to her body, and his jaw twitched. Why had he picked that dress out for her? Everyone could see her through it.

Hades swept the flowers away with a hearty laugh.

Hecate enchanted Hades's two-pronged bident with the power to command moonlight into his realm for a time. The lower undying offered up more of the same—enchanted jewels, stolen art from above, a rare relic of power—and on occasion, someone would offend Hades with their gift and vanish with a flick of his lord's wrist.

Cerberus watched and detested them all. They came one-by-one to appease his lord with everything but loyalty. Muses and their ballads and poems, Furies and their prophecies and dreams; it made his ears ache. When Cerberus was nothing more than a monster, he never had to attend these festivities, he'd been free to do his job like Charon. But times had changed, and so had Hades's requirements of Cerberus.

This gift of manhood was not something he could turn his back on. His brothers, Chimera and Hydra, had perished like all the ancient beasts of old.

Cerberus was the only one left.

The only one except for his father, Typhon, who was imprisoned far below.

The last of the supplicants approached to offer their gifts, but Cyane hadn't stepped forward. He instructed one of his canines to prod her into action.

The music swelled, and those who had survived Hades's displeasure had become drunk on nectar and ambrosia and were enjoying the festivities freely. Cyane, who had been hidden behind the white curtains, shakily stepped forward.

Cerberus's hands tensed.

She held a cup in her hand, one he hadn't realized she'd picked up, and he watched her polish it off and set it on a table. His eyes narrowed, wondering what a gods drink would do to her.

She slowly made her way toward the dais, dodging drunken nymphs and daemons, flitting along like a lost maiden. Her chestnut hair fell in wavy curls down her back and arms, nearly bleeding into her white dress. Cerberus's jaw twitched, and he had stepped forward when another guest rammed into her but stopped when Cyane caught herself, straightened with an inhalation that captivated him and weaved forward.

Tipsy or not, she made it to her destination.

Cyane stopped a short distance away and looked straight at Cerberus, making his body grow rigid with want. Her eyes were dewy and lightly glazed. Her hands gripped the sides of her dress, and her mouth opened like she wanted to say something, but then she glanced at Hades before looking back at Cerberus in question.

She's asking me permission to come forward. Cerberus nodded stiffly. The thrill of her obeying him flushed through him, tightening his loins in a shocking, damning way. They pressed against his trousers painfully.

Damned! He didn't understand it. Not even goddesses and naked, wanton nymphs made him react like this.

She shifted on her feet. Her tipsy courage urged him to take advantage, to assert his control over the situation and send her away, but it also made him wary, curious. He could smell her fear, her slick. When she appeared as though she might run, Cerberus left his place by Hades and went to her.

If she ran, he'd have no choice but to chase her. He didn't know what he would do if that happened. Though something hard and shallowly buried inside him was increasingly delighted by the idea.

"Cerberus," she breathed when he approached, "I'm scared."

"You are a guest, there is no reason to be scared." He fisted his hands tighter to keep himself from reaching for her. "I won't let anything happen to you."

"And the others that vanished? Where did they go?"

"Wherever Hades decided they needed to be. Come." He tilted his head towards the dais. The sooner this day was done, the sooner he could take her back to the gatehouse and away from Hades, away from everyone else's eyes.

She stayed rooted in place. "My gift is bad compared…"

His curiosity piqued.

Cyane nervously tugged her hair. "Can you unsheath your sword?"

He eyed her, intrigued by her request. Did she want to share a gift with him to give to Hades? Cerberus's undying servitude and loyalty was his lord's, but Cerberus hadn't thought to share a gift. He tugged out his blade and held it firm between them.

Cyane's eyes flickered up and down its length, and pride filled him. But then she lifted a lock of her hair and pressed it taut against his weapon, slicing it off with ease. She held one curled strand while several wisps fell to the floor.

She clutched the lock of hair to her chest. "I'm ready."

Her gift.

He sheathed his weapon. The thrill darkened. *She doesn't plan to share her gift with me.*

He nodded, annoyed, and escorted her to Hades. Cerberus took his place at his lord's side when Cyane bowed before the God of the Dead.

Something else filled Cerberus, something he didn't like. He wanted to take his sword back out and slide it through Hades's back, push his lord's bloody corpse aside, and take his place.

"God Hades," she said, head still lowered. "My name is Cyane. I'm honored to be in your presence."

Hades leaned forward eagerly.

Cyane took in a deep breath before she continued. "I do not wish to dishonor you, but I have little to offer. Please take this lock of my hair, a piece of me, a part of my identity." She held out her open hand and meekly peered up at his lord. The curled, silken length of hair lay in the center of her palm.

Hades reached forward and took the gift with a smile. "Beautiful. I gladly accept your tribute, mortal Cyane, but your presence here is the greatest gift of all. Please stand."

"I don't understand?"

Hades didn't answer, instead, he played with her hair between his fingers, rapt in his one-sided game. Cerberus scowled furiously as Hades wrapped Cyane's hair around his middle finger, where it tied itself into a band.

Cerberus's hands twitched at his sides. Had he enjoyed Cyane's hair like that? He'd never taken off his gloves when he'd touched her, and although his fingertips were bare of material, he'd only felt her at their tips. His chest tightened for the piece of her he'd failed to take for himself.

Red threatened to cloud his vision.

Hades stood and approached the edge of the dais.

Cyane shifted uneasily on her feet.

Hades's voice boomed, "The Day of Gifts is coming to an end, let it be known that my queen and I are pleased with your tributes. This year, unlike so many years before, will mark a change that I have longed for—longed for hungrily as I await Persephone to descend and come to me freely. This year, unlike the countless that preceded it, I will receive the gift that I have always wanted. And this year, I will give a gift in return."

Hades looked directly at Cyane, and his smile turned terrible.

Cerberus stepped forward as the crowd roared. He reached out to Cyane and jerked her to his side.

"What's happening?" she asked.

He shook his head.

Hades's voice assaulted the air. "Let the Day of Battles commence!"

The large doors to the ballroom slowly creaked open. Everyone turned at once to watch them. The hush that had settled over the room was broken by giggles, whispers, and a few misplaced claps as excitement built for the surprise.

Cerberus's scowl deepened as he scanned the ballroom.

The Day of Battles always began after a pause. There'd be

a lining-up of fighters, and then they were chosen and pitted against each other in tests of strength. Those who did best rose in the hierarchy of Tartarus, while those who did poorly were humiliated until they could redeem themselves the following year.

But this year was nothing like those that had taken place before.

A giant head of a wooden horse appeared between the doors, monstrous and sharply angled. Smoke billowed from its nostrils as it pushed through the widening crack and rolled into the room.

Cyane pressed against him as the beast's head slowly rolled from side to side, considering all the guests in apt hunger. The rest of it remained solid and still.

When the horse finished passing through the doorway, it stopped at the center of the obsidian dancefloor. The doors shut with a resounding bang. The horse continued to creakily take in the partygoers that gathered around it and touched its enormous hooves with glee and curiosity.

"The Battle of Troy?" Cyane murmured with awe.

Hades turned around. "Very good, Cyane. The Trojan horse burned up in flames long ago, and like all dead things whether they were alive or not, ended up here in my realm. And like all dead things, it can be revived." Hades sat back down on his throne; his smile was gone. He played with the ring of hair around his finger. Cerberus gritted his teeth.

The hounds gathered around them from the shadows, surrounding the dais.

"I don't want to be here anymore," Cyane whispered beside him. "Please."

Cerberus glanced down at her.

"This is not for you, mortal, this is for them," Hade said, his voice carrying across the ballroom, bringing with it snickers and clapping. The clapping grew louder, drinks were spilled, and Cerberus unsheathed his weapon for the second time that hour.

The horse reared up on its hind legs and slammed its front legs down on the Arae before it. The claps transformed into screams as blood splattered across the floor. It thrust its head down, snatched up several daemons in its jaws, and crunched them between its blunt, wooden teeth.

Cyane shrieked, and Cerberus gripped her arm to keep her from fleeing.

Hades was the only one laughing now as everyone ran for the walls, clawing at them to get out.

"Why?" Cerberus stepped forward.

The horse killed the Arae behind him.

"We have to get rid of the old to make room for the new," Hades said.

"The gods will look upon this unfavorably," Cerberus swore, feeling Cyane shake against him.

"The gods? They're spared such deceit. Take in the scene, Cerberus. The horse is not bothering the gods in attendance. This is a place of death, of darkness. We've had too much life here that is not of my own making for far too long. How can we bring in new life when the house is full of meaningless swine?"

"Is that your plan? To bring in new life? Is that why Cyane is here?" Cerberus wrapped a protective arm around her as she clung to him.

"Hmmm…" Hades lifted his hand and eyed the ring made of Cyane's hair. "So many questions, and in front of the court." Hades's gaze shot to Cerberus's as the pounding of the horse's hooves beat down like a drum.

The crunch of bones and the snap of its jaw filled Cerberus's ears. The screams ebbed as the death count rose.

"I did not think you had the courage to confront me," Hades said. "Should I demand you to renew your tribute, old friend of mine? Aren't you hungry? I'm surprised you're not itching to join the Trojan horse in its feast."

Cerberus snarled. A part of him did want to join in. The part of him that Hades himself had buried deep under Cerberus's man suit. Copper scented blood filled his nose, making his mouth water, his teeth ache. If he opened his jaw wide enough, he could hear the screams of all the souls he'd devoured still trapped deep within.

His hounds, all around, salivated from the shadows, watching the slaughter with their own yearning.

Hades's twisted smile returned to his lips. "You do want to join it. Go ahead. This gift is as much for you as it is for me. You can leave the mortal with me. I promise she won't be hurt. It's been a long time since you've had a real meal, hasn't it?"

Cerberus clenched his hands, scanning the bloody ballroom as his hounds crept forward eagerly. Cyane cried silently against him.

"Unless she's stopping you? Interesting." Hades took in the mortal clutched rigidly against Cerberus. "Your choice—take her away or enjoy the battle. I'll enjoy it either way."

"This isn't a battle, it's a massacre."

Hades turned away. "Perhaps."

Cerberus peered down at Cyane, hunger hollowing out his gut. He tried to cup her cheek, to lift her face to his, but she wouldn't let him, hiding deeper into him. His gloved palm came away slightly damp, and his eyes narrowed upon it.

Her tears had gathered upon his armor.

He hungered for more than souls. Her tears looked delicious. The thrilling feeling returned to claw away at his insides, making him shudder.

I am *hungry.*

Starving.

He made his choice.

Cerberus pulled Cyane tight against his body and gathered the darkness around them. He slipped her away to safety just as his hounds rushed forward to join the giant, rabid horse.

Hades's laughter followed.

POWER

Cerberus held Cyane. She wavered on her feet, and he wasn't certain if it had to do with the nectar she'd drunk or being privy to Hades's evil nature.

Cerberus had taken her back to the gatehouse tower a short while ago, but she wouldn't move away from him, gripping what she could of his armor with hands that turned increasingly white. She silently cried and shook. The longer she continued to do so, the more he realized he had no idea what to do.

She wouldn't unbury her face from his chest, nor move away, and so he remained where he was and let her take what she needed from him.

He understood sadness and confusion. He even understood fear. He'd seen and even felt such things himself now and again over his long life, but comfort? Comfort was foreign to him. Comfort was something he'd only seen between his lord Hades and Queen Persephone and only on the rarest occasions.

Queen Persephone had cried often at the beginning of her reign. Though, eventually, her grief had turned to love.

Cyane's grip loosened upon him, and he lowered his arm.

Slowly, she removed herself from his side. He remained silent as he watched her reassure herself of her surroundings.

Part of him wanted to grip her in his hands again, to pull her back upon him, and feel her mortal heat seep into his armor. Another part wanted to force her back to her knees.

Such a strange thing...

She wiped her cheeks with the backs of her hands and looked back at him.

Her brown eyes were even more glazed then before. Tears were a beautiful adornment to her soft features.

She flinched when he reached up to touch her hair with the tips of his fingers.

"I don't want to die," she said, shuddering.

Sudden anger flashed through him at Hades's intentions. Just because he hadn't intended to kill Cyane at this time didn't mean Hades wasn't going to eventually. Cerberus never cared for the lives or souls of mortals beyond his scope of making sure they did not linger in Styx or try to return above. The gods and titans of Olympus adored and abhorred mortals equally, as they had often shaped the world as it was today.

Atlas kept the world afloat for them, holding a burden Cerberus could not fathom. Prometheus had defied Zeus to give them fire and was still punished for it.

Cerberus pinched Cyane's lustrous hair.

"I would like a gift from you," he rasped, still bristling at the thought of her death. Meanwhile, his hounds ate the corpses of the undying as they spoke.

CYANE DREW BACK. Cerberus's fingers pulled at her hair. They didn't let go.

Her eyes widened. "A gift?"

He's completely unfazed by the horrible bloodbath.

She could still hear the screams, could still smell the blood.

Her mind whirled around Hades's words… *This is not for you, mortal, this is for them.*

The only thing that had stopped her from having a nervous breakdown was Cerberus. He'd blocked it all. He continued to block it all. Every time she was near him, the world righted itself, just a little bit.

He had saved her again.

She was beginning to think he would always save her. A terrible, painfully buried part of her desperately wanted that to be true. But also didn't want it to be, because feared this growing dependence. It made her feel weak and disoriented.

She could blame the parents that had given her up, the ones she desperately wanted to meet, to confront—but that was weak, too.

Was it weak to allow someone control for a while? Even if it was her choice? Her tears threatened to return with her confusion.

She'd heard the exchange between Cerberus and Hades, even through the horrible chaos of noise happening around her. It reminded her that Cerberus wasn't a man, or not only a man, but an indescribable creature as well. Although it had been days since she'd been forced to glimpse his true form, it still lingered in the back of her mind, reminding her who she was willing to give up her control to.

Cerberus pulled and rubbed at the lock of her hair, his focus solely on the strands he held. "Yes," he said, low and grave. Like the request haunted him.

She knew what he wanted.

Her belly heated. She shifted back and forth on her feet as that heat pulled down between her legs, making her sex knot.

With a shiver, Cyane reached up and ran her fingers through her hair, pulling the strands from his grasp. The bed was right there... Would she survive taking a man like him into her?

This place was beyond her world, and strangely, death didn't feel as terrible here. Even though she'd seen those in the ballroom killed, had they really died?

She wrenched her eyes shut. *What is wrong with me?* Dozens of beings had just been slaughtered. She was in over her head, and she was just assuming that Cerberus was even interested in her?

But if he wanted a gift from her, she would gladly give it. Thanking him was the least she could do. "Unsheath your sword," she said softly.

He took out his weapon and held it vertically between them.

She pulled the strands of hair he'd been playing with taut, much like she'd done earlier, and lifted it to the blade. His eyes sparked a deep red as she pressed her hair against the edge. Cyane held the cut locks between her own fingers as he lowered and sheathed his blade.

She handed it to him and held her breath, wondering why he wanted something from her to begin with and what he planned to do with it now. He turned and went to the table.

She followed him to see what he was doing.

Cerberus laid her hair upon the table's surface and made short work of taking off his gloves. Long, white fingers, the same pale skin that could be seen elsewhere, were revealed. His hands were clear of marks and scars, almost porcelain in appearance despite the strength that seemed to emanate from them.

There was nothing horrifying nor monstrous about them. *Just hands. They were just hands.*

I want to see more! A selfish part of her almost snatched

her hair back, to hold it hostage until she got her way. But he picked up the strands before she could and wove them around his thumb, much like how Hades had done earlier. Only this time, it didn't fill her stomach with dread.

It made her...happy.

He began to draw his gloves back on.

"Stop, please." Cyane reached up and grabbed his fingers. They were icy cold. She gripped them tighter.

Cerberus's body went rigid before her eyes. His fingers twitched in her grip.

He slowly turned back to her.

"Why do you hide?" she asked before she lost the courage.

He gripped her hand back. "Cyane..."

She canted her head and waited for him to say more, but instead, he brought his other hand up to cup hers between them. His gaze moved from her face to look at their joined hands.

His skin grew warmer, as if her touch alone could bring the dead back to life. His thumb moved, tracing circles over her palm, sparking a tickling shiver deep inside. Then his thumbs trailed upward to do the same with her wrists.

A soft sound escaped her lips. She didn't mean for it to happen, she'd barely known what she was up against, but Cerberus's touch was like rich chocolate or a rollercoaster ride. *That made no sense*. His thumbs continued to move in circles, oh so lightly, over the sensitive veins of her wrist and doing terrible things to her insides.

"I hunger, Cyane," he said, his voice even lower and darker than before. He reached down and gripped her other hand, bringing it between them. "I don't know why you make me so hungry."

Her half-mast eyelids flared at his words. His thumbs slowly moved up the insides of her forearms, heading straight for the weak, sensitive spot of her inner elbow.

Before he reached that glorious ticklish spot, he clasped his fingers around her arms, raised them up, and held them away from her body.

"Let me touch you," he demanded. "I've never had flesh as warm as yours, that turns pink like a rose with a single touch. Are all mortals so warm?"

He watched her, his eyes blazing dangerously and…familiar?

Why were they familiar?

She blushed. "Will you hurt me?"

"I don't know."

His fingers started up their circles again, making her skin prickle with goosebumps. Cyane swallowed.

Give in. Give in and fall to your knees. Give in and worship him like the god he is. What was wrong with her?

"Then, I…don't know."

His eyes darkened.

His petting resumed, this time within the crux of her elbows—as if he wouldn't take no for an answer—and her mind blanked. Her eyelids lowered, her heartbeat hastened. His hands didn't stay there long, making her shudder, lulling her to give in to the caress he bestowed upon her.

She'd never been touched like this before. His long fingers and wide palms slid up her arms and over her shoulders, clasping her under the flimsy material of her dress.

"Now?" he asked.

Cyane shook her head weakly, a little dizzy, a little tired, and moved forward to rest her brow on his chest.

He raised his hands to cup her neck, his thumbs back in action, slipping softly over her throat, fingers brushing the sides of her neck. She swallowed, testing the pressure he exerted. His grip tightened…a little. This was wrong.

"Worship me, Cyane." His voice burning a hole through her pleasure before becoming apart of it, stirring her. Even if this was cruelty on his part, as he played with her excitement filled her anyway.

"Yes." It came out breathy and weak.

His hands moved down her neck, his fingers slipped back under the sleeves of her dress. He pushed the sleeves off her shoulders, and the dress fell to a soft pool at her feet.

His hands returned to her throat. Cerberus didn't push her back to indulge in her nudity, and because of that, she didn't feel the need to cover herself. His fingers fanned out to thread through her hair, eventually moving away from her neck entirely to comb her hair.

Another sound escaped her. He did it again, and when she held in the feel of pleasure, he seemed bothered by it. It didn't last. He pulled his hands from her hair and cupped her cheeks, rubbed her lips, even her teeth, with his thumbs. Then he went on to pet the shells of her ears, her hairline.

Heat built up inside her, making her core knot. Cerberus asked her to worship him, and yet she was the one being worshiped.

Or maybe he really is playing with me.

But he studied everywhere he touched as if each caress was new to him.

Her chest tightened.

He wasn't playing. Awe filled her. Was he...a virgin? She almost couldn't believe it. The thought alone was unbelievable. But...was he?

She stepped back and watched his reaction as his eyes dipped to her body. They moved upon her, and she fought the urge to shield her breasts, her sex, to turn away and hide.

She'd barely been good enough for a quick tumble with her one of the other foster kids, who'd snuck into her bed one night when their foster parents were drunk and asleep. How would she fare with a powerful deity?

She held her hands at her sides, worked to keep her spine straight and confident, fighting the urge to shy away.

She breathed in and focused on his eyes, which moved slowly over her several times. His bare hand came up and grabbed the hilt of his sword, but other than that, there was no reaction from him.

Cyane chewed on her tongue, her heartbeat fluttering, steadily increasing.

"This only makes it worse," he said.

She flinched, snapping her arms over her breasts. "I'm sorry. I thought when you slipped my dress off..."

"That I wanted to see you?"

Oh god. "Yes." Like how much she wanted to see *him.*

"I would rather feel you, Cyane. I see you, always."

Oh fuck. Blasted tears rushed to her eyes, and she swiped them away quickly. He pulled her into his arms before she could turn away, before she could grab her dress and hide. He brushed her tears from where they gathered.

Realization struck her.

After everything she'd wanted before, despite everything she'd seen, she'd submit, drop to her knees, and worship him, always.

Cerberus never had to ask her. Never again.

What else was there for one to do when one wanted a god?

And that god wanted her as well.

THE DAY OF BATTLES

Cyane moaned. His hands never stopped roaming her body. They started with her face again, catching her damning tears before they ran back through her hair, drifted over her neck, and whispered once more down her arms.

A horrible, wet ache grew between her legs. She wasn't a saint, nor a vestal virgin, but as Cerberus stroked her body, it felt like he was stroking her sex, penetrating her to the core and making her as hungry as he claimed to be.

Lust had been stolen from her by inept sexual experiences, and she had begun to question if she could sincerely desire. But now she burned with it.

She wanted him inside her, pounding and erratic, needed the power he had focused solely on her.

His hands slipped down and cupped her breasts. His fingers circled and toyed with her nipples. She moved as close to his body as she could without interrupting the touch of his hands on her.

He squeezed her breasts gently. "Do all female mortals have such heavy breasts?"

"No."

"Only fertility goddesses are endowed as such. They do not come to Tartarus. You have been given a gift."

Cyane reached up and gripped his arms as his squeezing increased.

She was suddenly aware of how her nudity faced his fully armored body. It emphasized his power over her. She slid her hands up to his neck, under the metal edge of his helmet, and licked her lips. "Take this off. Let me see you," she said.

"If I'm called away to protect the gates, what will protect my neck?"

"You could put it back on?"

"You may not like what I look like, Cyane."

"I don't think there is any face that would frighten me away from you. I've seen..." She swallowed. Teeth. Drool. Serpents and snouts. "Let me see more?"

He stared at her for a short while, and she thought he was going to deny her this request. The yearning in her grew at the thought of never seeing him without his armor.

Cerberus released his hold on her. Cyane inhaled and dropped her arms from his neck to curl them around her chest.

She was going to see him.

She was finally going to see what he was... The three-headed hound? The ancient nightmarish monster?

A simple man?

Not a skeleton. His hands and the peek of skin around his eyes and brow proved that thought false.

He bowed his head, gripped the sides of his helmet, and pulled it off. Thick, black, slightly curled hair poured out first, making her reach out to touch it... The locks fell away as he tucked his helmet under his arm and brushed his fingers through the strands to reveal his face.

Her lips parted, her eyes widened, and her chest constricted. She stepped back, horrified.

The memory of the horrendous slaughter from earlier, the unrepentant dealing of death, rushed back to her. How could she forget it so soon?

"Hades," she whispered, afraid.

CYANE BACKED AWAY FROM CERBERUS, frantically reaching for her dress. Anger cracked his heart. Was he so hideous that regret filled her the moment he revealed himself? He'd never taken his helmet off for anyone, not since Hades had given him a man's body.

No one had ever asked him to, nor would he have even if they had. He knew he was made in Hades's image, but his lord was known for his appeal.

"Hades?" he said. "I'm not Hades. Liar," he fumed, watching her tug back on the dress. The one he'd procured for her.

He strode forward and gripped the dress, tearing it from her body. It vanished back into the darkness.

One last piece fluttered to the floor to settle at his feet. Whatever it was, it didn't disappear with Cyane's dress.

She shrieked. The sound reminded him of the thousands of souls he'd devoured. It was their final cry before they descended into the abyss of his belly.

His eyes snapped back to her, and he grabbed her before she could flee. "Look at me," he ordered.

Cyane struggled but did as he dictated. He smelled her fear. "Please—Don't. I don't want this, not with you!"

Cerberus glared at her. "Not with Hades or Cerberus? You said there is no face that exists that could frighten you away from me, but that's not true? Is it?" His hounds emerged from the shadows to bare their teeth and watch.

They brought the soft scent of blood, fresh from the ballroom.

She flinched.

"Perhaps we should return to the shores of Styx and find out what other lies so easily escape you."

"Why?"

"Why? *Why?*" He narrowed his eyes and furrowed his brow. "I should be asking you that, Cyane. Gifts given to you go over your head."

"Why do you look like Hades? Are you him?"

She tried to pull away, but he wouldn't let her. He fanned his fingers out so he could hold her hair between them. The heat of her panic made him realize how cold he truly was, how desperately he needed her warmth.

"Is that why you reek of fear?" he asked.

"Are you him? Is this a trick?"

His annoyance grew. "No." He hissed. "I'm not him. No being, no matter how powerful, would pretend to be a lord of one of the three realms. Hubris is the wellspring of war."

Cyane grabbed his wrists. "You're not him."

"I'm not."

"Then why do you look like him! Is that why you hide yourself—so he and you can change places?" Her words spilled out. "How will I ever know you're you? I don't under-stand, make me understand."

Cerberus let her go, and she quickly pulled a blanket from the bed and covered herself. The warmth he craved, denied in one simple action.

"I look like him because he remade me in his image. If you want to know why, you'll have to ask him yourself. *I* do not question gifts from my lord."

"H-he killed all those guests, they screamed for help, they begged, they clawed the walls. The devil I know above is the liar, and he lied to his guests," she whispered. "Hades feels like the devil. If I spoke too soon, pulled away too fast, it was because I trusted the man I thought I knew, not…"

"What am I to you now?"

Cyane shook her head.

His mood darkened, and he lifted his helmet to put back on.

"Wait! Please don't." She took a step forward and took his helmet from his hands. He watched as she placed it on the table beside his gloves. "I don't want your face to be hidden from me anymore."

Confusion bled into his anger. The hunger in his gut grew with each passing second. Her nakedness, so clearly visible under the blanket, her vulnerability, even her fear, did not deter this feeling. It made it worse. "You can't have it both ways."

Her shoulders shook, and she turned to face him, snapping her eyes to his face then away just as quickly. She looked down at his hand where her ring of hair wrapped around his thumb.

"That"—she pointed at his thumb—"will be how I'll tell you apart." Cyane picked up one of his gloves and handed it to him. "Hide it. So only you and I know where you wear my gift."

Cerberus stilled, his confusion only building. He took his glove from her hand and pulled it back on anyway.

"If you really aren't Hades, then you'll show me your hand whenever we meet," she said.

"I'm not a liar."

"But Hades might be?"

He should hate her for asking him to keep something from his lord, for forcing Cerberus to keep a secret from the one he was most loyal to. But the smell of her trepidation ebbed, and he was willing to do what he must. "You do not realize the gravity of the things you ask of me."

Cyane curled her arms back over her chest, her eyes downcast, and nodded.

Despite her lie, and considering her reaction only reminded him that mortals were known for their deviousness...the ring was the first tribute he'd ever received.

The feel of her hair pressed tightly between his glove and his skin was *right*. It was precious to him now.

He began to understand the obsession that many of the gods had for the lower beings that dwelled on their world. Humans were strange creatures. They dictated so much of what the realms did, and in return, they forgot about the gods that served them...gods who only wanted to be served in return.

The revelation compelled Cerberus to reach out and explore Cyane further, to lay her out before him and see if she was warm everywhere. To find her imperfections that so clearly told him she was not one of his kind—the very flaws that made her captivating.

But death, the Underworld, and Hades himself were not easy things for her kind to handle, and he watched as her gaze drifted from his exposed face. She couldn't keep her eyes on him for more than a moment. It frustrated him, and he worried he may harm her in resentment.

Cerberus frowned.

He ached, staring at her, unable to do anything but. Cyane's submissive posture rushed his veins with blood.

It would be so easy...

She had yet to lift her eyes back up from his feet, and the ache he endured gathered in his loins, testing him.

CYANE SHOOK UNWILLINGLY.

She'd forgotten that the same being that made her feel

safe was also a creature that took demands and requests with ease. His anger reminded her that she was alone in a place meant for the divine. Tension seized her. She searched for the courage to look back at Cerberus but feared his face and the confusion it wrought.

His eyes bore into her flesh, and she tightened her arms against herself. A bloom of warmth rose to her cheeks as the tension held. The intimidation. The unease. The pounding, waiting ache of her sex that still wanted to take his power inside her and ride it straight into hell.

I can't take it anymore. She met his gaze.

Cerberus's eyes glowed with fire. His lips twisted and parted. She inhaled sharply. This time, her eyes could linger on his face a moment longer.

"Eat," he ordered, waving his hand outward. The table where his helmet and other glove sat was now covered in a variety of fruit. "And get some sleep."

She glanced at the bed to find it even more luscious than before, with several of his hounds sitting atop it, watching her. Their eyes equally as bloody, as ruby red as him. They truly were his.

"You will not return to the ballroom until this new day is over," he said.

A final gift. "Thank you." Her voice came out a croak.

The tension grew again, and his gaze bore into her naked flesh, threatening to root her back to the spot. Cyane gritted her teeth, exhaustion flooding her being. She unrooted her feet, bypassed the table, and climbed into the bed, putting herself between the hounds. They settled around her as she slipped under the blanket and pulled it to her chin.

She peeked out from under the blankets to find Cerberus. He appeared as tense and uncomfortable as she was.

She wanted him to come to her, to finish what they'd started. In the dark, at least. His face made her stomach turn even if it was an ethereally handsome one. She didn't have the courage to beckon him, didn't even know if he wanted her the way she wanted him.

Warmth was all he spoke of… though she still could feel the phantom touch of his palms sensually exploring her chest.

When the room felt like it ought to erupt into awkward, tension-fueled flames that screamed for their bodies to come together, the darkness rushed in around him, and he disappeared. Her heart fell as she searched the shadowy corners for his presence. His helmet and glove were gone.

Cyane slipped farther under the blanket, wishing the darkness would take her away too.

A SOUL, A DRINK, A FIRE

CERBERUS RETURNED to the ballroom to find that Hades and the resurrected Trojan horse were gone. The only ones that remained were those who drew power from the carnage that was left behind and those who mourned the dead.

Hecate, who cried over her Underworld Lampade nymphs and followers, the Keres who sought the souls that lingered, and the few servants that cleaned the mess the higher beings ignored.

The sheer curtains that remained were soaked with blood, turning them into crimson, wet ribbons that the surviving lamiae tore with their fanged teeth.

Cerberus turned around as one of his hounds approached him with a fresh wraith of a soul. The hound dropped it at his feet, and Cerberus knelt to suck it up into his belly. Some of his hunger abated.

But it was not as satisfying as he needed it to be.

"Sweet Cerberus, I've missed you."

He stiffened as Melinoe's arms drew around him to hug him from behind. Any remaining warmth he carried from Cyane was replaced with ice.

"Melinoe," he muttered, detaching himself from the goddess's embrace. He turned to face her. She still wore the black dress from earlier. She was accompanied by an entourage of ghosts screaming and crying behind her, ones that didn't disappear when looked at directly. He wasn't the only one who'd scavenged from the remnants of Hades's entertainment. "Where is our lord?"

The goddess's eyes darkened. "How should I know? I assume he went to that hidden study of his."

Cerberus moved to leave.

Melinoe grabbed him. "Why does my father ignore me? Why does he hate me so much?" Tears filled her eyes as Cerberus shook her off him again. Her grip, despite its iciness, was far too similar to Cyane's for comfort.

"I can't answer that, ask him for yourself."

"But you know! I know you do! If anyone knows Hades's mind, it can only be you. Please... sweet Cerberus, my love. Tell me what you know."

Love? The word coming from Melinoe's lips sounded like rot. He knew the answer to her question, as did several others in the court, Hecate included. But a creature that disgusted Hades, even a royal goddess, disgusted all his followers, too.

"You're the only one who talks to me, you're the only one who listens when Mother isn't around," she whispered.

Melinoe reached for him again, and he drew the darkness toward him, vanishing before her touch could spoil his mind. Hades's daughter quickly fell from his thoughts as he arrived in his lord's study.

Hades sat in his usual chair by the fire, where only embers burned, with a cup of nectar in his hand. Cerberus moved to sit down across from him.

"Three more days until my queen descends," Hades said.

"Yes."

They sat in companionable silence, watching the fire, close to dying, but never quite guttering out completely. It continued glowing, often sparking embers of frustration as Hades's will kept it alive.

The subtle heat that it gave off made Cerberus long for warmth to return to his body. If he threw his hands in the hearth, would he purify Melinoe's touch and make Cyane's return? He pondered it for a while, but decided not to risk the ring he wore around his thumb.

Fire wasn't his friend after all. The dark gloom and flowing waters of Styx were the forces that embraced him. He was drawn to water, not fire.

Cerberus pulled his gaze from the hearth. "You may have new enemies. At this very moment, Hecate mourns the loss of her followers."

Hades swirled his drink. "When a god gives a gift, it will always make others jealous—or worse yet, feel entitled to my attention. Besides, Persephone never liked having so many carrion-eaters around."

Cerberus bristled. Persephone didn't like death at all, especially murder.

"So the gift was ultimately for our queen," Hades said, leaning back.

"It was as much for her as it was for you." Cerberus reached up, took off his helmet, and set it on the floor by his seat.

Hades's gaze moved to his face, and his mouth curled into a smile. "As handsome as ever, my friend. Our mortal guest has changed you. How very fun."

"She challenges my loyalty."

"Sex has a way of doing that, doesn't it? I've always thought our dear, delectable Aphrodite might be the most powerful of us all."

Cerberus's head tilted. "Sex?"

"Sex, the joining of two bodies, the battle of give and take, the horrid twisting thrill that clouds one's mind as they seek to dominate or be dominated. To take control or to relinquish it. Sex brings the highest men to their lowest and the lowest men to their highest. Gods, mortals, animals, none are spared this dilemma. None are immune to Aphrodite."

The thrill I feel, the hardening in my loins.

"Have you taken our mortal to your bed? I know you watch her constantly and that she sleeps in your haven."

"No, I have...not."

Cyane's imperfect, curvy figure filled his head. It took an immense amount of willpower to keep himself from following her into the bed, from feeling the rest of her. Her long, wavy brown hair begged his fingers to toy with it, and he longed to cup her fertile breasts in his palms.

"Do you not want her for yourself?" The question burned his throat with distaste. Hades would never share, *never*, and if he did have intentions for the mortal like Cerberus thought from the beginning...

A picture rose in his head of Hades seducing Cyane as Cerberus guarded them. He imagined himself as Hades, and the possibility filled Cerberus with as much displeasure as it did exhilaration. Cerberus and Hades were the same in physical form, but to picture Hades having her, while he couldn't...While the mirror-image played out... Cerberus wanted to rake his nails down his face and destroy the connection.

He understood now why Cyane fell away from him. Why she'd reacted with so much fear.

He tightened his hand into a fist and grazed her ring of hair. *No wonder she insists on seeing her tribute. Trust?* What was trust but a lie with a visage like his? Cerberus's face wasn't his. It had a history that wasn't his own.

Hades smiled slowly. "Why? I've already told you why. She's here to serve."

Cerberus flashed his teeth. "Who will she serve?"

"You've changed."

"Have I?"

"I must confess," Hade's smile dropped, and he sipped his drink. "I didn't see this outcome when I planned to bring the mortal here. But now I feel magnanimous, and since I know you will never betray me, I will not take offense to your questioning. Or the curiosity that plagues you regarding my actions.

"I may be supreme, but I suffer the same wiles of desire as everyone else. We have more in common than you think, and whoever you fuck, I get to fuck too, my brother. It's quite a delicious notion, sharing my flesh with you."

Cerberus stiffened angrily.

"A new god has not been born in ages, not since the mortals turned their back on us and chose to believe in false gods. This decay on our kind has been frustrating." Hades scowled. "The goddesses deny us their flesh. I had no choice but to steal and coerce my queen, and look what that has given me." He waved his hand. "Nothing. Nothing but villainous lies, treason, and power plays."

Hades handed Cerberus his half-drunk cup of nectar, and Cerberus took it, swallowing the rest. He played with hellfire and needed the liquid to soothe.

"Melinoe is eager for your affection," Cerberus muttered

"My...*daughter*," Hades hissed, snake-like, "is nothing more than a nuisance. I will not fuck my children as my brother does. Melinoe doesn't matter in the grand scheme of things. She's nothing. Will never be an heir. My queen will give me heirs, true heirs. I have picked her, and my choice is final. I have waited long enough for her affection to return, and Cyane—that mortal—will be what Persephone needs to bare her cunt to me again. Her cunt to *me*! Me! And not her father Zeus! Even if my brother took her wearing my face!"

The embers burst from the hearth into screaming flames, illuminating both Hades and Cerberus with shades of golden red.

Questions filled Cerberus's mouth, but he swallowed them like he had the nectar, nodding instead.

Hades's breaths were labored with rage. "Cyane is to serve me. She is a means to an end, like all mortals, so do what you will with her, but know when the time comes, she must come to me." He sighed wearily as if all the weight of the world rested on his shoulders. And perhaps, in a way, it did. "Leave me now Cerberus, before I change my mind."

Cerberus grabbed his helmet and stood. "Thank you, my lord." He meant it. He drew the darkness to him.

"If I had given you a woman's body, would you have given me an heir?"

Cerberus's brows furrowed at the question, then he nodded. "I would give you my life."

Hades's smile returned. "We would've made a monstrous god, the likes of Typhon, you and I. Perhaps it's best you always remain within the body I have bestowed upon you. Yes."

A new, full cup of nectar appeared in Hades's hand. He turned back to the fire.

This time when the darkness consumed Cerberus, he wasn't stopped.

THE WORSHIP OF A MORTAL

He watched Cyane sleep.

Her chest lifted and fell with each soft breath. His hounds curled around her on every side, protecting her as they protected the gates of the Underworld. They were him, after all, always feeling as he did. Through their snouts, Cerberus smelled her womanly scent, and through their sharp eyes, he saw her because they still belonged to him.

Now I know this thrill, this terrible hunger. Hades's words drifted in and out of his thoughts. He finally understood some of the motivations for Hades's actions, and that eased Cerberus if only a little. But it also made his belly burn with acid and his jaw ache.

I should tell her, prepare her. She will serve better if she knows what to expect.

Cyane's head fell to the side with a muted sigh, baring her neck.

He unclenched his hands and removed his gloves, setting them on a small table next to the bed. He caressed the ring of her hair and turned back to watch her.

If he told her, he'd be telling her she'd never be free of this place. He'd once offered her freedom in return for following him, and he hadn't meant to lie. He wasn't made to be devious, but these circumstances had changed him.

Hades had been correct in his observation.

Cerberus pulled off his helmet and set it beside his gloves.

Her eyes twitched behind her lids, and he leaned down to study them, wondering if she dreamed of him or if nightmares filled her head. Either way, he wanted it to be of him, only him, and not his lord.

Cerberus reached out and cupped her neck.

Her eyes snapped open, mouth parting, and she jerked up under the blankets, pulling them to her chest with sudden, startling fear. Beautiful.

"C-Cerberus?" she gasped.

He showed her his hand, and her gaze flickered from it to his face, her pulse grew wild under his palm. She gripped his wrist with one hand, holding the covers up with her other one. An eternity seemed to pass before she lowered her guard. She swallowed under his hand and licked her lips.

He released her and unbuckled the leather knot at his shoulder.

Cyane sat up straighter as he released the buckles along his armor. Like his helmet the day before, it had been ages since he'd removed it. He took off the chest piece, feeling the cool air of Tartarus drift across his skin like a long-awaited lovers touch.

He made short work of his vambraces, boots, and pants until he was as naked as Cyane. His cock sprang heavy, jutting from his groin. The soft glow of gloom fell upon their skin.

"What are you doing?" she whispered.

The hounds, with their labored breaths, filled the room with their panting. They were free to react in the animalistic ways he worked to contain. He sent them away, back to the shadows where they could guard from a distance.

Some gods loved to fuck in animal forms, delighting in the taboo, but he wanted to come to her this first time as a male, one she equally feared and submitted to. Cyane showed no submission towards his hounds.

Cerberus grabbed the blanket she held and ripped it from her grip. Her arms flew across her chest as her legs curled under her. Gorgeous brown waves fell over her shoulders and down her chest and arms.

He now understood his body's reaction, even if the sensation was new.

Cyane's eyes dipped, trailing over his body.

Cerberus knew what she saw. He knew what Hades's male form represented, his might and absolute power. A lord did not represent the extremity of dominance without appearing the part.

His mouth watered in response to her unease as she studied his body. Her eyes darted to his hand, to the ring wrapped around his thumb.

'Cyane is to serve me. She is a means to an end, like all mortals, so do what you will with her.'

Hades was in his head, always.

"I've returned to feel you," he said, placing his knee on the bed.

Cyane, grabbing a pillow from behind, slipped it in front of her, covering herself as she moved back. "Why?" she whispered.

"The warmth you gave me has left. I'd...like to feel that way again." He wouldn't move closer until she gave him the answer he was looking for. "Let me touch you." He didn't tell her that their time together might come to an end, that his hunger for her had to be sated now or they risked losing the opportunity.

He only told her what he desired. He waited.

A strange sort of fear filled him, one that warned she may turn cold if he took what wasn't given. Death was often taken, and it was always frigid.

He overcame the urge in his shaft and stepped back from the bed. "It's your choice."

A short time passed before she made her decision. She loosened her grip on the pillow. "Are you certain it's me you want?"

How could she ask that? Did she not see his need? Feel it herself? The smell of her arousal was thick in the space between them. He only wished he could take her while she knelt at his feet, while she submitted to him with downcast eyes. "Yes," he said eagerly. "I'd kill a thousand men for you and lay their heads before you."

Her eyes widened. "Okay."

Her breathless voice made his mouth water.

Cyane reached out her hand, and he took it, sliding into the bed next to her. Cerberus drew away the pillow and shifted so he was atop her. Cyane's unusual sunlit scent captivated him. Fresh and new and so unlike the dark chasm he knew.

He held himself up on his elbow as he pushed her legs down with his free hand, forcing her body to align with his. She was tense, but not with resistance—with something *new*. He tucked her arms beneath his chest, petting her as he adjusted her to his liking, finding enjoyment in little hairs that lifted from her skin and the soft sounds that fell from her lips.

The blunt dagger of his cock rubbed over her thighs and pelvis. It was the coldest part of him. He pressed it between her warm legs, which were tightly together, and groaned as he forced the increasingly painful appendage in. Her nails bit into his chest. He didn't understand her rigidity.

"Let me in," he rasped the order.

Cyane's chest rose and fell against his, but she did as he'd bidden and parted her thighs, giving him a slip of space. He pressed his hips forward, sliding his cock into the gap...

Cerberus closed his eyes in reverie and groaned.

Trembling, Cerberus opened his eyes and looked down at where they were connected. He groaned again.

"You... The heat." Words escaped him. The heat flooded him, hurt him, and begged him for more.

Overwhelming.

"More." He didn't recognize his own voice.

Cerberus drew back his hips when the heat became too much, only to realize his horrid mistake as he slipped from her. Cold. He pushed back down between her thighs. His gasping increased, and his arms strained to hold himself up into a position to push in and out while keeping her perfectly in place.

If she moved and took away his pleasure, he didn't know what he'd do.

Pressure released from his cock's head, and his mouth fell upon Cyane's neck where her pulse raced erratically. His back arched as new sensations ricocheted through him. The pressure-pain built again, and his tongue licked her pulse.

He thrust.

The bed moved underneath them. He slipped his hands under Cyane's shoulders and held her tightly to him. Sweat decreased the friction of his thrusting, and the need for more consumed him. He pushed in and out of the gap between her thighs with harder, quicker jerks.

The pressure in his loins grew so heavy he thought he might be losing his mind. A roar tore out of his throat, and his grip on Cyane tightened. Going mad.

Pleasure exploded through him, and he shook, the pressure dissolving suddenly into near-blissful waves. He groaned and rasped as hellfire erupted within him, his body jerking in a way he couldn't control. On her, over her, like the thousands of couplings he'd seen from a distance.

He thrusted several more times, slipping between her wet thighs, feeling beyond warm, and instead, feeling excruciatingly *hot*. The closest he'd felt like this was after battling the titans long ago, but even that paled in comparison.

His body continued to shake even after the momentous eruption left him. His breathing relaxed, and he loosened his grip on Cyane, helping her settle into the bed beneath him. Her hands fell from his body, and he rose up to take her beauty in.

She breathed heavily, her chest rising and falling rapidly like his. Her eyes were wide, and he couldn't place the emotion on her face. Surprise? He lifted further up, slipping his member from between her thighs.

"Are you hurt? Did I hurt you?" he asked.

She shook her head. Shock maybe?

Her thighs were dewy and wet and slicked with his seed. He reached up and touched his brow, feeling the dampness of sweat there as well.

His eyes lingered on the hair at the crux of her legs and then her breasts before finding her face again.

His heart raced, his cock grew hard again. He found the more he tried to figure her out, and the longer she lay beneath him, the more the feel of her skin on his acted as a trigger. He waited for her to speak, to say something, but she just continued to study him with that strange, stunned expression.

He'd experienced more pleasure than he ever had in his life, had finally understood why Hades thought Aphrodite may be the strongest god of them all, and...

She has nothing to say?

Anger filled him. "What is the matter, mortal?" Cyane had

been privy to him when he was most vulnerable, and she was not pleased?

Her lips parted, and his gaze dropped to them. It made his cock twitch.

"I…" Cyane began.

"What?" he snapped.

She blushed. "You're a virgin?" Her voice was barely audible, almost as if she was afraid to ask.

A virgin? He never considered himself anything but the son of Typhon and Echidna, brother to Chimera and Hydra, guardian of Tartarus's gates, and ally to Hades. *Virgin* just didn't fit with that. Females were virgins, not males of his ilk.

"No," he gritted. "I only wish to be warm."

She nodded slowly. Her legs moved against his as she rose up on her elbows.

"I make you warm?"

"I make you warm, too," he fumed, sliding a thumb across her brow where her own sweat had gathered.

Cyane nodded again, still watching him in that strange way. "Are you warm now?"

His back was cooling down, his cock the same. Its pressure returned, its near-painful rigidity.

"No," he growled, falling upon her again.

CERBERUS GRABBED her legs and spread them wide, pressing his body hard against hers, near suffocating her in the bed. This time when his cock landed, it hit her sex, sliding hard and heavily against it.

Shock still filled Cyane. She couldn't grasp what exactly was happening between them. Part of her mind still lingered with sleep and the tipsiness that refused to leave her since the nectar she drank so long ago... At least it seemed long ago.

He rammed his length against her again and again, his grunts filling her ears. "What is this?" he growled at first. "What hell is this?" He moved over her, lifting himself up to look at where he rubbed, glanced at her face, and then pushed back down over her as if he needed to feel her completely against him.

She smiled at the naive chaos behind his actions.

His shaft shifted angle just a little, and suddenly, he was moving vigorously over her clit. Her breath hitched, and she pressed her thighs together to hold him near her. Wetness gushed from her—from him—she had no idea, but despite the shock, the longer their rocking continued, the more the sensation within her grew.

He was a virgin, even if he wouldn't admit it. And she was about to be his first. Any nervousness she felt before about being inadequate was gone.

The smell of sex filled her nose. Her nostrils flared.

She hooked her legs over his thighs, digging her heels into the muscled backs of them, and shunted upward as he thrust down. He was so hard, and his muscles moved like boulders.

Their pelvis's slammed together, and she flung her head back.

"Yes!" She cried.

A grunt. "Yes, what?"

"Don't stop!" A harried gasp.

Cerberus pushed back up onto his elbows and grabbed handfuls of her hair. His eyes were a fever pitch of violent, unrestrained red.

Cyane lost her breath. They were so beautiful, so uncanny. Sweat dripped from his face to land on her brow and on her cheeks. She licked it, salty and delectable. Their noses bumped, his tongue swept out to lash her skin like an animal. Her mouth parted, hoping it would find its way into her.

He battered her clit, and her sleepiness fled. She was fully awake now.

She couldn't fill her lungs, couldn't find her breath.

Honor filled her almost as much as lust.

Cerberus still hadn't breached her, and she was dying for him too. She reached around him and dug her nails into his back. His hips bucked into her. A guttural noise filled her ears.

Shaking, she begged. *Please, please.* She pulled her legs further up his hips, her bliss so close. *So close!*

His teeth scraped across her face, his tongue everywhere. Cyane gripped him with her thighs as much as she could. Everything was wet between them now. Wet and hard, and her legs kept slipping across his skin. It was infuriating and delicious.

He moved up slightly, and she shifted with him. He rammed back down, and whether on purpose or by accident, his tip found her entrance.

Cerberus slammed home with his next rut.

A scream tore from her throat. Cyane's eyes wrenched shut.

He stilled above her.

Cyane clenched around him, her body tense, pulsing, fighting him off—fighting him out—but he didn't move. His cock filled her, stretched her, bringing both pain and bliss.

Her sex constricted, again and again, her climax growing hard and violent. It wanted to erupt from her, like a screaming fiend. Her nails clawed his back, her hips shook from side-to-side, and her hold on him tightened as each gripping wave shot through her.

He remained still. She didn't have the ability to open her eyes and find out why.

She didn't know how long she fought beneath him, trying to simultaneously push him aside and keep him planted firmly within her. She rolled and shattered and shook, fighting for breath as much as her freedom, unable to understand...

What was happening to her?

A godly being was fully seated deep inside her. Even with her very limited experience, Cyane knew this wasn't what sex should feel like.

"I can't!" she heard herself screech again and again, and yet he didn't move, and she didn't let him go.

Her eyes shot open—finally! She found him gazing, disbelieving, down at her. Snakes, snouts, teeth, and brimstone smoky breaths filled her vision. She wasn't covered in sweat anymore but awash in drooling saliva.

"Cyane? Cyane!" she heard Cerberus say from somewhere very far away...

But darkness called her, and she surrendered to unconsciousness.

GODDESS OF NIGHTMARES

Cyane woke suddenly, shooting up in bed. Her hands flung up to her neck to feel her racing pulse and then skimmed her skin, moving hurriedly down her arms and chest. A whistling sound filled her ears. Her gaze snapped about as she pulled her legs under her.

She was alone.

I don't feel alone.

Cerberus wasn't on top of her, or beside her, or watching her from a distance. Even his hounds were missing, but she still sensed him all over her. Her sex still fluttered continuously, feeling so painfully full, like he was still there.

She reached down to find nothing amiss.

But he was still inside her, she knew it—the stretch and burn from his sudden penetration remained. The heaviness of his shaft was probing heavily deep within, making her wince, making her moan. Her body fought, working to understand the overwhelming pressure.

Cyane closed her thighs tight and writhed on the bed. Her nails ripped at the sheets. *Oh, god, please!*

She pressed her palms back to her chest where her heart pounded so hard she thought it might burst. Minutes passed as she tried to calm herself. Aching and needing. Dampening the sheets with more of her essence.

And despite feeling him all around her, still inside her, she was alone.

The whistling sound grew louder through it all, eventually pulling her out of her torment.

Cyane pushed herself back up, falling back down twice with pleasure before she was able to stand. She staggered to her feet. Her legs bowed as she found her footing, knowing Cerberus's cock was still seated deep within her, somehow.

She didn't know how, but her mind didn't linger, pushing through her physical confusion. Nothing was normal here.

The whistling in her ears refused to be ignored.

Another chiton dress was laid out for her, and she worked it over her head. The weightless material fell to the tops of her feet.

Perhaps it was a consequence of taking a creature like Cerberus inside her body. Something wet licked her cheek, followed by something warm nuzzling the same spot. Teeth brushed the place afterward. Cyane pressed her hand to her skin and rubbed the sensations away. He was still with her!

Her gaze shot everywhere searching for Cerberus but couldn't find him.

Her eyes drifted to the table where a loaf of bread and fruit were laid out on a platter. She wandered over to it and picked up a grape.

Still not hungry.

She set the grape back down. She moved to the bath where tendrils of steam plumed softly into the air. Cyane dipped her hand in the water, and it came out slippery with minty oils. She wiped her hand dry on her skirt.

Thrust, lick, groan. Her hips shot forward, and she clasped the side of the tub, screaming with pleasure. Her hips jerked several more times, moved by some unseen force. Her inner thighs grew slick.

It stopped, and she collapsed to the floor, resting her brow on the side of the bath. She waited for the next onslaught, but it didn't come.

A crash like a giant wave startled her. Several more followed after it, jolting her body each time. The sound came from outside the room, from the terrace. She pulled herself to her feet. But as she neared, she noticed Hades's castle was missing, and the odd crashes grew with the sound of whistling.

What the? Styx and its current of souls were gone too. It was replaced by a wild black and red ocean in every direction. The waves hitting the tower below were the source of the noise.

She'd heard stories from the nuns that hell was by the ocean, was in the ocean, deep, so deep underground that the easiest way to get there were the trenches. She'd never believed it, until now.

I always loved the water... Cyane inhaled deeply, biting back fear. She bit back receding clenches of pleasure as well. Was she going to face Poseidon now?

A series of crashes below made her scoot forward. Coming out of the gatehouse was a short, rocky beach, much like the entryway to Tartarus.

A woman with long white hair grinned up at her. Her hair whipped around her face.

The whistling sound?

"Melinoe?" Cyane called out, her brows furrowing. The goddess was the last being Cyane wanted to see with slick running down her thighs.

Within the next instant, she was standing on the rock

beside her. Cyane stumbled on her feet, finding footing, even as Cerberus was *still* within her.

Melinoe grabbed Cyane's hands. "Sweet Cyane, I've finally found you."

Cyane's belly churned. The smile was kind, genuine, and yet it filled her with unease. It didn't make sense, it never made sense. How could kindness feel so terrible? Melinoe had been as good to her as Cerberus, but every time she encountered the goddess, a frigid chill told her to stay back.

"You were looking for me?" Cyane asked. "Where are we?"

Please don't notice Cerberus fucking me invisibly!

"We're still in Tartarus, just far past my father's castle and where Styx lays. This place is endless, like each of the realms. Earth has space, Poseidon has the abyss, and well, Hades has this. There is more water under Gaia's flesh than there is upon it." Melinoe swept her hand out.

Cyane glanced out at the riotous waters with a shiver.

"But once you're within it, you're not with Gaia anymore," Melinoe teased.

"This feels wrong," Cyane said.

Melinoe circled her arms around Cyane and hugged her tightly. Cyane couldn't stop staring at the waves, and the red foam it created on the rocks. *Blood.*

"I've been searching for you, but I couldn't find you in my father's castle. He often likes to keep his playthings hidden away, but I know where he hides them. You weren't anywhere in the darkness until the festivities began. I did not think you'd be Cerberus's prisoner. He's never taken a prisoner before."

Cyane turned her face to Melinoe and pushed out of her embrace. "What?"

"They're never going to let you go."

"H-how do you know that? Do you know why I'm here?"

"I don't."

"Then how can you be certain?"

"Hades has never let a mortal go, never. But I can help you. I know you're searching for your parents. I can help you, my friend, but would you do a small favor for me?"

Cyane reached up and felt her chest where she usually stashed her note, but it wasn't there. Fear crashed down upon her like the waves around her, pounding her ears. She'd even given up on her attempts to leave, needing to believe this dream, that this place would all eventually come to an end.

Cerberus wasn't a trickster, he'd told her himself, but had he ever really expressly agreed to help her leave after the festivities? Cyane wracked her brain but couldn't remember, not exactly.

Where was her note? She gripped the material of her gown in distress.

"It's not there, is it?" Melinoe said.

Tears, blasted damning tears, sprang to Cyane's eyes. "I can't find it!" When had she lost it? How could she forget to keep tabs on it? The note had been with her her entire life. The thought of it being gone, of the only connection she had to parents disappearing, filled her with more terror than anything she'd come up against so far.

Melinoe took Cyane's hands forcibly into her own and squeezed. "It's not too late. I can help you if you help me."

"How? What do I need to do?"

"Find out why Hades hates me so much. Find out and tell me."

Cyane's body shook. "That's it? That's all I need to do?"

"Yes, sweet Cyane, ask him and find out, then tell me. I'll help you escape if you so choose. I will be eternally grateful, and having a grateful goddess on your side is no small gift. A deal. A deal between friends?"

Cyane, wet now with ocean spume, slowly nodded at Melinoe. "Okay."

Melinoe smiled. The chill returned ten-fold upon Cyane.

"My dear, sweet friend," Melinoe said, "it's time to wake up."

Before Cyane could ask what she meant, Melinoe released her hands and pushed her into the ocean.

She didn't have a chance to scream before it consumed her.

THE DAY OF DEALS

CYANE SHOT UP WITH A SCREAM, arms flailing outward. The taste of mint filled her mouth, and she spat it out, yet the smell lingered in her nose.

"Cyane?"

Her eyes fixated on Cerberus, naked and perched in the water before her. Concern marred his face, as did lust, and it threatened to smolder her anew. His pale, muscled body was a welcome sight.

Cyane pulled her gaze from him before she melted. She was back in his room—her room. They were in the tub.

Cerberus cupped her cheeks, forcing her eyes back on him. "What happened? You left me, and I didn't know what to do. You said baths were good for humans, so I thought this would help."

This wasn't the ocean.

"A nightmare. I had a nightmare," she whispered.

Cerberus frowned. "A nightmare? What kind of nightmare?"

Cyane shook her head as she recalled her conversation with Melinoe. She didn't know if it'd been real, but something kept her throat tight. "I was drowning again... I was back in Styx," she lied. "I was drowning, and you weren't there to pull me from the water."

But in a way, he had, hadn't he? Cyane curled her arms around her stomach, feeling a little ill.

Her lie was a dangerous confession in itself—she was afraid for Cerberus to know that she'd made plans with Melinoe. If he found out her deception... *He knows when I try to leave, when I want to leave.*

Don't think about it! Nervousness clawed at her throat.

With his hands still cupping her cheeks, Cerberus leaned closer, studying her a little more than she liked... "I will be there to pull you from the waters. Always."

"Even if I were dead?" she mumbled.

He cocked his head. "Even so."

"Don't say things you don't mean." Melinoe's words filled her mind once more. "A mortal has never been saved from their fate."

A crack formed in her chest.

"My mortal will." He lowered his hands to her waist and drew her into his arms, into his lap, and then settled back on the opposite side of the basin.

My mortal will... Tears formed in her eyes, and she burrowed her face against his chest. It was mildly cold again, but she didn't mind. The water was hot.

How could I leave him? Give this up for a near impossible chance to confront parents who had left her with nothing but a note?

She'd only known him for days—*days!*—and she was already reconsidering everything. What if she made her way home only to face terrible strangers or worse...no one at all. Would she ever be able to live again after all she had learned? *Could I get a job, save up money, and find someone to love after this?* Start a family? Adopt her own children, and wake up every morning, already dead inside, knowing their inevitable fates?

Cerberus's fingers stroked her arm before they tangled into the strands of her wet hair and played with her locks.

Time is different in the darkness...

She nuzzled his chest harder, wanting more than anything to disappear.

"Why do you do that?" he asked her.

"Do what?"

"Press your head to my chest?"

The crevasse in her chest grew, but with it, warmth. "It brings me comfort. Your heart is in your chest, it's where all of our emotions begin and end. Being near yours helps to distance me from mine."

"Mortals are strange."

"Yes... Yes, we are. Would you like to try?" She glanced up at him, finding him staring down at her, pondering.

Cerberus shook his head. "I feel many things and most of them I don't understand. I don't want to distance myself from them until I understand since they all belong to you."

Now that crack in her chest burst into a chasm.

"Oh." Even such a simple response was almost impossible for her now.

As if it couldn't get worse, Cerberus curled a finger around a tendril of her hair. "But perhaps later, when I do understand them, I would like to press my head to your chest."

Cyane wiped her face to hide the growing wetness in her eyes. She wanted to give him a gift, another one, a grander one than the ringlet of her hair around his thumb.

"I have another gift for you, Cerberus, if you'd accept it?" she whispered, moving over him now to straddle his hips. She placed her hands on his shoulders and his bulge jerked between them. He'd been hard the entire time, but it didn't seem to matter to either of them until now.

"The Day of Gifts is long over," he said, slow enough to bolster her confidence.

But he didn't stop her. *He wants this. He's curious.*

"This has nothing to do with that. This is between you and me, like every interaction we've had, that we will ever have."

"Then do not wait, mortal, give it to me," he demanded, the hunger she now knew so well growing in his thirsty gaze.

She placed her dripping hand over his eyes. "Close your eyes."

"If you deceive me, this will go badly for you."

"Just close your eyes! It's not like I can even hurt you if I tried, and I have no intention of jumping out the window and running. You'll like this."

He stiffened. "Then make it quick. When my eyes are closed, *all* of my eyes are closed."

Cyane sighed, pursed her lips, and removed her hand from his eyes to confirm they were closed. Her gaze dipped to his slightly parted, beautifully bow-shaped lips that shouldn't exist on any man, ever.

And they were hers. This gift was hers as well. *No matter what happens.* She'd own this moment.

She inhaled softly and leaned forward. She pressed her lips to his.

Cerberus's eyes snapped open, and she shuddered, rubbing his mouth. She closed her eyes as his darkened. She didn't want him to stop her, to question this until she was done.

Cyane moved her lips softly at first, slowly back and forth over his, until his mouth loosened to meet the softness of her own. She slid her hands up to cup his neck, the back of his head, and pressed forward, pushing her chest against his.

The aroma of the minty water was eclipsed by Cerberus's heady scent. Like everything about him, it was overwhelming, and even though she was currently tentatively in control, his scent stole her senses.

She flicked the tip of her tongue out to taste him.

And like the abyss, his mouth opened to swallow her own. Cerberus's tongue shot out to slam against hers. The softness of the kiss fled as their tongues tangled. His hands, which now spanned across her back, slid up to hold her hard to him.

A strained moan escaped her, but he swallowed that up as well. She clutched his hair. He pressed and kneaded the muscles of her back even as the spear of his cock was trapped between them, pushing against her.

It was impossible to know how much time has passed since their last coupling—time really wasn't normal here—but found despite being sore from before, she still wanted him back inside her.

His tongue drove harder between her lips and explored her mouth, as demanding and heavy as his erection. Cyane slanted her head as much as he would let her and opened her eyes to look at him.

Cerberus feverishly stared back at her. Her aching sex knotted. He wrapped his arms around her, grasped her backside, and lifted her hard against him as he stood. Cyane grabbed onto him but there was no need—she was locked so hard between his arms that she couldn't get away. Cerberus walked them to the bed and laid her down. She whined when he ripped his mouth from hers to stand over her.

Gasping, she gazed up at him.

"I will be inside you again, mortal, but I need to know you won't leave me this time. I thought I killed you, and I..." His eyes streaked over her body, landing between her legs.

Embarrassed, she began to close her thighs. His hands

shot out, and he tore her legs open again. Spread wide open to his gaze, she shivered as butterflies assailed her. His eyes had not moved from her sex.

She dropped her own gaze to his bulging prick and wiggled uncomfortably. She couldn't believe such a huge, veiny shaped specimen had been inside her.

Perhaps that's why I passed out...

She sucked in her stomach. "You what?"

"I was about to tear this realm apart for your soul to slam it back into you."

She moaned. Why did that make her moan?

"You didn't hurt me before. I—" she struggled for the right words. "Being with you, like that, it was so sudden, unexpected. I wasn't prepared, not for *that*." Whatever it was. Cyane licked her lips as his hands gripped her thighs harder. "I don't think anyone could prepare to be with someone like you?"

His jaw ticked. "As they could with a mortal?"

She nodded.

"Have you been with a mortal?"

"Once—"

"Who?"

"It doesn't matter."

He leaned over her menacingly, releasing his hold on one of her thighs, and she drew away, as far as she was able. "Who?" he demanded.

"A boy," she hesitated as Cerberus's chill careened over her. "Another foster in the house I lived in when I was young."

Cerberus could do anything to her at any time. His constant control of all her movements was evidence alone.

But she knew he would never hurt her, and every time he used his absolute might upon her, she buckled willingly, near desperate to do everything he wanted. Wet. She was achingly wet for it.

Cerberus pressed his lips to her ear. Her throat closed after a gulp. "You will give me his name when this is finished between us, and I will wait for his soul to come to me to die another death."

Cyane shivered. "I don't want this to ever be finished between us."

The blunt head of his cock rubbed her sex. "Then you will never leave."

"Will you protect me?"

"Yes," he said with such adamance that it stole her breath.

"Would you..." She licked her lips. "Would you swear an oath to Styx on it?"

Cerberus's cock rubbed up and down her open sex, the hard ridge of his tip bumping across her clit, her aching core. She grew wetter by the second.

"I swore an oath to Hades to always be loyal to him," Cerberus murmured.

"I wish I knew what he wanted with me," Cyane gasped. "What the point of all of this is."

Cerberus lifted his lips from her ear and clasped her chin between his fingers. "Swear fealty to me, Cyane."

"Why?"

"What other god but me has given you everything?" He forced her to stare into his hauntingly red eyes. "You could belong to me, always."

Her heart fell into her gut, the air caught in her throat. At that moment, she loved and hated him more than anything. The delicious lick and burn of his erection hadn't stopped rubbing her, killing her with desperate lust to be filled by him again. It wasn't fair. None of this was fair. But nothing had ever been fair, not since the day she was left by her parents to face the world alone.

Her doubt that a powerful being like Cerberus could ever want her fled.

Swearing fealty wasn't everything, was it?

His breath fanned her face as he waited for her answer.

"I swear fealty to you, Cerberus." The words tasted right. She knew what he wanted from her. "I'll worship you. I worship you," she whispered.

His beautifully terrible face twisted with something she couldn't read, but it made her heart beat wildly, excitedly. Lovingly.

He pressed his mouth against hers and slammed home between her legs.

Cyane screamed in bliss.

CYANE WAS HOT. So very, very hot.

Something akin to gripping obsession consumed Cerberus. He was crazed with it, forsaking his duties, forsaking Hades, forsaking *everything*. He'd never felt so alive.

To think a mortal had done this to him.

A creature he once thought beneath him who were nothing more than bugs to be punished if they dared to fight the will of nature.

Cerberus thrust into Cyane relentlessly, and she only begged for more. Her female flesh gripped him, wetted his length, and strangled him into delirium.

At some point, Hades called him to the ballroom, but he went ignored.

Cerberus's monstrous, true form—stuck under his man-suit—was as free as it could be with this tender mortal, and yet his mortal screamed for it. Screamed and screamed, and hellishly begged with delicious noises that echoed in his once quiet sanctuary.

It was only once Cyane slumbered beneath him, that he lifted his mouth from suckling her flesh. There wasn't an inch of her that he hadn't tasted, and even the parts of her where she had resisted, had sparked with life under his attentions. He had filled his hands with her and driven his fingers deep into her mouth.

He wanted to know everything about his mortal servant. The right of gods was heady, and he was just learning to use his.

Still hungering, his bulge still heavy and uncomfortable, Cerberus brought the darkness to him and replaced the soiled bedding. He didn't let the shadows take his markings that covered Cyane's body—he wanted to keep them there for a while longer for him to enjoy. She'd marked him as well with her nails, and those marks he might keep forever.

When he was done he lay back atop her, keeping her where he liked her most and breathed her in.

Time passed while she slept. He passed the time kissing her skin. He vowed to one day wipe her memory of her former lover and feast on his soul as slipped his mouth over her.

Hades has done more for Persephone. Cerberus would follow his lord's lead and do the same.

The thought of Hades churned his gut, and the calling of the Lord of the Underworld struck Cerberus again. He was being summoned. And yet the thought of releasing Cyane from where he trapped her infuriated him.

He moved his lips upon hers one last time and lifted himself from her. She curled onto her side and brought her hands to her chin. He covered her with a silken blanket.

'Cyane is to serve me. She is a means to an end, like all mortals, so do what you will with her, but know when the time comes, she must come to me.'

Cerberus gritted his teeth. His hands tightened at his sides.

He walked to the terrace and glared at Hades's castle. It pained him, all of these emotions Cerberus was now cursed with. Hate was within him, and hate hadn't been there since Hercules chained him, forcing him to the world above.

But despite it all, he didn't hate Hades or even what might come to pass. He hated his inability to stop it, he detested that his loyalty was in question and that he understood Cyane's predicament better than he was letting on.

How could he claim to be loyal while also lying to those he was loyal to?

The worst thing that could happen wasn't her death. Death belonged here, death was easy for him to control and understand. *No, the worst thing that could happen is her loss of faith in me.*

Which could happen. If he couldn't protect her from whatever Hades planned to do with her.

Hades called him again.

The Day of Deals was nearly over, and Cerberus had one last thing to do before he confronted his lord.

THE GOD OF CROSSINGS

BACK IN ARMOR, Cerberus entered the ballroom from the shadows. His gaze caught Hades's from across the room. He deftly checked out his lord, trying to read him and know what mood Hades was in before Cerberus approached. Their eyes met, and Hades gulped back his cup of nectar, dismissing him with a nod to talk with the undying bowed in submission at his feet.

Although Cerberus had been temporarily dismissed, that didn't mean Hades still didn't want his hound by his side. But he turned away, taking those moments to set his plan into motion.

It was rare for Cerberus to not answer his lord's summons at once, but he believed the deal he could make was one that would please Hades. Even if it was shrouded with betrayal.

Cerberus scanned the ballroom.

He wanted to make this quick and get back to Cyane before she awakened.

The ballroom held far fewer guests, but there were still a hundred or so in attendance.

The strongest ones. He assumed. Or the quickest, the craftiest. The ones the undead Trojan horse didn't hunt, like the gods and demi-gods, and those like Tantalus, the eternal servant, who was serving timeless punishment.

Flowing strips of cloth still hung as curtains, but none touched the ground, having been torn away by daemon hands and teeth, consumed due to the blood they'd soaked up. Candles lit the room, clustered in thousands along the walls, giving what had been purple-white the appearance of dried blood.

The obsidian walls gleamed.

Soft music played so conversations could be had and deals could be made. The undying who remained dressed conservatively or manipulatively, depending on the deal they planned to make.

The smell of nectar was potent as basins overflowed with it, wetting the floor in slick puddles. Even those that didn't partake in drink carried it around where it soaked their clothes and sandals.

Cerberus judged through the eyes of his hounds while searching for Hermes. He found the golden god, blessed by Aphrodite (whom he now envied), speaking with Hypnos near Hades's dais.

Cerberus strode across the room towards them.

"One poppy is all I need," Hermes said.

"One from my dwelling could put half the mortals asleep. It'll cost a steep price for me to relinquish one."

"Was it not I who helped you with Hera when she needed Zeus asleep? Was it not I who brought Pasithea, a revered Grace, here to wed you? Have I not allowed the crossings of you and your offspring to the slumbering mortals above? You could not own half their lives with sleep without the power I bring," Hermes argued.

"All power is omniscient, even if it's yours, young god.

You did not allow something that is the right of gods far more ancient than you," Hypnos mused. "We have been at this all day, and my stance will not change. If you want a poppy from my garden, I will know why first." Hypnos regarded Cerberus and canted his head in greeting.

Cerberus nodded back. Hermes's lips curled in distaste.

"We are not done," Hermes gritted as the ancient god of sleep wandered away. Hermes turned to Cerberus anyway. "You and Hades's mortal guest have been missing all day. I feared that the horse may have swallowed her."

"Are you keeping tabs on me?" Cerberus didn't want to think of Hermes watching for Cyane, let alone himself, any more than what he wanted to ask anything from this god.

He'd prefer to break Hermes's jaw wide and eat the golden boy whole.

"Oh, don't sound so honored. There have been whisperings that some of Hades's brood wanted to leave after his grossly entertaining stunt. Who else could they make a deal with to escape Tartarus if not you? Even I can't cross a non-god from this place." Hermes looked around. "So where is she? Our mortal guest?"

"Safely away, slumbering as mortals do. She's not here."

Hermes shrugged, and the feathers on his boots and helmet shrugged with him. "There's something about her I can't quite place, but I swear I've met her before. That irks me. I'm not often so perplexed by a face, let alone a mortal's." Hermes and his feathers shrugged again. "My imagination does love to run wild."

Cerberus couldn't care less. "I have a deal to make with you," he said. He didn't like that Hermes thought about Cyane. When a god became fixated on something, their attention remained there until something else distracted them, and the fact that Hermes clearly fixated on Cyane annoyed Cerberus. She was not the winged god's responsibility.

Which made what Cerberus was about to ask all that much harder.

"A deal? From Hades's loyal hound?" Hermes guffawed. "I don't recall you ever making a deal with anyone but our dark and terribly murderous lord. You've intrigued me Cerberus, as only a bevy of naked nymphs can do. Spill it out, for I may die of curiosity in the next second!"

Cerberus could hardly keep his contempt for Hermes out of his voice. "This is about our mortal guest."

Hermes's gaze shot towards Hades. He lowered his voice. "Let us go somewhere else to speak."

"Follow me," Cerberus said, striding away from Hades's dais and towards one of the candlelit walls. There were shadowy places, but not many today. The Day of Deals was not to be a private event for the very same reasons as Cerberus sought privacy with Hermes.

Even though Hermes's sandals were silent, Cerberus didn't need to see if the god followed. When he got far enough away from the others, he turned to see Hermes was behind him, eagerly awaiting a little bit of mischief.

Cerberus scowled under his helmet. "I want you to take Cyane from here if something should befall her between now and Persephone's descent."

"And why would I do that?"

"Because she is innocent in all of this."

Hermes rubbed his jaw. "Innocence won't save her from us gods. Do you not know what Hades has in mind for her?"

"I don't feel comfortable with her safety," he admitted.

Hermes cocked a brow. "You care for her? You? The creature that has cared for nothing but nature's law and Hades, despite the body given to you. Our little mortal guest must be quite something, something more than is being let on."

Cerberus clenched his jaw and his hands, resisting the urge to ring them around Hermes's neck. "It doesn't matter what I think or feel, and Hades shares his plans with no one. She has sworn an oath to Styx and to me that she is not here for any reason of her knowing, that she's not here to cause harm. No one has ever trespassed into Tartarus who has not sought to upset this place or to steal from Hades. But she *has*."

"Oh, I think it matters greatly, Cerberus. Are you certain she is telling you the truth? Certain enough that you would stake eternal loyalty and your immortal life on it? If what you say is true, Hades is scheming, even killing his loyal followers with a smile, so why would I risk myself to help her? What do you have to offer me?"

"I will open the gates of hell for you, and only you, for this next mortal year so you might spy on Persephone for Demeter. You and Persephone's meddling mother will finally know what happens when she is beyond your view. Demeter would owe you if you brought her such a gift."

Hermes narrowed his eyes. "Not enough."

"I know you still burn that Zeus chose Hades over your suit for Persephone's hand, even if she was not your bride."

"You assume much! Aphrodite is my loin's torment."

"Perhaps I can procure a poppy from Hypnos. A poppy potent enough to make even Zeus himself fall into slumber."

Hermes sucked in a breath. "How do I know this isn't a trap?"

"I come to deal with you of my own accord, and I vow on Styx as we speak, Hades, nor any other being, knows of my objectives," Cerberus growled, feeling the vow hit him.

Betrayal, anger, and shame beat at him as well.

Hermes growled back. "If Hades ever finds out, he will make you pay. Make me pay. You believe this mortal woman is worth this?"

"Yes."

Yes. He hated how far he'd fallen in such a short amount of time… Frustrated that he needed Hermes for anything.

"She is not what she seems, Cerberus, regardless of any vows."

Cerberus countered, his patience wearing thin. "Will you make this deal or not?"

"For the price of a poppy, I will steal her from here and return her above—if something should happen between now and Persephone's descent."

Cerberus nodded once, stiffly. "Wait here," he ordered, gathering his shadows and slipping away to where Hypnos's cave and his garden of flowers were. No alarm bells rang, nobody questioned his intentions—the loyal lapdog of Hades.

He returned the next moment with a small poppy in his hand. "I will decide if she's in danger, not you. Watch for my signal."

Hermes took the small, delicate, incredibly powerful flower from Cerberus's palm. His eyes widened with hushed excitement. "I hope you know what you're doing."

Cerberus's jaw twitched as Hermes stored the flower away in his golden hair. He didn't bother answering as he strode from the winged god and retreated to Hades's left side.

He stopped short as he saw Cyane enter the ballroom, dressed in liquid gold. Melinoe romped by her side, holding her hand and pulling her forward.

"Ah, so you've finally decided to join me, Cerberus," Hades mused. "It seems our guest has joined us as well."

Cerberus fought the shock in his system, staring at *his* mortal, who'd been sleeping under him not that long ago. She was so beautiful that he barely heard Hades over the soundless gold reflecting the candlelight with dazzling effect.

Melinoe dragged Cyane through the puddles of nectar, making him shudder.

She looks like a goddess.

Hermes flew to Cyane's side just as she caught Cerberus's gaze from across the room. Cerberus tensed with lust, but then her attention was pulled from him far too soon.

"You're slow to respond," Hades muttered.

"I was caught up in my head," Cerberus said, unable to pull his eyes off Cyane. All his eyes, all his hounds were fixated on her.

"She makes a lovely addition doesn't she? Too bad it seems she's been targeted by my blight of a daughter. It really diminishes her beauty."

Even though he'd asked for the winged god's help. Cerberus gritted his teeth, his belly yawning open to eat. Eat, and then fuck. Then fuck again.

Hades continued when he remained silent. "Tell me what has caught up your head enough to ignore me? It was her, wasn't it? I suppose I can forgive you. The first time I tasted cunt, no one saw me for months. Was she good?"

"She was," he said, his mouth salivating.

"My damned!" Hades swiveled on his throne. "I never thought you'd actually go through with it. I would've brought a mortal woman down here ages ago if I knew they'd tempt you. Then again, you have fine taste. Cyane is extraordinary, isn't she? I could almost forgive you for ignoring me this grand day. *Almost.*"

Cerberus swore under his breath and looked at his lord. The hackles on his hounds rose. "I apologize, I was overcome."

"And yet you spoke to Hermes before joining me. Are you branching out? Eager to try a man next? So soon?"

Cerberus tensed with anger.

Hades's slow smiled was full of leer. "What is that saying

these newer mortals love to spew? *Go fuck yourself?* It has a new meaning, doesn't it, when it comes to you and me."

"Hermes sought a poppy from Hypnos's garden," Cerberus said. The vow he gave to Hermes, to Styx, did not state any retroactive deceptions. He hadn't lied. And who knew Styx better than Cerberus? He'd spent more years by the primordial goddess's side than anyone else.

Hades's smile dropped. "Hmmm."

"Hypnos refused."

"Delightful. Did you take care of it?"

"I made a deal with Hermes instead and gave him the flower."

Hades sat back and sipped his nectar. "Do you know what he plans to use it for?"

"To put a god to sleep." Cerberus had to guess. "I assume."

"Obviously. And what did you get in return?"

"Added protection for Cyane," he said vaguely. Despite the omission, the truth felt good on his lips, a reminder he was still loyal to Hades and always would be. He didn't wish his lord harm. "When I am not there to protect her myself."

Hades sighed. "I'm annoyed now. This all annoys me. I hate being annoyed." He waved his empty hand emphatically. "Cyane is not yours, she is mine, and her protection is *you* because you are also my protection. Have more faith in your abilities, hound."

"If I knew what was to be expected of her, things would be different," Cerberus snapped. He bristled at Hades's claim on Cyane. Cerberus saw her as his now. HIS. Her words of fealty and worship were binding.

"My bloody cunt! Can't anyone enjoy surprises anymore? Paranoia rules the gods, and while I once found that mightily enjoyable, now I grow weary of it. I will not let anyone, even you, ruin my plans." Hades's eyes slid to meet his. "You can never tell who is listening in. If our lady

Demeter can attempt to drown us in flowers, who else might have knowledge of my realm? One eye or ear is all it takes."

"Yes. My lord," Cerberus gritted, holding Hades's gaze. "That is true."

The tense moment came to an abrupt end when an undying approached the dais. Hades turned back to the task at hand—making deals.

Cerberus sought out Cyane, his hungry eyes landing on her immediately. The golden, shimmering dress like a spotlight, highlighting wherever she was in the ballroom. He wanted her to subject herself to him in front of witnesses, vowing loyalty in the limelight of that dress. Then he wanted to stake his claim in front of all higher and lesser beings alike and show them who she belonged to.

Her fealty was *his*. Her submission and servitude. Cerberus had been the only one to taste her, to feel her worshipful touch, to see her wide and innocent gaze upon him—her need so great, and it had all been his.

It bothered him that she was here. I *left her alone. Who, if not Hades, found and brought her here?* He didn't like others staring at her like he did.

Melinoe's grip on Cyane's wrist had not relented. His eyes fell to it hatefully.

That one touch from the blighted goddess infuriated him nearly as much as what Hades's mysterious plans were. His ideas on the subject were not kind to Cyane. Even Hermes's wandering eyes, scanning Cyane's flesh, didn't bother Cerberus as much as Melinoe's hold on her.

Let Hermes look.

If he touches her...

I can kill him, eat him. Oh, to eat a god. He always wondered what it would be like. He would enjoy it if it were Hermes. He would take his time and revel in the winged god's screams and wear his flying, blood-soaked adornments as a trophy.

But not Melinoe. He wouldn't dare devour her. The very idea of it threatened his stomach with sickness. Her presence alone was despised by all, her voice brought rot to the mind, and though hatred for the goddess burned deep, Queen Persephone may never forgive him for eating her only child.

The Day of Deviance was swiftly approaching. Cerberus stepped forward, intent on stealing Cyane away before it began.

"Stay," Hades commanded Cerberus before he could take another step. "We are not done speaking."

Cerberus turned to glare at Hades, barely able to hide his murderous contempt. He wished no harm to come to his lord but...what would it feel like devouring such a god?

I do have his face.

"You did not answer my summons multiple times this day. You'll be punished as I see fit."

NEAR TIPSINESS, with her feet drenched in the god's nectar, Cyane held onto Melinoe for balance. She hadn't even sipped the liquid, but the powerful scent of it made her world tilt. It was just a little, but enough to feel in her human body. Though her sex ached, her mind lingered on what happened between her and Cerberus.

The ballroom was so beautiful it glowed, and there was more light here than she'd seen since her descent, and *goddess*, how Cyane missed the light. Each little candle flame was like a golden star in the night sky, and their little sparks reflected off the liquid at her feet. Her dress, which at first she had been almost afraid to wear for its brilliance, was reflected back at her.

For once she almost felt like she belonged. *Fuck*, it felt good. Except Cerberus didn't accompany her—he was across the room, watching, protecting her from afar when she would like his cold presence beside her.

Relief was the best part. Every step she took with Melinoe through the hallways, she'd been afraid there would be nothing but rotting carnage at the end. Pieces of bodies strewn about, splashes of blood across the walls.

Cerberus hadn't been there when she'd awoken, but the whistling had. There'd been a knock, and she'd opened the door of the gatehouse to find Melinoe standing on the other side, the gold dress in hand and a giddy smile on her doll-like face.

Melinoe's smile hadn't lasted, faltering as she barged past Cyane, entering the room. Despite the bed being made, the smell of sex had lingered. Melinoe tore away the blanket Cyane used as a robe and ordered her into the bath.

Now the goddess wouldn't let her go.

Hermes peered down at Cyane, his haughty eyes narrowing on her face. He'd been talking for some time, but she hadn't been listening. She was waiting for Melinoe to let her go so she could go to Cerberus.

"So familiar," Hermes purred. "Who are your parents?"

Any good feelings Cyane carried, fled at the mention of her parents. "I—"

"She doesn't know who her parents are, don't you know? They abandoned her at birth," Melinoe tittered.

Hermes glanced at Melinoe, scowling. "Interesting."

"She was on her way to meet them before her arrival."

Hermes stepped back and canted his head. "Is that so?"

"Yes," Cyane whispered.

"They contacted you? After all these years, now?"

She didn't want to tell Hermes anything, didn't want anyone to know her shame, that her secret was now a very buried urge she kept deep within herself. *Cerberus would know, he would know if I considered leaving.* Not even Cerberus knew about her parents. Only Melinoe, and only because Cyane had spoken before realizing she was dealing with...*gods.*

"They left me a note," Cyane said.

"Sweet Cyane and I have that in common, the lack of our parent's love," Melinoe spat then smiled.

Hermes cocked a brow. "I could find them for you, could figure out who they are."

"You could?" Cyane's heart began to race.

Hermes grinned and glanced up at the throne. Cyane followed his gaze to where Cerberus stood. Tension filled every fiber of her body when she saw how he stared back at her. If only they could go back to the gatehouse—

"For a kiss, I think? I'll do it for a kiss," Hermes said.

Melinoe released Cyane's wrist to clap. "Yes!"

Cyane slid her gaze back to Hermes. She rubbed her wrist. She could feel Cerberus on her flesh, could feel the burning heat of his stare. Several hounds stepped forward from behind Hermes to approach her.

What he offered her was almost more enticing than what Melinoe had. *To finally know...*

Years flashed by her eyes as she recalled the countless times she'd searched for her parents, guessing, wondering. There'd been so many sleepless nights. For the cost of a single kiss, she could have a god find them.

Hermes, who wasn't bound by human law and order, who had abilities the best detectives couldn't fathom.

If I don't make it out of here, if I don't make it to Sicily in time... Or what if I do make it, but they're not there?

But this felt wrong, insincere. Hermes had no reason to help her, had no reason to know her business at all. The idea of even kissing him made her stomach churn.

I belong to Cerberus.

"Well? Don't you want to know?" Hermes asked. "A kiss is nothing to enlightenment."

Cyane had parted her lips to answer when Hermes vanished. A crash and clatter of falling candles echoed across the room, and then Cerberus stood in front of her. Her eyes widened with shock.

The chatter in the ballroom halted.

Off to the side, Hermes was slumped on the ground, his feathers and hair smoking. He pulled himself up, barking out in laughter, and brushed himself off as if the impact hadn't affected him at all.

Cerberus growled, stealing her attention. He towered over her with furious eyes. He reached out to touch her but stopped short, curling his fingers.

"I wasn't going to accept." Her stomach fluttered. She didn't know how much he heard, but he must've heard enough because her words didn't seem to settle him at all. Everyone was watching them. Even Hades.

She had a sudden need to tell Cerberus everything, about her parents and about her note. To tell him everything she'd failed to bring up, and explain why Hermes's offer had made her hesitate. But the eyes of the crowd were on them now, and words failed her.

Hades's voice roared out over the ballroom.

"What a grand way to start the Day of Deviance!"

The guests laughed. Cyane flinched. *Deviance.*

Hades grinned. "There is nothing more fun than sexual interaction, especially coercion."

Cyane flicked her eyes back to Cerberus to find his still on her—on her lips.

They belong to you, she wanted to say. *Only you.*

"Let's not wait another moment," Hades boomed. "Dionysus descends as we speak! Honor me with your compliance, and perhaps I'll be inspired to use your tricks on our Queen."

Guests cheered and raised their drinks, throwing their heads and cups back.

Luted, wild music began to play. Laughter followed.

The Day of Deviance. Her mind whirled with the implication. Each day so far had been literal. The idea of viewing another god, Dionysus most of all, sent a shiver down her spine. An excited shiver or not was yet to be discovered.

"Cerberus...what's happening?" she asked.

He stepped away at her words. *No!* Her chest broke open. She reached for him, but he moved farther away, to the other side of Melinoe.

Confusion forced her to drop her hand. Boredom filled what she could see of his face, and he turned towards the dais, hiding his expression from her completely.

She didn't have a choice but to follow his gaze. The sudden raucous of the guests vanished, everyone was watching the dais, too.

Several of Cerberus's hounds howled as a woman with dark hair and a spiked crown strode towards the dais, holding a flaming torch aloft. Hades stood at her arrival. Cyane had seen the woman before, during the day of gifts, but didn't know who she was.

A goddess. She had to be. The woman's aura was powerful. More so than most, enough to nearly eclipsed Hades. Cyane could feel her presence consume everything.

She glanced at Cerberus. Her breath shortened with fear. *Please look at me.*

His focus was entirely on the woman who now regarded them studiously. Even Hermes had turned her way.

Cyane wasn't afraid of the goddess staring out at them. She feared what was about to happen. Consequences for what happened between her and Hermes and the possibilities of more massacre were looming.

Why didn't he stand next to me?

Then the goddess spoke, and Cyane realized who she was.

Hecate.

"Herein lies the day before last, the final celebration before our Queen Persephone descends to the farthest realm. Our great queen and dearly beloved mother of spring prepares for her departure. Today, this Day of Deviance, we honor her with the act of creating new life, even in this darkest of places."

Hecate raised her torch and waved it once before her.

The ballroom changed before Cyane's eyes. The candlelit obsidian walls faded, and in their place were giant, tangled trees. The pillars throughout became trunks, sprouting all kinds of flowers from their bark. An earthy, heady musk filled her nose, and the floor softened beneath her feet. Rich dirt, thick pale grass, and tiny white flowers rose up everywhere.

Streams of moonlight streaked down from an impenetrable ceiling of branches and flowers. The basins remained, but the drink inside them turned a deep red. She watched the liquid bubble and swirl as more trees grew out from the ground.

When it was done, she thought she'd been transported to a forest glade at midnight. Little ponds emerged throughout filled with lily pads and darting silver fish. She half expected to see little fairies flying about, but none appeared.

Tartarus itself fled. Everything disappeared, even the uncertainty and doubt that she'd harbored vanished. Déjà vu hit her so hard that tears threatened to emerge. For the first time in her entire life, and with a sensation she could barely understand, Cyane thought she was home.

Truly home.

In all her travels across Europe, she'd never seen anything so beautiful, so magical, a forest perfectly undisturbed by civilization.

This is what I've been searching for. She reached down and slipped off her sandals. This was more than her parents or the gods themselves, this was *her*. All her. Cyane eyed the ponds, her mouth watering.

"I depart now to meet Persephone above and lead her home," Hecate declared.

The sound of her voice summoned her back, like she had never been alone. While the feeling of *home* dissipated, Cyane struggled to believe this was all an illusion.

The goddess stepped off the dais, now made of moss and stone, and walked calmly through the glade. The undying bowed and lowered their eyes at her passing. Her burning torch was a beacon in the shadows. She passed through the doors and was gone.

Cyane finally glanced back at Cerberus; he was holding Melinoe's hand, and the goddess was gazing up at him with adoration.

Cyane's heart twisted.

Terrible thoughts seized her.

He never offered me more than protection.

Maybe being kept in his room had been a way to manipulate her? No one had harmed her since she'd arrived. *Had he tricked me?* Something didn't feel right. Her chest squeezed tight, but her spine straightened.

I'm not crazy. I'm not.

Cyane stepped forward, forcing Cerberus to look at her.

THE DAY OF DEVIANCE

 Cyane said.

"There's nothing to discuss."

"Please," she begged, her voice softening. She refused to look at Melinoe even though the goddess stood next to him. It hurt too much. "Don't make me beg. Not here."

"Melinoe, leave us," he ordered, and Cyane's heart thudded with relief. The goddess bowed her head and moved away.

Cyane inhaled and waited until Melinoe was out of hearing distance before she spoke. "Something's changed."

Cerberus canted his head.

"Tell me what's changed," she demanded.

"I am, and always will be, Hades's servant. Nothing has changed."

"You held her hand. *Her* hand. You detest her, I know you do. I can't stand it." The words poured from her. "I don't know what's happening to me, why I'm even here," she cried, "but I can't stand this, any of this, not anymore!"

Cerberus grabbed her hand and roughly pulled her to a shady alcove of trees, deeper into the glade. She tripped after him. He released her just as suddenly and flung her around. His eyes sparkled with red fire.

"You make my life hard," he growled. "Harder than it should be. You're just a mortal."

Just a mortal? Cyane gaped. "You think your life is hard? Fuck you. Fuck you! You don't know the meaning of hard."

He went rigid. Power bloomed from him, and she stiffened.

Cerberus stalked closer, and Cyane stepped backward, her back hitting against the tree. "Little human, you and I are nothing more than pawns to beings much more powerful, much greater than us. The sooner you come to terms with that, you'll understand the meaning of hard."

"Something has changed! I know it."

Cerberus closed the distance, leaned close, and trapped her. Cyane eased back as much as she could, feeling the bark digging into her.

"Oh yes, something has changed," Cerberus said. "Many things have changed, more than I can keep up with. I'm trying to protect you, but you make that so very difficult. I wonder why I even try."

"I wasn't going to accept Hermes's deal."

Cerberus's hand came up to push into the tree near her cheek; the bark broke under his fingers. "What did he offer you? What did he offer you that I haven't? That I can't? Escape from this place? The affection of one of the beloved golden gods of Olympus? Flight?"

Information. Cyane lowered her eyes. But maybe the relief of having a single question answered would have been more terrible than its cost.

"What was it? Speak!"

"My parents," she whispered. "He offered to find out who my parents are."

The crunching of bark breaking ceased. "Your parents?"

"I've been searching for them my entire life. I was on the way to… I was following the only lead I ever had when I ended up here." She paused. "It doesn't matter."

He growled. "Why didn't you tell me?"

Cyane shook her head. "Would it have mattered?"

His hand moved to cup her cheek, and his thumb rubbed the delicate spot beneath her eye. The gentle touch was unexpected. She wanted to nuzzle into his palm as badly as she longed to bite it, hating that his same hand held Melinoe's minutes before.

"No," he said at last. "But I could help you find them if they are here."

"Dead?"

"If they are dead."

She closed her eyes tight, then nodded once before opening them. "Thank you…"

"For that kiss."

Cerberus stood back, and she heard it. Somewhere in the distance, the sound of giggles and lutes had grown, and the smell of wine filled the air, overwhelmingly strong. The background seemed to blur out of focus as she gazed at his striking form. She could feel the blood rushing through her as her heart seemed to beat in time with the whispering music.

Cerberus pulled off his helmet. Her body responded to the sight of his dark beauty cast in moonlight. The darkness shrouded him like his black armor, his pale skin an indication that he'd never felt the sun. His chest heaved once as if it drew in the scent and the sounds as well, and she remembered what that chest looked like under his armor. Toned, rippling, glorious.

My god. The only god.

Her sex knotted, and a light breeze fluttered the flowers

and leaves around them. Behind him, she saw dozens of his hounds prowling.

"Yes," she agreed breathlessly. *Yes*, she would do deviant things, deviant acts, for a kiss from him.

He lowered his face, but she pressed her hands to his chest.

"Your hand," she demanded.

Eager, the lust growing between them, he ripped the glove from his fingers and showed her the band of hair around his thumb. The next instant, his lips were devouring her, his body pressing her back up against the tree.

Cyane gasped, breathing in the heady air and his raw scent.

The giggles in the background turned to moans and grunts, even screams. Cyane's belly flipped. She wanted to join them. She grasped at Cerberus, her hands running all over his armor, his arms, from his large shoulders to the tangle of hair at his nape.

"I need you," she pleaded. A kiss wasn't enough.

He grasped the dress at her hips and tore it up her legs, hefting her up as she climbed him. She hooked her legs around his waist, uncaring of how his hard armor dug against her skin, hurting her. The hurt felt so good.

They reached down together and tore at his belt, shoving his pants down to release his already hard cock.

Cerberus rested his brow against hers and panted heavily over her face. Cyane took the warm air into herself.

"I belong to you," she moaned. "My dark god."

He responded back, mixing her name with an animalistic grunt.

A light, chilled breeze blew over her sex, and she clenched, hard and desperate. His hands grabbed her hips, tilted them forward, and he thrust brutally into her.

Cyane screamed and dug her nails into his scalp,

throwing her head back. Stars flooded her vision. She wrenched her eyes shut as he pressed her back against the tree with every forceful thrust, uncaring of her comfort. She held on, hugging his neck.

Each time Cerberus grunted her name, she clamped down on his enormous cock. It was a battering ram that speared through her desire and fucked her soul. It sent her straight from her body, taking it for his own.

She gasped to discover tears in her eyes. Blissful ones. She brushed them away to see Melinoe, staring at her from behind a tree. Their gazes met and Cyane shuddered, another shove into insanity taking her. She snapped her eyes shut, but the goddess was still behind her lids.

Cerberus grabbed a fistful of Cyane's hair and pulled her head back to reclaim her lips. He drove his tongue into her. His thrusts grew more brutal and quick, his tongue lashing inside her mouth.

He roared, pushing himself even deeper into her, grinding her onto him. Burning liquid burst inside her, filling her up where his cock couldn't go. His pumps slowed, his lips grazed her dewy cheeks.

He laid her on the soft grass and rose over her, adjusting his pants downward.

Cyane glanced to the side as he poised her to enter her again. Melinoe was gone.

"You didn't scream like you always do," he growled through ragged breaths.

Her sex still ached for relief even as she experienced more relief than she had in ages.

"I wanted to feel you," she said.

He petted her thighs. His deft fingertips caressed her slick folds. "I wanted to feel you, too."

New laughter filled her ears, dark and frightening, far to close. Cyane shot up, but Cerberus pressed her back down with his hand. A figure knelt next to them, appearing from shadows.

Hades.

"My lord," Cerberus muttered.

Cyane shoved down the skirt of her dress and curled her arms around her chest. Cerberus pulled her up against him, wrapping an arm around her.

Hades smiled with glee, roving his dark eyes over them. She pressed into Cerberus but couldn't look away from the God of the Underworld

Had he watched them too? Her lust fled as something sick took its place.

They're so much alike. Replicas, twins... Now that she could see both men up close, side by side, she realized their eyes were slightly different, as was their smells. Cerberus smelled wild and musky and untamed. Hades smelled like cold death. Not even the scent of wine in the air reached her nose, it was powerless compared to death.

Hades was nothing like Cerberus.

He was abysmal perfection. A vampire in the night. A whisper in the darkness that promised all physical delights for a terrible, horrible favor.

Hades's smile deepened as if he knew her thoughts. Cyane tensed and pressed her thighs together and a blush heated her cheeks as Cerberus's seed emptied from her to spread between them.

Hades's gaze flicked to Cerberus, and the suffocating pressure left Cyane. She sucked in a shaky breath.

"You ignore my demands once again, Cerberus," Hades said. "Perhaps you're no longer afraid of me?"

"Never," Cerberus's voice lowered menacingly.

Cyane peered up at him, her brow furrowing. Hades reached out with frozen fingers, caught her chin, and forced her to face him. He held her gaze.

"Your honesty delights me," he whispered, turning her head from side to side, studying her. "Cyane, did you know your paramour knows why you are here?"

Cerberus's body went tense.

Her fingers curled. "N-no."

"Cerberus was quite adamant about finding out, spewing his need to protect you, but I can see… you've already figured it out on your own. You don't need protection while you're here. If I deem you safe, you are safe, although pain might still find its way to you." Hades tittered then addressed Cerberus. "So my friend, were you protecting her from me?"

Cerberus didn't answer.

Hades drew her face towards him as if seeking her lips.

"I kept her away from all who would use her naivety against us," Cerberus growled.

Hades paused, his fingers still grasping her chin.

Cerberus continued. "I kept her to protect you, this realm, and the laws of nature against greater disruption. If you had but told me all of your plans, my choices would've been different. The world nearly died when Persephone was taken. The past will not repeat under my watch."

"But then she made an oath to Styx," Hades mused.

"Yes."

Turning his face to Cyane, Hades's smiled grew wicked. "Would you like to know why you're here, Cyane?"

She pushed her way out from under Cerberus's protective arm, distancing herself from Hades, from Cerberus too. She ached terribly from the rough sex, and her core trembled for release and mercy. Her throat tightened uncomfortably, knowing Hades might use this against her.

She glimpsed Cerberus; his face was hard, furious. *He knew, he knew but kept it from me.* She could see it now. The image of him grabbing Melinoe's hand returned like a demon, but it no longer made her upset.

It made her sad.

She'd avoided Hades all this time, thinking he was the largest threat; perhaps that was a mistake. Maybe a deal with the devil, the God of the Underworld, would've saved her sanity.

Cerberus's arm fell away from her, his hand rounded her wrist to hold her still.

I chose him willingly, despite everything. I'll always choose him.

She'd found home twice already today, once within the forest and flowers and again in his arms. *He* was her home.

Her heart cracked. *I love him.*

Cerberus may be the monstrous hundred-headed hound, the endless heads of serpents, the terrorizer of souls, but he'd become everything to her. Fangs, saliva, snouts, and slithering tongues. All of him.

Cyane shivered and faced Hades. "Tell me why I'm here."

THE NOTE

CYANE FOLLOWED HADES. Cerberus detested every step she took away from him. Hating it even more that he couldn't stop her.

They went to the dais, and Hades created a seat for her beside him, offering her a goblet of wine. She picked up her skirt, gingerly sat upon the seat, without taking the drink. Her eyes found Cerberus where he stood. They roved over his helmet, almost fondly. He'd put it back on before anyone could see him.

His jaw ticked, and his feverish hunger returned. It was always at its worst when he was denied her.

Cyane tore her eyes away from him and looked out over the forest glade with a shiver even Cerberus could discern from where he stood. He could smell her arousal, could smell his musk on her. His cock remained hard and confined beneath his armor, frustrated.

He'd planned to finish her off before Hades interrupted him. He'd planned to take her again in the grass, and worship her how Cyane worshipped him. While sex wasn't something he was familiar with, he was an eager student, and he wanted to forget everything he had ever lived for to use Cyane at his will.

An orgy was taking place around him, naked bodies writhing and fucking everywhere, everything. Nothing, not even the basins of wine, the trees, or flowers themselves were spared. Not even the dirt.

Dionysus danced around with crazed delight, pulling his maenads to him and then shoving them away. Whoever he touched, whoever his followers touched, were caught up in the erotic euphoria.

It put him on edge, it addled his mind. One trio of men stuffed their cocks into a single female. She gagged and giggled as she swallowed one of the cocks in her mouth. Another pair of females poured wine over their cunts, taking turns slurping it from the other.

A female vigorously rode a male from above, screaming and buckling. Awe filled him at the sight. He'd only ever taken Cyane, trapping her and her lust, had never even considered the idea of letting her take *him*.

Then there were the screams of stolen sex and torment. Disgusting Menoetes held down a small maenad and thrust into her. Tantalus cried as Dionysus poured wine over his head, wine Tantalus would still be denied, as nymphs caressed their breasts before him, turned on by his wails. Not all the screams were good ones. Even rape could create life.

The only ones spared were Cerberus, Hades, Cyane, and…Melinoe.

He found the goddess sitting alone at the edge of a pond, and with Hades's command still in Cerberus's mind, he went to her. His stiff erection died as he neared.

He searched for Hermes as he crossed towards Melinoe, preparing to signal that he needed his end of their deal upheld, but couldn't find the golden pest. Cerberus gritted his teeth. He wouldn't search for him, his hounds already found the god's scent somewhere deep within the trees, and it wasn't a good smell. Blood, feces, and semen.

Melinoe glanced at Cerberus. Naked naiads and maenads swam around a dead Arae male, touching and kissing his corpse, one which they probably drowned not long ago.

"Sweet Cerberus, what do you want?" Melinoe asked. Ghostly hands came up from the ground to pet Melinoe's skin.

"Nothing from you."

"Then why are you bothering me?"

Cerberus moved his eyes back to the goddess, surprised. Melinoe had never not wanted his attention before. "Hades deems it fit to punish me with your presence this day, goddess."

She laughed, but it was tinged with sadness. "You must've done something horrible for such a punishment. Tell me, is the punishment really for you or for him? To keep me away from him this day?"

"I wouldn't presume to guess our lord's mind."

"Try, if not for me, then for a promise that I won't approach my father this day?" Melinoe dipped her fingers into the water, and the nymphs jumped out.

"He did it for both then, as much to torment me as to ensure nothing ruins his day."

"Hmm."

The Arae's corpse floated and drifted to the middle of the small pond. The body began to convulse and shake, slow at first then wildly. A soul tore out from its body and transformed into a ghost. He screamed and wailed, moving unwillingly towards Melinoe.

The goddess flicked her fingers through the water, urging

the Arae's soul to her, and when he stood before her, his translucent jaw hung slack from such violent screams. Melinoe forced him down to kiss her.

Disgusted, Cerberus turned away.

When she was done, Melinoe shoved the ghost towards him. "Something to alleviate your torture."

Cerberus stared at the crying male and drew him closer. His belly yawned with hunger, his mouth grew wide beneath his helmet, and familiar sharp teeth split from his gums. Several of his hounds arrived as Cerberus grabbed the ghost by its neck and opened his human mouth beyond its natural limits. The Arae screamed again as it contorted and slipped under Cerberus's helmet to be devoured.

The soul's cries joined the hundreds of thousands of others inside him. It did little to quench the void.

Cerberus found Cyane when he was done with his meal. Nothing would ever be as good as her.

I get to devour her slowly, beautifully, lovingly.

Lovingly. A strange word to enter his head. He hissed.

Melinoe tilted her head. "Was it not enough?"

"It's never enough." *I want Cyane, by my side, not Hades's.*

This truly was punishment.

"How did you find her?" Cerberus asked.

"Why does my father hate me so much?"

"I don't know, perhaps the same reason everyone detests you, goddess."

Melinoe wiped her fingers on the grass and stood. "But you do know. I know you do. End my eternal torment, and I'll end yours. I'll never bother you again. We made a deal, your dear Cyane and I."

A deal? "You assume I can't withstand your presence, I lived for eons before you were brought into this world, I will live countless more after you're gone."

"I offered her freedom," Melinoe taunted him with a whisper. "Tell me what I want to know and my deal with Cyane will be broken. Besides, she won't make it above before her mind dies, then she'll be mine forever more."

His hand shot out to grip Melinoe's neck before he realized what he had done. "What did she offer in return?"

She didn't fight him off. "I want an answer to the question I've been asking, the same one even my own mother won't answer."

"You're the goddess of nightmares." He squeezed, wanting so badly to snap Melinoe's neck. "The goddess of insanity. You're mere existence hurts."

"I'm powerful."

"You're a curse."

"The longer you stay beside me, the worse it will become, sweet Cerberus. Tell me, tell me, and I'm gone. Tell me now, and Cyane's deal is broken. The longer I'm near her, the worse it will get. The more she encounters me, the more her thoughts will melt. She's not a god, she's mortal, and she's susceptible to me. I've already stroked her mind on several occasions. She won't be able to recover what sanity she's lost. Mortals are weak, and I can't stop it. Tell me, and I will never go near her again."

Fury unlike never before filled him, fury laced with mania. He jerked Melinoe up then threw her to the ground. She scurried back with a laugh. "I'm hungry too, sweet Cerberus. Grab my neck again and take me like you took her!"

"You'll never go near her again?" he snarled, kneeling over the goddess. He didn't eat living beings, detested blood, but he'd make an exception.

"Never. I promise. I swear an oath on Styx. I will never go near Cyane again."

His mouth burned. "You're not Hades's daughter. You're the product of rape. Zeus, Persephone's own father, raped her after giving her to Hades. He stole Hades's heir. Your mother can't look at you without pain, and Hades knows you are the curse of Persephone's pain. You, Melinoe, exist as punishment, and not even Olympus wants the darkness that follows you."

The goddess was never supposed to know, and now she did.

He'd betrayed Hades again.

Cerberus was beginning to realize he'd do anything for Cyane. *Lovingly.* The word was too close to love. His kind didn't love…did they? He was the last one left of his breed.

The goddess's eyes widened. She sank back into the dark grass, and her eyes closed with a shuddering breath. Cerberus rose up, but not before he dipped his hand into the pond to get the feel of Melinoe off of him.

"Thank you," she said at last without her usual despair. "Thank you, sweet Cerberus."

A genuine smile teased Melinoe's lips. The first he'd ever seen her have.

She drew in the darkness and vanished, keeping her end of the bargain.

He searched the area, but no longer sensed her. Melinoe was gone. None of his hounds had her scent anymore. Pressure lifted from his chest.

His head cleared some, but not enough. It would never be enough. Not anymore, not after everything that had happened.

He stepped back into the forest and watched Cyane and Hades from the shadows. She sat in Persephone's spot, perhaps a little further back, and a little to the right. She was in his Queen's seat, where no one had ever sat besides Leuce, a nymph that his lord had also stolen from above. Persephone turned Leuce into a white poplar tree upon her discovery of their affair.

Just because one thorn in his side was gone, didn't mean his promise to protect Cyane became any easier.

'Cyane is not yours, she is mine.'

'I belong to you.' Cyane's voice eclipsed Hades's.

Hades's love for nymphs wasn't a secret, but it had been rarely entertained, incredibly so. Cerberus studied as his lord's gaze lingered on the writhing maenads across the glade.

Cyane is a mortal, not a nymph. Hades had neither touched nor wooed her, where the women of his past—if they didn't come willingly—were taken against their will.

If Persephone saw Cyane sitting there, would she know that?

The Day of Deviance was nearly over. He tore his eyes off of Cyane and drew the darkness to him, hating himself for leaving her in such a place alone. Dozens of his hounds moved to stand guard around the dais. If something should happen, he would know. He would return.

Cerberus stood in the gatehouse room once more, alone for the first time since Cyane's arrival in his haven. Loneliness from those previous days returned quickly. He glanced at the bed for a split-second, picturing her there. She faded away. He was turning towards the terrace when something caught his eye.

A white scrap of cloth?

No, a piece of paper.

It didn't belong. He knew everything that was in this room. Not one thing in this space had been placed there by anyone but himself...or Cyane.

Cerberus reached out and touched it. The note smelled of Cyane, even more so than the bed. It smelled like power and history, endless travel and tears.

There was nothing like it here in Tartarus. It was a thing

from above. The only items Cyane had with her were her clothes, and those had been promptly destroyed.

He picked the paper up and flipped it over.

'Dear Cyane, come to Thesmophoria on your twenty-fourth year. We await you in Syracuse, Sicily. Your father.'

He recognized the handwriting.

THE QUESTION BEST LEFT
UNANSWERED

GAZING OUT FROM THE DAIS, Cyane thought she'd found Cerberus, but then the shadows shifted once again to shady foliage. The potent reek of Dionysus's wine and the pounding tribalized music put her on edge.

She couldn't look at the bodies around her for long without her stomach feeling the urge to succumb to its own violence. Cyane tangled her fingers in her lap and pressed her thighs together tightly.

Before her was a glittery pond where a single female bathed. A naked male watched from the shore. They played a game, chase and retreat, a form of foreplay.

Guilt filled her for watching such a sight, but it was far easier to focus on them than the sounds in her ears, the brutal orgy, or Hades, who sat barely a foot away, acting as though he'd forgotten she was there.

And now I'm wetting the seat. Unwanted desire still beat in her. Cyane wrenched her eyes closed with embarrassment.

"How are you enjoying the entertainment?" Hades asked.

Her eyes snapped open.

"It's...interesting...my lord." *It makes me feel sick and terri ble. It makes me want to run. It makes me want to hate everything about this place.*

It makes me want to join in.

"Yes," Hades mused with a little more mirth then she cared to hear in his voice. "Every year I'm awed. You would think if you'd lived as long as I have, and have seen what I've seen, not much would phase you anymore. Yet today always brings a surprise."

"Some of your subjects are being hurt."

Hades turned towards her. "Do you feel for them? Would you stop their hurts if you could?"

Even from the corner of her eye, his presence was all consuming when his attention was on her. "Yes."

"Even though this day has happened each year for count-less years?" Hades raised one ebony brow. "Everyone came here knowing exactly what would happen, the dangers they were putting themselves in, as well as the vast pleasure, and they still choose to come. Some choose to be hurt. They seek it. They need it. Some come to hurt others or for revenge from past years."

Cyane licked her lips. "Why are you telling me this?"

"To tell you not to care so much." Hades laughed. "They didn't have to come. No one is here against their will."

She tangled her fingers even tighter in her lap. "Except me..."

Don't look at him. Don't look at him! She didn't want to see Cerberus in him. *I want Cerberus, not him.*

The woman in the pond splashed at the man on the shore, stealing Cyane's attention. She wondered what it would be like to be them right now. They appeared so carefree and happy, enjoying their voyeurism without shame. It's not like she was voyeuristic, but she'd switch places with the nymph in a heartbeat to be free of...*this.*

"Cyane, even you came here with free will," Hades purred.

Cyane paused. "I followed you for answers."

"Hah! Yes, yes you did. But I mean here"—he waved his arm out—"to my kingdom. You couldn't stay away. You were given all the freedom of the world above, yet you still came here willingly."

She stiffened and turned to him, flinching when she saw Cerberus for a split-second. "What do you mean? My boat capsized. I was on the way to Sicily for—"

"Thesmophoria?"

"How did you know?"

He leaned over the arm of his chair and lowered his voice. "What do you think this festival is? It's not like the mortal one above, which is all women honoring my shrew of a sister, Demeter, where they beg and pray for good harvests and fertility. That bitch brought you winter and starvation without a care in the world for your meager mortal lives. She's as selfish as they come."

"And you kidnapped her daughter without consent and kept her here to be your queen, I'd say you're selfish, too," Cyane snapped.

Hades's smile turned wicked, and she turned back to the couple playing at the pond. They were gone.

"Zeus gave me consent," Hades spat, "and if Zeus gives his consent, there is no other consent one needs. He rules everything. Even me."

A stocky, wizened man flashed in Cyane's head. Long white hair with crows feet framing the side of his eyes. His leering gaze was ancient and full of lightning. The image disappeared, and she realized she was thankful to be sitting next to Hades. How was that possible?

"It doesn't matter," she whispered. "I didn't come here willingly."

"Yet you carried my note for twenty-four years."

Her stomach sickened. *What?*

Hades continued speaking.

"You read it nearly every day once your young mortal mind could comprehend words. You, Cyane, were the most eager of all to be here. Even I could feel your desire from so far below."

The air stole away from her lungs. "No." Shock dominated her mind, and her hands untangled from each other. "You lie," she stammered.

"If only life could be that easy for you."

"No," she said again, heart thumping painfully in her chest. Maybe if she said it enough times, it would be real. But Hades reached out and touched a tendril of her hair, petting it with fingers that were now so familiar. It made her want to vomit. *No, please. Please, god no.*

"Yes," he said softly, terribly. "You turned out perfect. Persephone will be pleased."

Cyane jerked back with a cry. "Don't touch me!" She moved to stand, but Hades clamped his hand on her shoulder. Her struggles were nothing against his strength.

He forced her back down. "You will sit, and you will listen. That's why you're here, aren't you? To watch others fuck with the man who is the closest thing you have to a father?"

She cried out again, shaking now, trying not to hear what he was saying. She didn't want to hear it. Didn't want to know anymore. If the note came from Hades...

My whole life...

"We don't have much time before my Queen arrives, and once that happens, we'll both be too busy to even look at each other, let alone speak. You're going to help me, Cyane, because you exist for no other reason, and you will serve obediently, because I know of your treachery to escape this place, and I know what Cerberus would do for you." Hades chuckled. "He's committing even more treason as we speak!"

Cerberus. She couldn't find him among the trees, the orgy. His hounds walked in and out of the treeline shadows. She caught the gaze of one and held it, finding a modicum of courage. She swallowed down the bile in her throat.

She didn't want to believe Hades. It wrenched her mind, but if what he said was true, then…

Her fingers twitched to claw out her eyes.

"If you want to ensure Cerberus's safety, you will listen and you will obey. Understood?" Hades's voice slithered into her.

Cyane nodded.

The moans and guttural grunts of countless orgasms filled her ears, but none were enough to eclipse Hades's voice.

"Good." He released her shoulder.

Cyane slumped as though all her strength had been drained. Her skin was frozen where he'd touched her.

"It was no small feat to bring you back to life, so you owe me a great debt. Not only did I have to collect your soul from the world above because, well, you'd never truly died, but Charon was also not thrilled to leave his ferry to travel inland."

"My—soul?"

"It matters not. You were dying, and I've waited a long time for it to happen, but it still wasn't fast enough. The mortals above honor you to this day, and their worship was enough to make you linger.

"You see, I'm an incredibly patient god, one of the most patient of my family, but after hundreds of years waiting for you to die so I can bring you back to life in your former form, well, I grew restless."

She didn't understand what he was telling her. The possibility of leaving this place and returning to her life before was crashing and burning with each word he spoke. She desperately needed to believe this was all tricks and lies—even when something deep inside told her it wasn't.

I'd already succumbed to my fate here. The fate that a normal life above, a reunion with normal parents, was impossible, and had been for awhile.

"Are you really my father?" she whispered.

"Not in flesh or blood, or godly gifts. I would never sire a mortal. I couldn't, even if I fucked every child-bearing female above. Not that I would. Only Persephone holds my lust these centuries. In terms of giving you life...I suppose I am responsible for your existence, but I would never claim you as a child."

"Why?" she rasped.

"You're no heir."

"I mean...why did you bring me back to life?" Cyane couldn't even remember her childhood to well, let alone an entire *previous existence* as Hades seemed to be insinuating. "Why bring me back to life and leave me alone? Why sign your name on a note as father and do such a terrible thing? Why go to all this effort if I'm beneath importance?"

"Ah, so many questions. More than most would ever dare to ask me in a given year. It's refreshing. If not willful and annoying." Hades took a long drink from his cup. "I suppose." Even his swallows weren't masked by the music and lovers.

"I came all this way. I deserve to know."

"Deserve? How you entertain me." He tittered. "I left you because a mortal doesn't belong here, and to raise one amongst the dead, well, it would've ruined my plans. You had to be left above, and as such, alone."

Cyane breathed. "And what if I ignored your note, or lost it, what if I never came?"

"It was enchanted to remain with you, never to wrinkle, never to deteriorate, designed to haunt you. And if you never came, I would've had to repeat myself and steal you from above. Which would not have been ideal. Predictability is a bad trait for a Lord to have. Predictability is weak."

All these years she'd obsessed over that note, wondering and searching, letting it rule her life, letting it rule every decision she had the ability to make—had she ever really been her own person? Was she really even a person at all?

Hades was acting so nonchalant to her torment.

Where was Cerberus? She needed him now more than ever. Would give anything to have him there beside her. Even if the protection she needed was protection from herself. But he wasn't there, and even death couldn't save her.

Cyane grew numb.

If I died, I'd end up right back where I am.

Cerberus's hounds stalked the sides of the room, but there was still no sight of Cerberus. *Had he known?*

No, he couldn't have. He nearly killed me, made me swear to Styx before he even considered trusting me...

He had known *something*, according to Hades. Something that Cerberus hadn't told her. She shoved the thought from her head, needing to deny it.

Hades hadn't answered the most important question of them all. The one that her life now depended on—

Dionysus appeared before them, a bevy of women behind him, some hanging from his limbs. He bowed to Hades and offered him the cup of wine he held, then bowed to Cyane with a smile that made her want to drink her thoughts away and dance until she passed out.

She reached forward and stole a drink from one of his naked followers and gulped it down.

"Well, well, well, my Lord Hades, your guest of honor is not only beautiful and deliciously weak, but a joy as well!" Dionysus laughed.

"She is all those things and more," Hades agreed.

"I am not weak," she whispered, but both gods ignored her.

I need another drink.

Dionysus bowed once more, this time with less flourish. "I hope the party is to your liking?" he asked of Hades.

Could Dionysus see her torment? Could everyone else?

"You've outdone yourself again. It's a marvel what you and Hecate can accomplish when you work together."

"I humbly thank you to the bottom of my casks." Dionysus grinned. "Which have no bottom that I have yet found!"

High-pitched laughter filled the air. Cyane flinched, not finding it funny at all, not since her stolen drink very much had a bottom, and she had found it all too soon.

"Will you remain to greet our beautiful Queen Persephone on the morrow?" Hades asked.

"I would be honored, my lord. Will this new beauty of yours be with us?"

"She will be at the front of the procession. After me, of course, but I fear I will lose Persephone's attention once she sees Cyane."

What? Cyane's eyes snapped back to Hades, albeit unwillingly. She didn't want to meet the Goddess of Spring, not like that, and not so soon. If she knew anything about the goddesses of Olympus, it was that their jealousy and possessiveness were not a thing to incite.

Was that the answer to her question? Was that Hades's intention all along?

Was she being used to incite jealousy?

A new cup of wine appeared in Dionysus's hand. He offered it to her this time. "Here mortal, drink to your heart's desire tonight. The morrow will be interesting, indeed, and I am even more honored to be in attendance."

Cyane took the cup, and the other one vanished. She gripped it with white fingers.

Hades scoffed. "Leave us, Dionysus. I won't have you corrupt Cyane's mind this night. We are not yet done talking."

"Yes, my lord." Dionysus bowed again. He turned to the women behind him with an exuberant dance, and they all tumbled into each other with perverse delight, their laughter far less happy and more dangerously gleeful. Cyane couldn't help but think it was because of her.

She peered down at the wine in her hand and set it on the floor beside her, no longer wanting it. When the giggles disappeared, and Dionysus departed with his lusty broads, she felt Hades's attention return.

Cyane ignored them as best she could. *I could still find Melinoe, find Cerberus, and get the information the goddess wanted.* Maybe Cyane would take her chance at running—if she had the help of a goddess—but something niggling told her not to trust Melinoe. Especially not now that the goddess witnessed Cerberus having sex with her.

Even a blind zombie could tell the Goddess of Nightmares had feelings for Cerberus.

Cyane bit her tongue and steadied herself, turning to Hades. "What do you plan for me?" It hurt asking.

The corner of his devilish lips curled upwards. "Nothing."

"Why then...why am I here?"

"To serve," he said, offering no comfort.

"Serve how?"

"You are here for one reason and one reason only." Hades's voice slithered into her ear, dark and full of warning. "Your very existence depends on that reason. The fact that you haven't even inquired about your previous life sits ill with me, but know that it was because of you that Demeter discovered I took her daughter."

Because of me?

Hades turned fully toward her. "I do not easily forget nor do I easily forgive, Cyane. I gave you a new life for one purpose, and one purpose only—to ensure I have an heir."

The music roared, and Cyane's hands went slack. The cup she thought she put aside was returned to her, now empty. Had she picked it back up? Had she drunk it without realizing? Her mouth tasted of wine.

"Rest and be ready tomorrow," Hades said. "Your service begins tomorrow."

Her world grew dark. She welcomed it.

It was better than being here.

But Hades's voice was clear despite that descending darkness; just before oblivion swallowed her, she heard him say, "And Cyane, father or no, I'm not without mercy. You'll realize that soon enough."

THE HOURS BEFORE

SomEONE CARRIED HER. The feel of plated armor dug into her side, but then it was gone, and she was placed on something soft and warm. Warm bodies moved to lie next to her, and a familiar scent filtered into her nose.

Dog.

Not just a dog, but a hellish hound. Cerberus's hounds. They warmed her sides. His one-hundred heads that were no longer apart of his body. Cyane burrowed into the bedding, into the hounds. She wanted them to consume her, hold her, comfort her like the countless times she'd burrowed into a bed in the world above.

But the taste of wine was still in her mouth, and try as she might, she couldn't forget all that Hades had told her.

Rest and be ready, he'd said, when he'd really meant, *Come to terms with your situation or cease to exist.* Oh and, *Do it outside my presence.* She curled up on her side and squeezed her eyes even harder shut.

"Cyane," Cerberus said her name somewhere beside her. She didn't want to face him, didn't want to see his face so soon. She wished she'd engorged on wine all day so she could truly be unconscious right now. Not temporarily put here by an evil god.

I don't have parents.

Her fingers gripped the blanket beneath her.

I don't have control.

Her heart thundered.

I'm nothing but a means to an end...

A sad, agonized wail escaped her.

A hand rested softly over her head, then lifted enough to pet her with chilling fingers. She shrunk away from them and cried, heaving into the pillow.

"Please go away," she begged between aching breaths. "I don't want to see you."

"We need to talk," Cerberus said without remorse, making everything worse. "But I will don my helmet if hiding my face eases your pain."

His hand left her head, and she heard him move beside her. Everything made her sick—even him. She needed him to just go away, even though at the same time she wanted to crawl into his lap and submit and beg and pray. Not just pray, she realized, but pray to him. Pray for darkness, and offer herself up as a sacrifice, to show her fealty.

Hate, sickness, and love. Was this what loving a god was like?

"This note. I know—"

"Did you know?" she snapped. If Cerberus was going to force her to talk, he was going to deal with her anger. Cyane lifted her head to glare at him, thankful and annoyed she was looking at his helmet instead of his face. "What did you know? Did you know Hades is the reason I exist?"

"No," he said.

"Did you know I was reincarnated, that I was someone, *something* else in another life that crossed your god?"

Cerberus started, and she could see the shock in his eyes. It made her feel a little better.

"No," he said once more.

"Did you know my very existence isn't my own?" She wanted to scream, but most of all, she wanted to forget. "That every choice I ever made was because of some unseeable god pulling strings from afar? That nothing I've ever done or felt means anything?"

Cerberus lowered and knelt beside the bed. "No," he whispered. The word was soft and low and hollow behind the shield of metal over his mouth. "I knew none of this."

God, how she wanted to believe him.

"I'm nothing, nothing. *Nothing*." Cyane pressed her palms to her eyes and heaved, feeling the air refuse to fill her lungs. *Nothing.*

Cerberus took her hands and drew them from her face. He sat on the bed and pulled her to his chest, and she cried again, unable to stop. The gentleness of his gesture made it worse, but she pressed herself into him, needing everything he would give her. Needing him.

"You're not nothing," he said, his arms banding around her. "You are everything."

Cyane tried to steel herself and force the pain away. It was easier, horribly easier than facing the truth. Believing her parents hadn't wanted her, hadn't kept her, hadn't given her anything but a damnable note was better than this. She'd thought nothing would be as sickening as being unwanted, forgotten. She'd been wrong. And now she hated Hades so much, hated him to the very core of...what? Whatever she could claim as herself, because fuck, she didn't even know if her soul was hers anymore.

"What did you know?" She gripped Cerberus's armor tight, holding onto him like a lifeline. "Tell me."

His fingers brushed through her hair. "That you were brought here to serve."

His softness irritated her. "You knew that?"

"Hades would tell me nothing else."

Cyane pulled away and wiped her eyes. "I'm never leaving this place, am I?"

"No. You're not. Unless—"

"How long have you known?" she asked. "Since we slept together?"

"Since the Day of Battles."

"Since before we slept toge—that was…" Days ago, although it could've been an eternity. "And you didn't bother to tell me? You let me believe I still had a chance? That there was still a chance for…" Her voice hitched, but her anger rose. "I had no idea why I was here, and you knew." Cyane couldn't look at him, couldn't bear it. She looked at her wet hands instead.

"Cyane—"

"Don't," she snapped, pulling away. "I don't want to hear it. I have hours before my time is up. I want to be alone now."

"There is still a chance for you to leave."

"What?"

"You can still leave." Cerberus sat back and faced the terrace. "I made a deal with Hermes."

She wiped her eyes again, not quite believing what he was saying. "Why?"

"Whether you believe me or not," he said, still gazing out the terrace opening where Hades's castle loomed like a diseased finger in the distance. "I promised to protect you, even if it's against my loyalty to Hades. I didn't know why you were brought here, nor what plans he had. My lord does not share much with anyone, not even me, and I'm the closest he has to a confidant, but he did tell me you were here to serve. If I had seen the note sooner…"

"Why do you serve him? Why do you care so much for such a terrible man?"

"He's not so terrible." Cerberus turned back to her. "My father was terrible. My brothers were terrible. Even my mother, the Mother of Monsters, was terrible. They wanted to destroy, to challenge, to go against the ways of nature and sow chaos, a fate worse than death, upon everyone. If it weren't for Hades finding me, leading me away from them, I may have become like my family. Hades offered me retribution and life, a purpose. A purpose that used my talents for destruction to instill order between the living and the dead. What you see as terrible is nothing compared to what the other gods of Olympus are capable of. What history and humanity are even capable of. I am honored to serve Hades, but it is a choice I made myself."

"I don't want to serve him," she whispered. "He's not my god."

You're *my god.* She wanted to say but didn't.

"I know, Cyane."

The words broke her heart. This time when he reached out to caress her, she let him.

"Will you come with me?" she asked.

His hand dropped. "No. I don't belong in the light."

"We can manage," she said. "I can show you so much more. There is real goodness above. I'm good. There are dark places above as well, so we could find such a place and make it ours. A sanctuary where it's just us."

"I don't belong with mortals. I may look human, but I'm not. Goodness is not easy on me, the souls of the dead sustain me, the hounds need the shadows to thrive. Parts of me will die in the light, parts of me I cannot lose. And, say we did this without incurring the wrath of the gods, that we found a place where a smaller version of me might live, what would happen to me when you died? What would happen to you?"

"We can make it work. I know we can."

Cerberus shook his head.

She grabbed his hand and squeezed. "We can change."

He squeezed her hand back, and suddenly they were in a dark tunnel far different from anything she'd seen before in Tartarus. Cyane stumbled, and Cerberus caught her, keeping her upright. A rushing river flowed beside them, and far, far upriver, diminished by distance, was a weak light.

Moonlight.

She'd known it as sure as she knew her own face. There'd been moonlight below, light from the river, even candlelight, but none of it had been real. None of it was like the small beam ahead. She stilled.

He's letting me leave.

Cyane gripped him tight. This was happening too fast, all of it was. From Hades lecturing her on her existence, the hopelessness, and now this. The loss.

Why couldn't she have remained unconscious?

"I can't change," he said, "Not like that."

She turned from the moonlight. "Of course you can change, we can all change. With every day that passes, change is happening."

He cupped her face within his palm. "Someday you will die, Cyane, and if I'm above who will be here to await your soul's final journey? Who will stop Hades from pursuing you when he finds out you're gone? Mortals don't belong here, they never have, and they never will. This place isn't for the living. It's for those who created it."

"But you belong with me." She blinked back tears and leaned into his hand. Freedom was before her, everything she knew lay just beyond. *He did this for me. Despite his loyalty to Hades.* It hurt her heart. Her life hadn't been great before, but it hadn't been terrible. *It'd been mine, and no one else's.* Now that life was being offered back to her, she didn't know how to take the first step.

"And you belong with me."

"Then ask me to stay," she pleaded. "Tell me to stay. Tell me it will all be okay." Cyane insides crumbled when all he did was look down at her with removed emotion.

He's not going to tell me it'll be okay...

He's not going to ask me to stay, and he won't come with me.

She bit back tears.

She reached up and pulled Cerberus's helmet off, needing to see him, aching for something from him. His dark, curly, shoulder-length hair tumbled out like tussled silk, his deep, red eyes, swirling with a myriad of color, stared at her, and his mouth parted slightly.

She leaned up to kiss him.

A soft, sad goodbye. Warm and cold collided for a lingering second, neutralizing each other one last time.

Cerberus pulled away from her far too soon.

"Wait here," he said, and before she could ask why, he disappeared into the darkness.

Cyane curled her arms around her middle and shook, glancing behind her where the tunnel led deeper back into the Underworld. Only a few yards could be seen before the darkness consumed everything. She shivered. It still frightened her, yet at the same time, she didn't want it to go away. After being within it for so long, it wasn't all that bad... It was just *different.* Another part of life. One that everyone would eventually belong to.

She turned back to the light, and for the first time since she'd fallen, she wondered about her few friends and foster parents. The people that were still in her life above. The social workers that cared for her wellbeing, the professors that taught her, even the nuns. They returned to her like a beaconing, warm aura of familiarity.

I like to swim. The moonlight slowly brightened. *I like chocolate-chip cookies. Books. Trees, the forest.*

A noise sounded, and she pivoted to see Cerberus appear with Hermes. Her shoulders dropped. The golden-esque god greeted her with a smile she couldn't return. His winged adornments fluttered.

"Hermes will lead you where you want to go," Cerberus said.

Pain. "Where I want to go?"

"When you reach the top."

Cyane glanced between the two men, having no idea where she wanted to go.

"The deal you made?" she asked, softly.

"Yes, the deal."

Hermes lifted into the air. "I will hold up my end of the bargain."

"I made a deal, too, with Melinoe," she said, having forgotten until that moment. Both men's faces shuttered at the mention of the goddess's name. "I haven't kept it." Will Melinoe come for her?

"You made a deal with...*that?*" Hermes spat.

Cerberus shook his head. "It's been dealt with. She was given what she's been looking for."

Cyane's eyes widened, then she nodded. "Thank you," she whispered, wanting to reach out to Cerberus again but didn't know if he'd accept it with Hermes there. Their interactions had always been private until the glade.

"Well, are we going?" Hermes muttered. "The day is almost over, and Persephone and Hecate will be coming down this way soon. I'm assuming you don't want to be seen? I certainly don't want my fair Goddess of Spring to see me breaking Hades's law. I'd like to return next year."

Cyane turned to Cerberus. He hadn't put his helmet back on. She hoped he'd be okay with Hermes knowing his face. Cerberus's countenance had changed since he'd returned with the winged god; he was acting as though they had already said goodbye.

"Please come with me," she begged again. *Know my pain.* She needed him to hear her plea for him, to give him that last opportunity to choose her. "Please."

He didn't respond, he didn't move at all. She couldn't wait any longer and didn't care who or what saw. She flung herself against Cerberus one last time and hid her face against his armored chest. The smell of worn metal filled her nose.

She held onto him desperately, and eventually, his arms came around her one last time and held her, too.

"Lovingly," she thought she heard him say, gripping him like her soul depended on it. His hands fell from her back, and she quickly drew away before she decided to stay and serve Hades, just to have the chance to see Cerberus. To be near him.

"We'll meet again," she said, growing numb. Then she whispered so low she barely heard it herself. "Ask me to stay. Please ask me to stay."

"Come," Hermes said softly, holding out his hand.

Cyane waited for Cerberus to stop her from making this choice...but he remained silent.

Heart breaking, she stepped back, turned away from him, and took Hermes's hand. He pulled her toward the shoreline, headed for where the light grew brighter with each step.

And when she glanced back, there was nothing but darkness to greet her.

Cerberus watched Cyane walk away, watched as the light haloed around her, swallowing her as she returned to its embrace.

A prickle coursed down his back—Hades called him—but Cerberus couldn't move, resting his hand on the hilt of his sword. What was one more defyment in the grand scheme of things? No punishment was worse than this.

It'd been so long since he'd seen the light. Its glory wasn't meant for him though, never had been, and never would be. Hercules had once forced Cerberus into it, and it had blinded all his hundreds of eyes. The loss had sent him into a rage and he'd had no recourse to the thousands of evil mortals who kicked, stabbed, and prodded his body.

That torment was nothing compared to the hollowing ache in his chest. It built with each step Cyane took.

But she is meant for the light.

Not here.

Not where Hades would use her. Not in the one place Cerberus couldn't ensure her complete safety.

Hades would break her, warp her into a dark creature. And Cerberus couldn't have that. Not now that he knew the lengths of what his lord had gone through to bring her here. Hades had plans for her. Plans Cerberus didn't know.

So sweet, so easy to pluck and possess.

He wouldn't be able to bear seeing Cyane destroyed, plucked and possessed. Especially by anyone that wasn't him. He'd kill anyone who tried.

She twisted to glimpse him, and he stepped back into the shadows. She still wore her golden dress. She sparkled like an angel. His hand tightened around his weapon's hilt.

When she stopped searching for him in the dark, where she'd never be able to find him, she turned away, and Cerberus had an epiphany. Love. That's what his feeling worming through his chest was.

We will meet again.

Cyane and Hermes became dots on the horizon, near gone now in the light.

Even in death, she'll never be mine. He could at least guard her soul, take her where she needed to go, but ultimately he would have to let her go a second time.

Cerberus put his helmet back on and turned away.

PERSEPHONE, DEMETER, AND HECATE

SHE THOUGHT the light would blind her, but it didn't. The smell of soil, grass, and flowers filled her nose. Cyane breathed in deep, having forgotten it all even in such a short amount of time. It helped a little with the growing void in her chest.

They neared the end of the tunnel, just visible at the end of a short rise. She could see brief glimpses when the ferns that blocked it swayed.

He wasn't there when I looked back. She'd hoped Cerberus would stop her, wanted the primordial near-god of him to save her, not leave her. She'd been prepared for many things, but losing him, and so quickly after everything? She hadn't been prepared for that.

You belong with me. Yet, he had done nothing but urge her to go. Now that she was right at the threshold of the realms, she wasn't sure she even had any choice in the matter.

She was sick of not having a choice. Cyane gritted her teeth despite her sorrow. She was sick of the illusion of control.

When they reached the entrance to the cave, Cyane hesitated. *What happens when you come back from the realm of the dead?* Hermes was waiting for her, holding the foliage that obscured the opening to the tunnel to the side and looking less patient by the second. She only had two options. *Really just one option,* she sighed.

Cyane took the final step.

Hermes helped her through the crack of the entrance, pushing the rest of the vines back. The once great river of Styx had become nothing more than a brook, babbling over rocks and stones.

Cyane straightened in the growing dawn light. She hadn't realized how cold and numb she'd been in the Underworld until the warm air blew across her flesh. Her stomach growled. She swallowed, feeling incredibly thirsty. Normal aches and pains assailed her. Everything returned.

Cyane rubbed her arms against the onslaught of feelings, of her bodily functions returning. God, was she hungry.

"You've crossed over," Hermes said, drawing her attention. He no longer appeared as a gilded, winged god, but like a handsome man aged into his forties. He wore jeans and a shirt which hid his once-bare chest, and even had light blonde scruffy beard. "It's not always easy leaving a timeless place."

Cyane glanced down at herself. She still wore her gold gown and sandals. "Where are we?"

"Northwest of Taygetos mountain, near the plateau of Tripoli—depending, of course, upon the names of this time period. Greece, to make it easier. The Alpheus river, or part of it I suppose?" Hermes kicked at a rock. "The entrance to Tartarus changes."

Cyane pulled up the vines they'd just crawled through, finding nothing but a small hole where the water trickled. "Oh." She frowned. *Oh...*

"You won't find your way back, not without help."

A soft cry and a rustle of bushes sounded nearby, startling both Hermes and her. He grabbed her wrist and pulled her away from the brook and behind a thick copse of trees and bushes. He pressed a finger to her mouth as the noises grew closer, and they both knelt to watch through the leaves.

Three women appeared and walked along the brook, stopping where Cyane and Hermes had been standing moments prior.

"My beautiful, fair as the morning sun, a budding flower at first light," Hermes murmured like a love-sick puppy.

They were incredibly beautiful women. Hecate Cyane recognized, though she no longer wore regal regalia, but instead a long black skirt and matching vest with puffy white sleeves pouring out of it.

Beside her was a woman with blonde hair pulled back, wearing worn jeans and a loose-fitting green top that hung low on her heavy breasts. Her arms were bare and slightly tanned, gold bangles circled her wrists, and there were gold chains draped from her neck. She held the hand of a third woman who looked very similar, if not a little younger.

Demeter and... Cyane gasped, the sound making Hermes narrowed his eyes upon her in warning.

Persephone.

The women spoke with each other, but Cyane didn't hear any of it.

I know her! The revelation nearly made her stand up and rush to the women without thought, but a hand clamped down on her shoulder.

The paintings in Cerberus's room came back to her suddenly. The very paintings she couldn't look at for more than moments without having to turn away because of the pain that filled her head.

Persephone wore a dress similar to Cyane's, the only one of the three that looked like a true Grecian goddess, but

Persephone's was a pale yellow, a soft chiton that clung and accentuated the maiden appearance of her. That was the difference between Demeter and Persephone, one had the aura of a mother…the other, an eternal maiden.

Persephone beamed with fresh radiance, blue skies, and soft sunshine. It was impossible to look at her without being filled with love. The kind of love that needed protection at all costs because it could so easily wilt.

"I know her," Cyane whispered in awe. That feeling of pure love filled her. It nearly eclipsed everything, all that she had been through, everything with Cerberus, even the horror of the Underworld and Hades. She knew Persephone so deeply, so fully, that it made her throat close and her chest tighten.

Hermes's hold on her tightened, but she barely registered it as she stared at the goddess.

Hecate raised the vines for Persephone as Demeter hugged her daughter fiercely, tears pouring down her cheeks. The young goddess hugged her mother back but quickly untangled herself from the embrace. A bright reassuring smile pulled at her bow-shaped lips, however, Demeter wasn't having it and crumbled to the ground. The grass and weeds around her dried up and browned.

Persephone turned to Hecate, lifted her dress, and climbed through the vines. Hecate followed with a splash of water, and as quickly as they had arrived, they were gone.

Demeter was left behind, sobbing, and killing the plants around her.

Cyane had the urge to go to the great mother and comfort her, to promise she'd stay by Persephone's side and protect her, but when she went to move, Hermes stopped her from doing so. She choked back a displeased moan as his hand pressed against her mouth, stifling it.

"She will not like being seen this way," he whispered. "And her wrath has the power of winter."

Cyane's heart raced, uncaring, but she stopped trying to move.

Demeter, in her lovely glory, rose to her feet, wiped her cheeks, and sneered at the cave entrance. She turned away, and a large, muscled man with white hair appeared out of nowhere. He grabbed the back of her neck. Demeter sighed, and they vanished.

Hermes released Cyane with a grunt. "Glad we weren't caught."

"Why?" Cyane picked up her skirt and went back to the brook.

"Demeter would've made me go with them. She so likes to use her agony to get what she wants."

A powerful urge overcame Cyane to follow Persephone, but when she swept the vines aside, the cave was gone. Only rocks and running water had been hidden behind the green curtain.

She turned back to Hermes. "I know her."

"Doesn't most the world?"

"No, I mean, I really know her, like I've known her forever. I love her, I don't know how or why, but I love her dearly. Enough to..." Cyane trailed off, glancing around her. "Enough to die for her."

Hermes canted his head. "Like you love Cerberus?"

She sucked in a breath, "Yes," she said. "I love him, too." But it was a different type of love.

She surprised herself, admitting that now. She loved Cerberus. It wasn't just the power of him that had brought her to her knees. But *love*.

Had she made the right choice? Her throat tightened. Could she go back? Would she even be able to? And if she did, would Hades forgive her? Would Cerberus? Or would she be punished for leaving?

She needed to know, needed to know why she adored Persephone. It was important. Why had Hades gone through such extreme lengths to bring her to Tartarus? *I was someone else in my last life. I'd done something to make Hades hate me.*

What was it? Cyane searched her head, but nothing came to her, nothing that would help her. All there were, were memories of this life, and nothing more.

She looked back at Hermes who was brushing the dirt off his jeans. "Hades said he'd waited for me to die," she said. "That my soul lingered above and would not leave. That he had to come up himself and take it and reincarnate me so I would come to him."

Hermes's head snapped up. "He said that?"

"And more." She grabbed him. He tried to pull away, but she held on. "You told me you recognized me. You said it several times. Look at me, not as a mortal, but as something or someone you may have met that wasn't."

"What else did Hades say?"

She bit down on her tongue, but spoke anyway. "I angered him somehow." She thought back on all that Hades had told her. There was more. Something that would help. *I shouldn't have drank the wine.*

Maybe I am weak. Cyane tried not to let the awful thought take over her, not again. "I'm to serve him. To make sure he has an heir."

Hermes's eyes widened. "A god hasn't been born, not for ages. The goddesses do not have children anymore. It is our punishment for betraying their trust and going astray. How would you help him do such a thing?"

"I don't know." And she refused to dwell on it because she knew if she did, it would only tear her insides out. "Who am I?" she begged.

"I don't know."

"Think!"

Hermes's jaw ticked, his nostrils flared. "I don't know!"

This time when he pulled away, tearing her hands off of him, Cyane let him go.

Then she recalled something. She brought her hands up and pressed her palms to her brow. "Hades said...he said I helped Demeter discover where her daughter was."

Hermes hissed. "That can't be, I was there, I would remember—"

Cyane looked up at him.

He stared at her, his mouth parting slightly, as his eyes flickered over her hurriedly. "There was a naiad, a naiad who gave me a belt. The belt Persephone wore the day she vanished. Her name..."

"What was her name?"

"How could I have forgotten," he breathed, pivoting away.

"What was her name?" she urged, asking again.

"Ciane."

"My name."

"But she was transformed. She wasn't a naiad, not anymore, she was—"

"What?"

"A pond," he said. "I only met her the one time, but I saw her play with Persephone from a distance when I used to, erm, watch the goddess."

It had to be her. It had to be. The name wasn't quite the same, but it was undeniably close. And Hermes had said he recognized her, although he couldn't place from where. "Can you take me to this pond? Does it still exist?"

"I don't like going there anymore." He turned away, and Cyane felt like she was losing him, losing him right when she was so close to finding out the truth and understanding why.

Hades had brought her back to life, but for what? Why

did she have any purpose in his plans? He kept reminding her of her lowly status, that she was nothing in comparison to a god.

"Why?" she asked.

His eyes shuttered. "It was where my beautiful maiden was last seen, where I lost her to the dark and depravity of"—he spat—"Hades. He stole her. Stole her purity, and the flowers of this world died with Demeter's agony. My beautiful Persephone, raped by such a man."

"Did he…" Cyane tried to imagine it, imagine Hades, as depraved as the spectacle of the day before. "Did he truly rape her?" It made her sick. *Poor Persephone.* But the goddess had smiled, had seemed almost eager to leave her mother's embrace and return to the dark. Even so, anger and a terrible sadness filled Cyane to think that such an innocent, beautiful creature like the Goddess of Spring had been subjected to that.

The grief, the pain, was familiar and old, as if a friend returned from her past, one that had been dead.

I know her. Did Cyane truly know her? Cyane's heart screamed she did, but there were no memories. Even now, as she wrung her hands into her dress waiting for Hermes's answer, she wasn't sure.

"He tore all that was innocent from her and took it for his own, without allowance, without appeal."

"But Persephone was brought home?" God, why did she care? "Take me to the pond, Hermes. Please."

"She was rescued, but her sentence was final. There was nothing anyone could do once Zeus decided."

"She didn't seem upset to descend?"

"Because she is innocent and believes Hades is good," he scowled.

It didn't make sense. "And yet you were celebrating with him these past seven days."

"Don't think to question me. Mortals do not command me. Now that you're free of Cerberus's protection, I could do all manner of things to you, and no one would help you," he dictated, rounding on her. "More than you could imagine."

Cyane stiffened but kept her feet rooted. She was in the sunlight and wasn't going to be intimidated by him, didn't even think she could after all she'd been through. "The deal you made was to take me where I wanted to go, God of Crossings, and you have yet to do anything but escort me down through a tunnel to a place I could've gone myself."

A sneer tugged Hermes's upper lip. His beauty diminished with a single gesture.

Cyane continued, "Don't you want to know? Want to know what Hades has planned? If not for my sake, then for Persephone's? If I helped you once, you know where my loyalties once lay." She hoped she sounded convincing. She couldn't hide the racing of her heart that seemed to grow louder with every passing second. She was sure Hermes heard it. "Help me remember, and I'll always be in your debt." She lowered her voice. "I'll be eternally grateful." She threw the same words Melinoe used on her, at him.

"Grateful, we'll see. Take my hand, Cyane." He threw his hand in front of her face, almost threatening her with it. "If you are who you think, Demeter and I owe you a debt, but if you're not… You'll be left there with nothing but that flimsy dress on your back, stranded."

Cyane swallowed. She reached up, took his hand, and didn't care for once about her own wellbeing.

THE FINAL DESCENT

Cerberus returned to the ballroom where Hades awaited him atop his dais. He tapped his foot, rapped his fingers, and scowled with an angry frown on his face.

My face. Cerberus shook the thought as he approached his lord. The reminder of their shared face only filled his head with recent memories of Cyane. It hurt to think of her, knowing he would never see her again. It hurt to think of what he discovered in her arms, only for it to be taken away. He'd treasure the memories he had and paint her on his wall. So she could forever be immortalized in his haven.

He rubbed the place her hair still wound over his thumb with his forefinger. It was all he had of her.

That, and her note.

The ballroom was empty. The others had yet to arrive for Persephone's descent, and he had a feeling he knew why.

Cerberus stopped before Hades.

They stared at each other for a length of time. Hades licked his lips and eventually sighed.

"You've angered me, my friend. A great deal of anger is

not what I should feel when I ought to be exuberant and anxious for my wife's return. Yet, I feel nothing but fury, and I know it is because of you." Hades looked around, raising one ebony brow. "Cyane is gone. I no longer sense her presence, and I can't help but feel it has something to do with *you.*"

Cerberus reached for the note which rested in his armor and handed it to his lord. "Why didn't you tell me you were her father?"

Hades scowled at the note. It burst into flames as if it had never been more than a simple piece of paper. Cerberus dropped it as it turned to ash and ember between them.

"I share my mind with no one, not completely, not even you—despite our great many conversations. You know this, hound," Hades spat.

Cerberus glared. "You don't trust me, after all we've been through."

"Trust? You dare to speak of trust? I trusted you like no one who has ever existed in this realm or the next, this life or the after! I trust you more than my sweet, honest wife, whose loyalties are, and always will, be strung between Demeter and myself. But I have every right to take my trust away, especially after you ruined what should have been a grand celebration that I had planned for decades."

He was no longer bothered by Hades's anger. Somehow, Cerberus realized nothing, not even his lord's fury, compared to watching Cyane walk away.

"I did enjoy your celebration," Cerberus said.

"A little too much! I told you to enjoy the celebration, not dismantle it! You did far more than enjoy!"

Cerberus scowled. "If I had known your intentions for Cyane—"

"Is that your excuse for disobedience? I know you enjoyed

your debauchery, but she is a mortal—a weak mortal. I can help you find a replacement. The nymphs of this world are delicious, many of them maidens yet themselves, but if you want something more innocent to spoil..."

"Cyane is irreplaceable." he snapped. "She was something else before you stole her."

"Oh, so she told you, did she?" Hades glanced up at the ceiling, his hands shaking. "Who knew she'd grow so fond of a monster like you in such a short amount of time."

"You steal too much, Hades," Cerberus fumed. "Every time you do this, it never ends well. Minthe, Leuce, Persephone."

Hades surged up from his chair. "Don't you dare."

"Would you not hear the truth from me? Or would you rather Zeus say as much?"

The ballroom darkened round them. The candle flames throughout the room danced back and forth as if a wind whipped them. Cracks filled Cerberus's ears as the stalactites from above elongated and sharpened. Several fell upon the floor with a *boom* and shattered.

"I've been too kind to you, my friend," Hades whispered. "You dare to act childishly, speaking out of turn when you don't know the truth of what you speak of."

Despite his enraged lord, calm filled Cerberus. Did the way Hades spin it really matter? The outcome would have been the same either way. The thought alone of Cyane being used and hurt made him want to kill. "Then for all the damned souls, enlighten me! I love her."

"She was not yours to love!"

"Neither was Persephone."

They scowled at each other. Twins, in nearly every way.

Hades spoke after a pause. "I would never have thought you could love someone more than me."

"Nor I you."

Stalactites fell continuously now. They stared at each other, neither one willing to back down. Somewhere, far below, something enormous and destructive moved beneath their feet, awakening, just a little, disturbed by what was happening above.

Typhon.

"You will not like what love will do to you," Hades said as the floor trembled.

"It has already done more than you know."

Hade's face softened, throwing Cerberus off guard. It wasn't a look he'd seen before, especially one he'd never imagine being directed at him. Within the next instant, Hades's face went stony and cold again even if the hate was gone. The change was enough to fill Cerberus with unease. There was comfort in knowing what to expect.

Cerberus wondered if his concerns were the same for Hades when it came to him. Expectations, on both their ends, had died like out-of-season flowers this last week.

The tension left Hades, and his shoulders fell. "I'm beginning to feel I've cursed you with this new body rather than give you a gift. I cursed both of us."

Cerberus had thought the same thing before the celebration began. But now, with Cyane and all that had happened between them, even the bad parts...it was an experience they had shared with this body. It was something he wouldn't trade for the world.

"No, my lord. This body hasn't been direct, nor easy, but I wouldn't go back to the creature I was before. I cherish all that you've done for me. Despite the confusion, despite the pain, despite the *hunger.*"

Hades scoffed. "And you show your thankfulness with betrayal."

"Cyane was afraid of what you planned for her," he gritted. "She swore fealty to me—to me! I could not let you destroy her, so I gave her my protection, as a god should. As all gods have to their mortal servants. I may not have been a god before her, but I am one now. Because of her."

What softness between them evaporated as quickly as it had emerged. Hades's face darkened. "And what about your oath of loyalty to me?"

"I wouldn't let her be used as a vessel for your children!" He settled his hand on the hilt of his xiphos sword.

"A vessel?" Hades cackled, his eyes growing bright with amusement. "You think I would lower myself to lay with a lowly mortal when I could have any female in my realm? No, she was supposed to be a gift! A gift of mercy!"

Part of the ceiling crashed down beside them, but neither looked towards the crumbling destruction ensuing around them.

Cerberus took a step towards Hades, burning with rage. "Lowly mortal? I'm done with these secrets. And what gift of mercy? You've slaughtered more in the last week than you have in millenia. What mercy do you have? Mercy of death? Mercy of servitude? Mercy of secrets and half-truths? Tell me!"

As Cerberus drew his sword, his hounds closed in on all sides, and raw power pumped through his veins. Tartarus, feeling the build of Cerberus's power grow, shook the realm in anger.

Hades turned pensive for a moment before he lowered to a crouch like an animal. "A mercy of love."

A flood of silently screaming, tormented ghosts appeared around them.

Melinoe's stench filled the space between Cerberus and Hades, and their scowls snapped to the goddess who dared to invade a private conversation.

Melinoe's eyes widened at the scene they presented, but

she quickly fell to the dusty, stone-ridden ground to genu-flect before Hades.

"What do you want?" Hades roared as he stood back up.

Cerberus dropped his sword back into its sheath but kept his hand tight around the handle.

"Speak before I banish you for a thousand years at Typhon's side!" Hades snarled.

If Hades did not kill her, Cerberus surely would.

Melinoe's head jerked up. "Cyane is gone."

"You think I don't know that?"

The goddess's eyes flickered between Hades and Cerberus. "Don't punish Cerberus for my offense," she said, stunning them both.

Cerberus growled. Why was Melinoe taking this? Was it because he gave her what she wanted? Was a putrid goddess like her so easily pleased?

Hades flung his hands into the air. "I'm surrounded by liars." He turned back to this throne and dropped into it. "And plagued by insanity! What have I done to deserve this?"

Melinoe stood. "I made a deal with Cyane in exchange for her freedom. Her end of the bargain was satisfied, so I let her go. Cerberus only sought to be loyal. Do not blame him for my mistake, please."

"And what did you get out of it, dear daughter?"

"I know," Melinoe said with a quick breath. "I know everything."

Hades cupped his brow and massaged it with his fingers. "It wasn't out of loyalty, Melinoe. It was to protect the mortal."

Confusion marred the goddess' face.

Hades turned back to Cerberus. "Protection?" Hades whispered, lowering his voice with warning. "You will be punished."

The giant doors to the ballroom creaked, and the subtle

smell of new flowers filtered through the air. Cerberus quickly moved to Hades's left side and knelt. Melinoe fell back to the floor where she chose to remain off to the side, her palms before her, fingers outstretched.

Hades jumped from his throne and strode hurriedly toward the two women entering. He made it several steps before he came to a dead stop.

Persephone, in glorious sun-dappled yellow, once the Goddess of Flowers and now the Goddess of the Dead, shyly wrung her hands as she made her way towards Hades. Even from where Cerberus knelt, he saw his queen's eyes rove over the destruction in the grand room. Curiosity and worry flitted over her face, as well as excitement, reserved for when her eyes landed back on Hades.

Innocence—the kind of innocence one gave their life for eagerly—radiated off his queen. Cerberus had never enjoyed more than contentment for a job well done as the celebration came to an end, but not this time. Jealousy seized him as he watched Hades and his stolen queen reunite.

His lord—now tense with excitement—grabbed Persephone and embraced her, burying his face into the hair bunched at her neck.

She pushed out of his arms, and looked at Cerberus. He stiffened wondering what his queen thought at that moment.

Usually, there was fan faire, flowers, and all the gods of the Underworld here for her return.

"My queen," Hades said with adoration.

Persephone looked back at him. "What have you done?"

Suddenly, a burst of energy split the space, a power that did not belong so deep in Hades's kingdom. Cerberus snarled, rising up. What now?

Hades grabbed Persephone and pulled her towards him, and Cerberus rushed to protect his lord and queen.

The scent of Hermes's magic met his nose as Cerberus's hounds rushed forward.

But every single one stopped as the God of Crossings appeared, for by his side was a sobbing, wet human that Cerberus knew all too well.

PERSEPHONE'S ABDUCTION

CYANE FELL to the ground with a retch. Traveling with Cerberus had never induced such intense vertigo. But with Hermes, her head whirled until she was releasing nothing but bile and spittle from her empty stomach.

Hermes stepped away with a sound of disgust.

She swallowed down another wave of nausea and wiped her mouth with her hand.

They were on a water bank, with reeds and brush all around. In the distance, there were walkways and bridges where only a few people hung around. Everything was overgrown and wild, but kept well, as if the proprietors cared a great deal to keep the integrity of the site intact. Cyane glanced up to see the sun rising in the sky. Morning.

Hermes leaned upon a nearby tree and fingered a strange plant. "The only place in the world where papyrus still grows wild," he muttered, as if that had any relevance at all.

Cyane looked back towards the calm water directly before her.

Nothing happened.

She dipped her fingers into the water. It was cold.

Still nothing.

"Well?" Hermes said from behind her. "Was it worth it?"

She pulled her hand from the water and stood, turning full circle, feeling nothing but the morning chill on her arms. "Is this where you received the belt?"

Hermes pushed off the tree. "I don't know. The geography has changed. Last time I was here, it was more of a meadow and less of a swamp, I think? Ciane's pond was much smaller."

Cyane peered out over the water; it went on far past her view. It was a small pond no more.

She rubbed her arms with her hands, suddenly uncertain.

Maybe I'm wrong. This place didn't give her any feeling at all, not like those subtle ones she experienced in the Underworld, and nothing like the deep certainty Persephone had made her feel. It didn't compare. There was nothing but emptiness.

"Well, mortal," Hermes came to stand next to her, walking through the brush. "I've done my part."

"You have," she whispered.

She saw him glance at her out of the corner of her eye. "You're not going to argue with me? How surprising." His head tilted as he visibly checked her out.

"I thought…"

"You hoped," he corrected.

"I hoped," she repeated. The words hurt to say. She rasped them out anyway. "I hoped I'd understand. Finally understand."

Hermes cupped the side of her face with one hand and turned her towards him. He leaned down and pressed his mouth to hers. The kiss was soft and supple, and full of talent, as if he'd done it a thousand times, with a thousand different women, his every movement was poetry. His lips moved, his tongue dipped into her mouth to slide over her own stiff one. He tilted her head, and she let him, allowing him to deepen it.

She didn't kiss him back.

He wasn't Cerberus. He wasn't her god. So, no matter how good it was, or how it felt, it only brought sorrow and numbness, and terrible longing. It did nothing but fill her thoughts with hounds, fangs, lashing tongues, and serpents.

She said a quick prayer to Cerberus in her head, begging him for forgiveness.

Hermes released her and pulled away. Their eyes met. Tears slipped down her cheeks.

"Goodbye, Cyane," he said.

Then he vanished, as if he'd never been there at all.

Cyane fell to her knees with a cry.

Alone. Always alone. Always to lose everything she loved most. The tears fell harder, violently, uncontrollably. A pounding wave of them that wouldn't stop. Pain filled her chest, tightening it. She dug her fingers into the grass and dirt. Her head fell upon her bent knees—the weight too much for her to stay upright. The beds of her nails filled with soil.

Wet, moist soil, that called to her. This didn't feel like the call of the grave, but instead the call of a well-worn bed.

A feeling. Something. It was weaker than anything she'd known in the Underworld, imperceptible compared to the power of Persephone. Something felt right. Every inch she moved kindled a secret fire within her. A vague sense of belonging took her over—so different and strange—and she desperately reached out to latch on before it too could abandon her.

She found the strength to crawl to the waterline, pulling herself along until the cold waters enveloped her, easing her entrance. As she descended into the lake she perceived noth ing. The water was neither warm nor cool. It felt like she was relinquishing her senses, one at a time.

The tears, so heavy now, sunk her to the bottom. As the water cradled her she felt at peace. She didn't struggle as it filled her lungs. She curled her arms around her knees and waited as the light faded around her when a long-lost memory emerged.

LAUGHTER, delight, and all nature's purest and most beautiful scents and sounds assailed the air.

Ciane lay on the edge of a brook, her bare feet in the water, with her naiad sisters to one side of her and the Goddess of Spring on the other. Dressed in flowers, colored by her friend, Ciane lounged, gazing up at the blue sky and dappled clouds.

"What should I name this one?" Persephone plucked a new flower from the water's edge. It was gray, for the goddess had yet to give it a color.

"Gerry!"

"Sisette," another suggested.

"Phrecosse."

Persephone placed the flower back into the soil where it took root again. "Gladiolus," Persephone proclaimed, "for it reminds me of a sword. A beautiful weapon."

Ciane dropped her head to the side and smiled as her friend colored the new bloom pink. Her naiad sisters giggled and awed over the new creation, which quickly sprouted up and bloomed in the grasses around them. Ciane didn't observe the spectacle; she eyed her dear friend instead.

There was no one she loved more. They were inseparable. Demeter rarely trusted Persephone with anyone, except for the maiden nymphs and naiads who adored both goddesses in accordance with the mother goddess's ideals. They shirked all masculine things, finding only joy in the beautiful, innocent creations of Gaia and her powerful descendants.

And Persephone gifted the world with flowers.

Oh, how Ciane adored her. Everyone adored her, how could they not?

An unusually chilly breeze fluttered the new flowers around them, and Persephone glanced up.

Ciane lifted onto her elbows. "What's wrong?" she asked.

"The warmth fled," Persephone murmured, gazing off into the distance where grassy meadows rolled. "But it is back now."

"We can't control the wind," Ciane teased.

Persephone smiled softly Ciane's way for a brief moment before turning her attention back to the hills beyond. "No, we can't control that, but it is strange, is it not?"

Ciane shrugged. Persephone stood, and grasped her delicate skirts up to step over her newly created Gladiolus. The goddess walked away, as if in a trance, towards the meadows. Ciane pivoted to watch her.

No one seemed to notice but Ciane. She pulled her feet from the water, even though leaving it felt wrong, like a loss of limb, and followed her friend. Once she stepped away from the flowers, the cool breeze returned to steal the warmth from her exposed flesh. She hesitated and glanced back at her sisters, debating rejoining them in the safe water.

She turned back to Persephone to see the goddess disappear over the crest of the hill.

My goddess? Ciane's face fell. She cocked her head, hoping Persephone would reappear. When she didn't, Ciane picked up the skirts of her dress and went after her.

The hill wasn't high, but the grass was long and it rubbed her soles in a way she didn't like. Dirt clung to her skin where the water from the brook hadn't dried, and Ciane stopped twice to wipe her feet clean. When she made it to the top, she found Persephone on the hillside beyond, kneeling in front of a narcissus flower.

One of the few blooms of Gaia her dear Goddess of Spring had not created herself. A rare bloom that didn't belong.

The breeze returned and whipped Ciane's skirts around her legs. It blocked out the distant sounds of laughter and play from her sisters.

"Persephone," Ciane called, worried now. Now they had wandered too far away from the others. Demeter would punish them all if the mother goddess found out. Ciane stumbled down the hillside when Persephone didn't answer. Her footing even more awkward and uneven going down.

Persephone leaned over the narcissus, breathed in its scent, and shut her eyes as if in a trance. She squeezed the stem with her fingers and pulled the flower from the dirt.

It wouldn't give.

"Goddess, wait!" Ciane yelled. The sunlight overhead disappeared behind broody dark clouds, and the air turned frigid. Her dear friend was completely oblivious.

Persephone opened her eyes, frowned, and tugged the flower harder. The ground split open where the roots should've been.

"*No!*" Ciane screamed, horror filling her.

Persephone's screams joined hers as the goddess stumbled back from the widening opening, her legs slipping over the edge. Ciane watched as Persephone crawled, trying to pull herself from the gap, turning over to her front to grab at the tall grass.

Their eyes met as Ciane let herself fall, tumbling the rest of the way down the hill. A sharp snap in her leg made her shriek, but she ignored the pain as she reached for Persephone's outstretched hand.

"Help me!" Persephone sobbed, stricken with terror.

The gap roared ever wider, eager to swallow the spring-time goddess. Ciane had a deathgrip on her friend, her other hand snapping out to curl around the goddess's upper arm. She pulled with all her might as Persephone tried to find footing on the crumbling ledge.

"Don't let go! Don't let go!" Persephone cried.

Ciane cried at Persephone's begging. It filled her with agony. Her goddess should never have to beg. Fueled with anguish, ready to give her life for Persephone's, Ciane braced her feet on the dirt, and pulled her friend from over the edge.

Persephone rounded her arms around Ciane, covering her with sobs, as they scrambled back from the edge. Ciane fell back on the grass, holding her friend to her chest, burying her fingers into the back of her dress.

The goddess's tears drenched Ciane's dress. "Thank you, thank you." She said the words over and over through fearful gasps.

The ground's trembling slowly abated.

Ciane tightened her hold on Persephone. "I've got you," she whispered trying to comfort her, comfort both of them. "I love you," she said, finding the strength to glance down at her hyperventilating friend.

But Ciane's eyes fell upon an awful man. He was decked in dark regalia, standing in a broken chariot led by poised skeletal horses, floating over the abysmal hole they'd just escaped. He wore a helmet decorated with long horns sticking out of its sides. From the peaks of those horns, streaks of transparency trembled over him, over his black chariot, and on the deathly quiet, undead horses. Their eyes filled with blood-red flames.

Hades.

Ciane's mouth fell open in horror.

He reached over the chariot's side and grabbed Persephone's ankle.

"No!" she shrieked.

Persephone was pulled from Ciane's grasp, but Ciane's fingers caught in her dress and were wrenched painfully into the fabric when she didn't let go. The dark god pulled harder, trying to free Persephone from Ciane's death-grip. Persephone fought and struggled between them.

"Release her. She is mine now." Hades ordered, yanking Persephone hard against his chest, and pulling Ciane up with her.

"Never," Ciane hissed, even as she was tugged part way into the chariot with them. She grabbed at Persephone's belt.

"Ciane, don't let go," Persephone cried. "Don't let him take me!"

Persephone's dressed ripped, the sound of tearing fabric slicing the air.

Ciane was thrown back, and her body hit the hillside with a thud, knocking her head hard upon the ground. Shrieks filled her ears as she forced herself to her feet to stumble after her friend. But when her blurry, star-exploding gaze focused, she saw the hole in the earth was already closing up, Persephone's voice growing more distant by the second.

She fell to the ground, making it several steps, but got back up. If she could only get to the gap before it closed, she still had a chance to save Persephone. Tears filled Ciane's eyes as she hobbled towards it, falling again and again, watching the gap vanish more with each second.

Ciane reached the edge right as the earth healed itself. She fell to the ground and ripped at the dirt beneath her. All that was left was the single narcissus flower offering only innocence of the sinister role it had played in this tragedy.

I failed.

Agony stole her soul as her life died to dust. *My goddess, I failed you.* Everything she cherished, all the beauty and delight on Gaia paled to ash. It was nothing without Persephone. Love itself fled.

Ciane curled onto her side, bringing her knees to her chest, holding the one piece she had left of her friend—a torn belt, riddled with holes where her nails had ruined it. She brought it to her lips as her body melted away.

She gave herself over to her heartache and turned to water.

HOME

A HAND GRABBED Cyane's arm and yanked her from the water. She gasped, crying out, remembering everyone. Remembering *everything*.

The pain of it nearly killed her.

Sobbing, Cyane found Hermes standing over her, with mild annoyance splashed across his face. He rolled his eyes and yanked her arm again. Wind rushed around them, and in a blink, she was out of the water and lying on hard stone. The sunlight was gone from above.

Beyond Hermes were familiar obsidian walls. Her throat burned, and she rolled over to choke out the water in her lungs.

"Who is this?" a slight voice asked.

Hermes released Cyane's arm, and she curled them around her stomach, bowing over, unable to lift her head, still overcome with failure. She had failed her goddess, her dear friend, her purest love, and even though time had passed, despite her new clusters of memories, of a new life given to her, and more time than she could comprehend, it still felt like it was yesterday.

"What's happening? Who is this, and where is the court?" the same voice asked again, this time with evident agitation. A voice Cyane knew so well, its sound fueled her pain.

"Persephone," Cyane rasped. Her wet hair covered her face and obscured her vision, but she swiped it aside.

Hades's sinisterly gleeful laughter rang through the ballroom, so loud it vibrated through her. Hades began to clap as a dark figure strode forward.

Cerberus. Her heart seized. *Don't.*

He bypassed her as she braced one of her hands on the ground to push herself up.

"You dare bring her back here?" Cerberus roared.

Hermes countered with a yell of his own. "She belongs here!"

The clash of metal against metal and the growls of rage from Cerberus's hounds filled Cyane's ears. She tried to turn to see what was happening, to plead for Cerberus to stop, that she wanted no more pain or death. But before she could move, cold fingers clasped her chin and forced her head upward and forward.

"Please don't hurt him," Cyane begged.

"You've come back." Hades smiled. "I'm glad."

"Not for you," she choked. "Never for you."

Persephone's voice rang out with a cry. "What is going on? Stop this fighting at once!" Persephone rushed forward and yelled at Cerberus and Hermes. "Is this how you honor me?"

Cyane inhaled; the smell of blood filled Cyane's nostrils.

The sound of fighting continued despite her queen's orders. From the corner of her eye, Cyane could see Cerberus, blurred in a miasma of darkness she'd only seen once before. Fangs, serpents, snapping snouts, and all beat Hermes to the floor. The winged god had a staff in his hands, and was blocking what he could of Cerberus's unrepentant violence. He was losing.

"Not for me, never for me," Hades taunted with a whisper only Cyane could hear. He wrapped his cold fingers in her hair, drawing her attention back to him. "But always for me."

Cyane slapped Hades's hand off her, and the dark god's laughter returned, making her insides shrivel up. She twisted to look at Persephone who stepped forward. Cyane drew the courage she needed from her long-lost friend.

The goddess, eyes alight with anger for being ignored, turned to Cyane.

Their eyes met.

"Persephone," Cyane whispered.

Love filled her. Despite everything, it filled her soul and drowned her thoughts, drowned out the fighting. It pooled from her eyes and coursed through her body. Cyane's flesh prickled with long forgotten delight, of perfection and cool waters under the bright light of day. Of fields of flowers and laughter that was anything but wicked. Persephone had the power to make every nightmare a dream, every dark place spill with light. She was perfect. Beloved. She stole Cyane's torment away with a single look.

"Ciane?" Persephone said, confusion marring her face. "Is that you?"

Hades yanked her arm, forcing Cyane to her feet.

"Yes. It's me." Ciane wasn't her name anymore, but it didn't matter. Persephone could call her whatever she liked.

Persephone stepped forward; her eyes flickered from Cyane to Hades.

"A gift, my love. For you," he said. "I've returned her from her woes of losing you so that you may be together again."

Persephone's face bloomed into the most beautiful smile Cyane had ever seen. She heard Hades's breath hitch beside her.

The fighting ceased, but Cyane couldn't take her eyes off of her friend, so afraid that if she did, Persephone would once again disappear into the darkness.

Cyane nodded, agreeing with Hades, understanding now what his claims of mercy had meant. Her hatred for the God of the Underworld could never compete with the adoration she held for his wife.

Persephone rushed forward, enveloping Cyane into her arms. Cyane burrowed her nose into her friend's hair and smelled the flowers of the world.

They cried together.

"You're so...so wet," Persephone breathed.

Cyane's arms tightened around her, shaking with joy. "Haven't I always been?"

Persephone laughed. "Yes."

"I love you," she said.

"I love you too, my dearest friend."

A DEEP SIGH

CERBERUS STARED after Cyane and his queen as they walked hand-in-hand out of the ballroom. Hades followed them to the foyer but stopped, letting the women go.

Cyane hadn't glanced Cerberus's way, not even once, not even when he was about to kill a god for her. He had been ready to start a war.

But he didn't mind. Seeing Cyane's face when she'd embraced Persephone was gift enough for Cerberus. He finally sensed that she was safe. If his queen loved her as Cerberus loved her, Cyane was the safest being in all the realm. No one would dare touch something their beloved queen held so dear. Not even Hades.

Hermes lay, bloodied and broken, on the floor under his boot. Cerberus wiped the blood off his mouth and kicked Hermes away toward Melinoe. She bent down next to Hermes with a strange look coming over her face. Hades turned back around and eyed the fallen god with boredom.

Cerberus flicked his xiphos clean and sheathed it. He wanted to shirk his duties and go after Cyane, even if it was just to fill his eyes with her once more, to convince himself that she was really back, and to remind himself she was safe despite the crisp salt of her tears in the air. But he didn't. He chose to scan the ballroom and consider the destroyed ceiling that had crushed the once slick black floor.

The ruin was a testament to his and Hades's unfinished business. Business that needed to be settled before Cerberus could steal Cyane away to his rooms and reacquaint himself with her warm flesh.

Hades tilted his head for Cerberus to follow, and they silently made their way to Hades's study, Cerberus several steps behind. He deftly withdrew his hounds to return to the gates and begin another year of servitude because—if he knew Hades as well as he did—the God of the Underworld would never give Cerberus his duties back without a return of their age-old trust between them.

Trust that couldn't be broken by something as small as a fight, even if that fight had been on the brink of a violent match for power, all over a situation Cerberus could now see that they had both made disastrous miscalculations over.

A short time later, they sat in their respective chairs and Hades brought the hearth fire back to life. It burst upward, excited, unlike the two Underworld-weary companions before it.

Hades sighed. "Is Hermes dead?"

"He'll survive." Cerberus's gaze roamed over Hades, reading his lord's countenance. He struggled to place it, especially when he realized he thought Hades might be...satisfied. "It will be some time before he heals."

Hades laughed low. "Melinoe will enjoy his company. It'll keep her busy and out of our lives...for a time."

Cerberus shrugged, leaning back. "She's out of my life forever. It was part of our deal—for the truth."

"You didn't bother to consult me before making such a bargain?" Hades's eyes darkened. "I won't tolerate not having anything between her and me going forward. I do not like her bothering me."

Cerberus smiled, amused. "I suppose we'll have to discuss that at a later time, my lord. For now, let's enjoy the satisfaction of not only breaking Hermes but that, as he recovers, he becomes a shield for both of us when it comes to Melinoe. If he ever recovers."

Hades glowered. "You're enjoying yourself."

"Aren't you? Your plan has come to fruition, has it not? Cyane is here, and Persephone clearly loves her. And everything she loves, you protectively cherish." Even Cyane. Cerberus ran his finger over his lips.

"Ah, my friend, but she still must serve. She still must accomplish the task I've set out for her. If she doesn't..."

"You'll do nothing because Persephone will destroy everything you seek so dearly."

"You think I fear my wife's hate?" Hades laughed. "She has hated me, she has loved me, she has felt everything under the sun and more for me. She would get over it."

"But the difference is the gift," Cerberus stated, leaning his elbows on his knees. "How many more could you give her, how many gifts are better? How else can you receive the gift you've been seeking from her? After all these long years? She will not accept a queendom, power, nor obsessive devotion. She will not take the birth of life in a realm of death, the breaking of nature's ways to grow all her favorite flowers and foliage here. She does not need love, nor family, nor purpose. She has all of that already. And most of all, she does not want jewels, clothes, or material possessions.

"Giving Persephone back someone she loves... Now that is different. That is what you did, did you not?"

"My damned, you have become so amusing!" Hades threw his hands up in the air.

Cerberus's eyes darkened. "It is true, is it not?"

Hades settled his palms on his knees. "Perhaps it is true, perhaps it's not. You would know the value of Cyane, wouldn't you? Better than anyone. But you forget one thing, if I do not receive the gift I seek, I can still hurt you, take out my wrath upon you. You may be right about Cyane, and I cannot fault you on that matter, because the love between her and my queen is what I hoped for, but you...your flesh is punishable."

"There is nothing you could do to me," Cerberus said, staring at the fire, "that hasn't already been done."

"Cyane has sworn fealty to you, has she not?"

A delicious shiver shot through Cerberus. "Yes."

He pictured her kneeling at his feet, either in vestal white or naked and vulnerable, waiting for his command. The delicious vision couldn't linger as Hades filled Cerberus' eyes with a darker image of himself.

"I suppose she loves you? As much as a mortal could love another?" Hades asked.

Cerberus looked Hades in the eye. "I wouldn't assume."

"But she cares?" Hades smiled. "She sought you out relentlessly during the Day of Deviance, only to find you gone. Her eyes roved the guests when she should have been paying attention to me, minding her own mortality."

A thread of regret spiked through Cerberus. He'd left her to face Hades alone, even if his intentions were for her protection. His hounds or not, Cerberus should've been by her side. Even if it angered Hades and brought Melinoe closer.

Hades must've seen the regret on Cerberus's face because he continued. "The loyalty of mortals is fickle, and the value of her fealty has yet to be seen. For now, she has the love and affection of a long-lost friend to keep her attention. But I may be lenient on your punishment, if you ensure I get all I yet want."

"A godly child," Cerberus gritted. Hades's opinions in regards to Cyane's affections mattered less than dirt to Cerberus.

"My wife's acceptance into her bed."

"One in the same."

Hades shrugged. "You are still loyal to me, are you not?"

Was he? He knew the answer before he finished asking himself. He sat back and trailed his eyes over Hades's dark, familiar body. Hades's scent was better known to Cerberus than that of his father, better than even his own scent. Hades would always be more than a lord to Cerberus, more than a friend.

"Yes, I am eternally loyal," Cerberus said, feeling the terrible truth of that statement settle over him.

An almost imperceptible softness fell over Hades's features; something only Cerberus would ever see, something he knew Hades had no idea he gave away.

Hades loved his hound as much as Cerberus loved his lord.

"Then you will attend me tonight, my brother." Hades closed his eyes and settled in his chair. "You and Cyane."

<hr>

CYANE LAY in the grass next to Persephone, the goddess's laughter a sweet song in her ears. Persephone had taken them to a garden somewhere deep within the castle. A secret place that shouldn't exist in the Underworld. Flowers grew here that Cyane had never seen or heard of before, they had been created for this place and this place alone. They stole away the smell of Tartarus and replaced it with floral musk and a little bit of spice. It suited the ever-present gloom.

Cyane adored the flowers because they showed her Persephone as she was now but still as herself back before her abduction, mixed together to give a little life in the one place where there shouldn't be.

Sorrow had all but vanished from Cyane's veins, and the result was almost too much for her to bear. She'd never experienced more jubilance and mirth. Knowing Persephone was alive and well, and just as happy, if not a little more bitter, a little more grown up, was the greatest gift of all.

They both were now, having grown up since they were last together.

But there was something missing in Cyane's heart, something that made her rise up on her elbows, again and again, to peer around the garden and its high walls. There was no roof here, and she figured this was a courtyard of some sorts because along the sides, the needle-like points of the castle's design could be seen reaching the faraway cavern ceiling.

Her eyes scanned the garden. Again. She was searching for Cerberus. She was desperate to be with him again but also...nervous. He hadn't stopped her from walking away, and now she had unexpectedly returned. She had no idea where they stood. Doubt and paranoia filled her the longer she dwelled on it, the longer he stayed away.

Persephone pressed a flower to Cyane's nose. Cyane smiled as she breathed in the new scent her goddess was proud of.

Persephone gave Cyane meaning, she fulfilled everything she thought she had been searching for. A friend, family, a way to contribute to something larger than herself. But Cerberus... He gave her love, darkness, and obsession.

Persephone was Cyane's goddess.

Cerberus was—and always would be—her God.

Cyane sighed. Not even one of his hounds appeared to steal her breath and impose upon her and Persephone.

Persephone replanted the flower and leaned over Cyane. "What's wrong? Have I done something?"

Cyane's face fell. "No! You could do nothing but fill my heart with happiness."

Persephone smiled but it didn't reach her eyes. Cyane sat up as her friend curled her legs under her and toyed with the grass at her knees. Cyane didn't want Persephone to be sad, not on her account.

"It's Hades, is it not?" Persephone whispered before Cyane could reassure her.

Silence fell between them.

Cyane took her Persephone's hand. "He wishes only to make you happy. I understand that now, after everything. I understand his motivations now and can't fault him." She inhaled because it was true. Even if the dark god frightened her still. "If I had his power… I may have done as much, if not more, to make you happy."

"He loves me," Persephone whispered.

Cyane squeezed her hand. "He does. Do you love him?"

"It's complicated. How can I love someone whose purpose is to kill and keep all that I create?"

Cyane licked her lips and reached for Persephone's other hand, holding them up between them. "When he took you," she said, the words paining her to say, "did he hurt you?"

"I thought he did, at the time." Persephone's eyes met Cyane's. "I thought when he stole me from my mother and from all I'd known that I'd learned what hurt was. But I was naive and had no idea what I had with him until my mother found me, and Zeus ordered me above again to end Demeter's terrible winter. I learned what real torment was then. I returned to find you gone and discover how dearly I missed Hades." A tear appeared in Persephone's eye.

Cyane frowned, feeling tears rise in her own eyes. "Will you tell me what happened?"

"You don't know?" Persephone stole her hand away and wiped her cheeks.

"I don't. I suppose…turning into a spring immortalized me…but left me deaf to all but the mortals who visited my waters." Those distant memories were hard for Cyane. They were timeless in a way that even the darkness of Tartarus couldn't compare.

"Zeus, realizing my misery, came to me one night that first spring. He disguised himself as Hades and ruined me for all time for my Lord of the Dead."

Cyane swallowed thickly. She had no idea what to say to Persephone. Instead, she reached forward and wrapped her dear friend in a hug and held on, held her as if the very same hole that separated them the first time would return at any moment to pull them apart again.

"I'm sorry I wasn't there," she whispered.

Persephone pressed her face into Cyane's hair and cried. "How can I be with Hades when my own father has destroyed me so?"

Sudden, unabashed anger filled Cyane. "Destroy? Zeus could never destroy something so pure."

Sobs filled Cyane's ears as she held Persephone to her, wishing she could take all the goddess's pain away.

She looked up to see Cerberus standing at the edge of the garden, watching them. His helmet was off, and Cyane's breath hitched. Beside him, farther behind, hidden in the deeper shadows of the castle's walls, leaned Hades.

Cyane's gaze snapped back to Cerberus. Her lips pursed and her body heated, overcome by the predatory gleam in his eyes. It was aimed at her, smoldering and hot, flaming her from the inside out. There was a splash of blood on his face, smudged across his mouth, and it reminded her of the animal he truly was.

She should be afraid, but all she wanted to do was crawl to him, press her brow to his boots, and pray she still was and always would be his. His eyes sparkled, diabolically demonic in the gloom, and to her strange relief, the want was clear in his gaze. But with a godly sniffle, Cyane was reminded that Persephone was the one in her arms.

Stiffness surged through her spine. She buried her fingers into Persephone's fallen hair, gripping her hard. Her own tears dried up as she held her friend, staring at the men who stared back at her. Hades's eyes were filled with warning until they moved to Persephone where they softened with longing and hunger. A hunger Cyane clearly recognized, having seen the same in Cerberus's gaze many times before.

Hades's words came back to her.

'I do not easily forget nor do I easily forgive, Cyane. I gave you a new life for one purpose, and one purpose only—to ensure I have an heir.'

She cupped Persephone's cheeks when her friend's sobs ebbed. She understood Hades's motivations now, but she still didn't like him, and hate for the God of the Dead could easily return. She hated that the words she was going to say to Persephone were the same words Hades expected Cyane would say. It made her feel villainous, even if they were what Cyane truly believed.

Cyane wiped Persephone's tears away with the pads of her thumbs. "Hades does not feel that way about you," she said gently, keeping her eyes level with Persephone's. "He does not think you're tarnished nor ruined. I see the way he looks at you, like—" She was about the say the way Cerberus looked at her, but caught herself. "Like he'll go to the ends of the universe and back to prove his love," Cyane choked. "He'd commit any evil, any terrible act, if the outcome put a smile on your face."

Persephone sniffled. Oh, how beautiful she was, even when flushed with tears. "How can you be so sure?"

"Hades would not go to such great lengths of bringing me here if he didn't care deeply for you. He told me himself,"

Cyane glanced behind Persephone and quickly looked back. "He detests me for fighting him, for...giving your belt to Hermes and Demeter, which..." It hurt her to say, knowing now all that had happened to her friend. "Which led to them finding you." Tears spilled from her own eyes. "I'm so sorry, so, so sorry."

Persephone cupped Cyane's face back. "Don't. You only tried to help me. You didn't know. I love you. Don't be sad on my part, not anymore. You've been sad, so sad for too long. I may not have know where you've been, but I have felt your agony."

Cyane pulled away and wiped her eyes, nodding. "I wish I could've protected you. It was my glory, my duty, and I failed."

Persephone laughed lightly, wiping her own tears. "Then protect me now. You're here now and that's all that matters. I haven't had a friend in so very long, not since you."

Cyane shook, excited, honored, and hurting all at once. "Hades wants you to return to his bed," she admitted. She couldn't keep this from her goddess, not after everything. Not after the honor and forgiveness Persephone bestowed on her.

Persephone's laughter died, her expression falling. "Do you really think he wants me?"

"Yes. I do." Cyane grabbed her friend's hands again. "He could've had any goddess give him heir, but he only wants you."

"Will you..." Persephone's voice turned grave. "Will you attend me? Make sure... it is really Hades who I lay with and not...someone or something else? I trust no one. No one but you in this."

Thoughts of Cerberus rose in Cyane's mind. She inhaled sharply. Zeus had taken the likeness of Hades, Hades bestowed his likeness on Cerberus. She and Persephone shared far more than Cyane could imagine.

Cyane straightened. "Yes." Conviction filled her. "I'll attend you."

Persephone's shoulders sagged and her smile returned—like the first rays of sunlight after a long and terrible night.

When Cyane looked up, both Cerberus and Hades were gone.

MELINOE LISTENED as Hades and Cerberus left the ballroom, but she didn't watch their retreat. Her gaze remained on the broken god at her feet.

She knelt at his side and eased one hand over him, fluttering her fingers a hairsbreadth above Hermes's bloodied chest.

Life clung to him, strong and fervent, riotously robust under his mauled exterior.

She smiled, pleased. She was already surrounded by so many ghosts. The last thing she wanted was another to add to her collection. Melinoe lifted her skirts and straddled Hermes's chest. He moaned softly as she covered him. He was beautiful, far too beautiful for the likes of her. But he was also alone and abused, and she couldn't have that. Not when she had the power to see him back to health. Not when she could offer him a place of safety while he slept.

She knew she wouldn't be able to keep him forever—the God of Crossings could not be caged—but while he recovered, and while his power was weak, she'd be able to enjoy his company. His warmth.

The last time she experienced warmth was when her mother held her when she was a babe.

When Melinoe sat tall up a short time later, they were in

her quarters—a dark place where she honored the old gods—Tartarus, Nyx, and Erebus—and their richly cataclysmic ways. Though they no longer took human form, they understood her like no one else and blessed her often.

Her haven, unlike Cerberus's, was large and spacious, with room after room, all draped in tapestries depicting her favorite nightmares. They were places she could enter at will and relive the events that had unfolded. Events she could draw a weak power from—enough to keep her starvation at bay.

Placed throughout her quarters were chains and cages. Most were empty—except for one or two that kept the ghosts of the undying that had wronged her greatly.

Melinoe climbed off of Hermes and crawled from her bed, where she had transported Hermes to rest. His godly blood soaked her sheets, but she didn't mind. Blood was not something that disgusted her—it intrigued her—and she leaned down to sniff the scent of it from Hermes's groin up to his closed eyes.

Her face fell into bliss, and she inhaled sharply. It wasn't his blood that pleasured her, but his masculine, living scent.

Melinoe licked her lips and drew up, slipping her dress off her shoulders. She lifted her legs to climb into bed next to Hermes but paused when she spotted a tiny burst of color between the strands of his tousled hair. She drove her nails through his hair and found a tiny poppy from Hypnos's garden.

Her breath hitched, and her heart thundered as she turned the small flower in her palm. She glanced back at the god languishing in her bed.

A smile stole across her face.

Melinoe pulled Hermes's lips apart, and he groaned. She stuffed the sleeping flower into his mouth, pushing it down deep into his throat. His throat bobbed weakly.

He will hate me when he awakes.

She kissed his brow anyway. "Sleep well, sweet Hermes. When you awake, you'll be in good health," she whispered.

Cerberus knows how to take care of me. She turned her smile upward, thanking him, loving him from afar.

She climbed into bed next to her stolen golden god, now hers for as long as the magical poppy would last. She settled herself comfortably against his side and draped her arm and leg over him.

Melinoe closed her eyes and entered Hermes's dreams, where she turned them into delicious nightmares.

THE FINAL DANCE

PERSEPHONE LEFT Cyane in the gardens hours ago. At least Cyane thought it had been that long, but as she watched the distant surreal cavern ceiling of the Underworld, the colors of Tartarus never changed. Not even slightly.

Creatures flew by now and then, cawing and cackling, but they never dived down close enough for her to see what they actually were. She was thankful for that. Their forms...weren't right.

She waited for Cerberus to come to her, and when he finally did, she still wasn't prepared.

Silent as a wraith, he appeared standing over her, blocking out the sky. Cyane's heart thudded hard at his abrupt appearance, and she tore the grass where her fingers rested at her sides.

His helmet was off, but his skin was now clean of blood. His face was stony and unreadable, and his eyes peered down at her, studying her. Heat flooded her body, and she waited for him to speak.

But he stepped back and offered his hand instead. His glove was already off, showing her the ring of hair he still wore on his thumb. She slowly rose up on her elbows and took his hand. It wasn't what she wanted as he helped her to her feet. She wanted him to kneel at her side and smile (had she ever seen him smile?) and cover her mouth with his own. She wanted immediate reassurance that he still desired her. That, even though he ultimately gave her what she wanted—freedom—that it hadn't been easy for him to let her go.

Because it hadn't been easy for her.

Cerberus drew his hand away and clenched it at his side. Cyane noticed.

"Come," was all he said as he turned and made his way towards the castle's shadowy passageway.

She watched him walk away, and her chest constricted.

She fell to her knees with a gasp. "Cerberus," she said, dropping her head and pressing her palms into the ground in submission. "I need—"

Cyane never finished what she was going to say.

Because then he was on her, behind her, pushing her to the grass, throwing her gold dress up over her head. Her chest was pressed upon the grass, but her butt hung in the air, her knees bent at an uncomfortable angle.

She tensed for an attack.

"Don't you dare, *Ciane*," he said low and raspily, his cold breath wafting over her exposed sex. "Don't ask anything of me this day. I want nothing but to take from you."

He knew. He knew about her previous life.

The warning in his voice sent a heady, dark whisper of need through her. A whimper escaped. Her core knotted.

She bit her tongue hard and forced the sudden stiffness from her body. But it returned quickly as his hands gripped her thighs, and his fingers pressed into her skin, pulling them apart, pulling her sex open. She knew he saw her clench, knew when she sucked in her stomach, it made her hips sway, just a little.

Embarrassed and delighted, unable to take a full breath, she wiggled further with anticipation, with dangerous craving.

A long, thin, rather inhuman tongue slid across her core. Several more joined it, twisting and prodding and licking *everything* as an otherworldly groan filled her ears, coming from everywhere, from every direction. It was unlike anything she ever heard from Cerberus before.

Fangs, serpentine tongues, smoke, and dripping saliva filled her vision. Hundreds of eyes, hundreds of hounds, all swaying in and out of a miasma of darkness, barely visible through the single strip of visibility her skirt offered to illuminate their frightening forms and movements.

Cyane brought her fists to her mouth to muffle her moans and squeezed her eyes shut, choosing to remain hidden under the drape of her skirt.

The tongues lashed, probed, and spun as they stroked and struck her, delving into not only her sex, but her breasts and backside too. They filled her mercilessly wherever they could, taking every intimate part of her and stealing it away.

"Warm, so warm," a deep, rumbling voice said, echoing on itself a hundred times over. She felt her sanity slip, and found the hold of the two very human hands holding her legs slightly up and apart.

His tongues circled her in waves, curling over her clit, slapping against the delicious part deep inside. A cry tore from her throat as she tried to press her legs together as every nerve ending was tormented maliciously.

She didn't want to come, didn't want to submit out in the open like this. But then teeth grazed her most sensitive flesh, the sensation unlike anything she knew possible.

Cyane buckled and screamed as a slurping noise filled her ears from behind, drawing out every jerk and jolt that seized her. A grunt. Then a sudden burst of frigid flesh replaced the exploring tongues, filling the space between her legs, and even as she fought to bring her legs together, to ride out the torturous waves, Cerberus's hard and unyielding cock thrust deeper into her.

She broke apart with another buckle, his hips pressed her hard into the ground. He leaned over her and pounded into her viciously, trapping her beneath him, riding on her body's twitching climax.

When she thought she couldn't take it anymore, wet pressure filled her sex, full of power, and Cerberus stopped with a guttural snarl. He pushed inside her one last time, deep and hard, groaning about his veins being filled with hellfire, then lifted off her. Cyane slumped limply to the ground, breathless.

Satiated.

Proven wrong again.

Feeling blessed, honored, haunted. And, perhaps, harboring a little bit of obsessive love.

Her skirt tore back from her face, and his hand returned to help her from the ground. Shakily, she took it, and he helped her rise.

"Are you ready?" he asked, studying her again, looking like he hadn't just fucked her soul from her body.

She licked her lips and lifted up on her toes to place a light kiss on his perfect chin. He shuddered. She dropped back down on her heels. He gripped her arms tightly.

"I'm ready now."

CERBERUS LED Cyane to Hades's chambers in silence.

He'd given her a new dress to wear. A handmaiden's dress for the sacred event. One of sheer, pale cloth that hung open between her breasts to where a belt stopped the split. Her skirts were made of the same material with parted slits up to her thighs. Little was left to the imagination. The only true covering was her hair, which fell in waves down her back, hiding her spine's beautiful curve from his view. The rosy hue of her nipples was visible through the front of her dress.

Cerberus cleared his throat.

He wore a simple, black himation that left his lower legs exposed. The cloth wrapped around part of his torso from his left shoulder to hang under his right arm, leaving half his chest exposed. He'd taken off the ring Cyane had given him in tribute and placed it on the table in the guardhouse, all while she watched.

His hands were to be exposed. Neither one of them wanted their secret to be as well. And unlike Cyane, whose face was there for all to see, Cerberus donned a simple mask made of twined sticks to shield his face. Queen Persephone did not know his face, and Cerberus planned to keep it that way.

Hades was pacing back and forth when they arrived, wearing a simple, black robe. He stopped and glanced their way, scowled, and returned to his pacing.

Cerberus strode towards him, leaving Cyane by the door.

The room was starkly ornamented, with only a single, large bed with overflowing blankets and pillows strewn atop it. Streaks of fire flared now and then along the obsidian walls, rising from the gleaming, cold floor. Streams of lava trailed across the ceiling like veins. Sometimes it looked like blood, sometimes it was as it should be—liquid fire.

The space was devoid of all else. No windows, no furniture, nothing. The fire, the dark walls, and the bed were all there was.

"Where is she?" Hades hissed when Cerberus neared.

"She will come, or she won't. All we can do is wait." Cerberus clamped a hand over Hades's shoulder. His lord's scowl deepened when a rustle of noise sounded. They both turned to see Queen Persephone enter the room.

Hades stepped forward, his breath hitching, muscles tensing. What little color Hades possessed on his face drained as his lips parted.

Queen Persephone wore a robe of her own, but hers was a pale yellow with embroidered narcissuses up its hem.

Amused, Cerberus wondered if he ever looked the same as Hades when it came to Cyane.

Persephone stopped in her tracks, her skin draining of all color as well, and quickly looked around. When her eyes landed on Cyane, she rushed to her friend's side. The women huddled together near the door.

Cerberus stepped in front of Hades to keep him from storming to Persephone and throwing her into his bed. Hades's scowl returned.

"Don't frighten her," Cerberus warned.

Hades swore, trying to peer over Cerberus's shoulder; Cerberus stopped him each time.

"I take orders from no one," Hades spat.

"You will from me tonight," Cerberus warned again.

Hades threw his hands into the air and turned away with a growl.

Whispers and low feminine voices came from the women. Persephone appeared as anxious as Hades, her slight hands moving everywhere, as if she didn't know what to do with them.

Cyane smiled. Cerberus's loins tightened and expanded, taking in Cyane's pretty, reassuring face.

If this night didn't progress soon, it wasn't Hades who would ruin it, but Cerberus. After all the things he witnessed during the Day of Deviance, Cerberus was eager to test them out on his mortal and discover the extent of her limits.

Cyane looked back at Persephone, and his queen straightened. The goddess turned slowly towards Cerberus and Hades and walked to the end of the bed. Cyane followed shortly after.

Hades pushed past Cerberus and stormed to stand in front of Persephone. His breaths were quick and ragged, harsh and hard. Cerberus couldn't imagine being denied Cyane's body for hundreds of years—seeing her but never able to love her. He pitied Hades, sick with lust of his own for Cyane even now despite taking her so harshly and desperately in the garden not long ago. He hadn't meant to be so mean, but he couldn't imagine her slipping away again.

Cerberus stared longingly at Cyane as the two of them stepped up behind the gods and placed their hands on their god's shoulders.

In tense silence, in erotic strain—with the scent of arousal and flowers filling the air—they disrobed their masters in unison, gazing nowhere else but each other, undressing one another with their eyes.

Hades dragged Persephone into his embrace and kissed her deeply.

The goddess's innocently wanton moans filled the space.

Cerberus and Cyane stepped back as Hades lifted his queen into his arms and carried her to the bed. There he covered Persephone's naked body with his mouth, running his lips over the curves of her flesh, reclaiming every inch of her.

Persephone—breathless and mewing—turned her head towards Cyane and reached for her. Cyane rushed to Persephone's side. She pushed Persephone's hair back from her face.

His queen, head tilted, asked with a hitch, "It's Hades, right? It's really my dear husband?"

Cyane glanced at Cerberus then down at Hades, who

suckled Persephone's breast, watching the women speak. Cerberus moved to the other side of the bed.

"It's him, my queen," he and Cyane said in unison.

Persephone slumped into the bedding with a satisfied moan and closed her eyes.

Hades lifted up and straddled Persephone, his large, godly cock resting on her stomach. "It will only ever be me, as it should only ever be me, forever." His voice grave and possessive.

Persephone reached up and cupped Hades's neck and brought him down to take his mouth.

Then, as if the eroticism and desire couldn't be more potent, Hades rose from Persephone and turned towards his hound. Cerberus's breath labored as his lord clasped his chin and brought Cerberus's mouth to his for a diabolical kiss. A surge of power rushed from Hades's lips to Cerberus's and within it, as their tongues connected, Cerberus felt a little more powerful, a little more at ease, and a little more excited. In the kiss, his lord gifted him with something new—but what it was had yet to be seen. Hades released him, peered deep into Cerberus's eyes, and rubbed the back of his hand across his lips.

Hades turned to Cyane, and Cerberus stiffened. His lord reached for her head, he was going to take Cyane's lips, and a flash of fury swept through Cerberus, but so did the residual excitement and power Hades had given him. Cerberus's hands dropped and fisted at his sides, tempering his reaction.

He didn't like what was about to happen.

But his lord was offering them gifts, not sex. And Cerberus knew, after the jokes and the threats that Hades would never lay with Cyane for respect for him and fear of his wife.

I'm her God. Not Hades. And Cerberus vowed to make certain Cyane knew what her fealty meant.

Hades gripped her hair in his fist, pulled her to him, and kissed her. Cyane moaned and met Cerberus's eyes, and kept them there for the duration. It went on for a little bit longer, a little bit harder, and a little bit rougher than Cerberus's kiss.

And when Cerberus was about to tear Hades and Cyane apart, he sensed the power exchange. The gift Hades gave her was palpable. Like Cerberus's gift, they would have to discover its dark secret.

Cerberus's eyes slid to Persephone. She watched them with a soft smile, her glorious pale skin pinkened with rose. When Hades's mouth left Cyane's, she moved between him and Persephone and placed a soft kiss on Persephone's brow.

Hades pulled Cyane's head back—his hand still tangled in her hair—giving her a stony scowl before fully releasing her and lowering himself back over his wife.

Cerberus and Cyane's eyes met, and Cyane rubbed her mouth with curiosity. They walked out of the room as the first rapturous moans assailed their ears. Before they'd taken a single step into the corridor, Hades's room vanished into the darkness where it would be lost to all but Cerberus, he pulled Cyane into his arms and whisked her back to his guardhouse haven.

"Mine," he rasped. "Hades's death was almost assured."

A gasp escaped her as he pulled her head back and took what Hades had stolen.

Soon Cerberus had her naked and writhing, straddling him as he lay on the floor, his hounds surrounding them on every side, giving him the audience he sought for this claiming. With her handmaiden's dress torn down from her shoulders, her breasts peeking upward in the cold air, she rode him—and only him—filling his ears with cries and blissful screams.

He may look like Hades, but it was Cerberus Cyane

mounted. Terrible, dark, immoral satisfaction filled him, and he came hard deep inside his mortal.

Tonight, two gods were born.

Tonight, they had served.

"Lovingly," he groaned as she collapsed onto his chest as her own climax strangled his cock.

"Lovingly?" she whispered back. "Love," she amended. Her lips formed into a smile against his flesh.

She fell asleep on him, and a rare smile tugged his lips up. He lifted her in his arms and moved her to the bed, where he covered her with his body and trapped her beneath him.

He never experienced more warmth, inside and out, never thought his existence could be so sublime—believing his servitude and his duty was the epitome of existence. Cerberus inhaled her scent and groaned. She belonged to him, she swore fealty to him, and for that, he would never let her go.

SIX MONTHS WITH CERBERUS

IT WAS weeks before Hades and Persephone emerged from Hades's chambers. Weeks of quiet, euphoric bliss.

Cyane missed her friend greatly but knew Persephone would be all right without her. In that time, Cerberus took her everywhere with him, showing her the hidden secrets of the realm of the dead and all its shadowy glory. He showed her the flowers and plants her queen had created, the halls of Hecate and her loyal followers, where enchanting singing could always be heard, Menoetes's fields of black cattle, and Pyriphlegethon, the forever burning river of fire.

But today wasn't quiet, nor euphoric. Hades had summoned them to the throne for punishment for their crimes.

Cyane wrung white-knuckled hands into the skirts of her dress, a simple beige peplos that hung loosely to the floor. She stood alone in the atrium, waiting to be called into the ballroom.

The large doors creaked opened far too soon. The ballroom slowly appeared before her. Her eyes landed on the

God of the Dead and her beautiful Goddess of Spring sitting on their thrones. Cerberus knelt before them already.

Cyane started. Hades wore the same horned helmet as he had when she'd first encountered him long ago, when he ripped Persephone from her arms.

"Come in, Cyane," Hades's voice bellowed through the space, hitting her like a punch to the gut.

I can do this.

Cyane straightened and took comfort in Persephone's presence as she strode to the dais. There were other gods of the court in attendance—Hecate, Hypnos, and the three Judges of the Dead she'd met her first day here. Minos smiled at her. She wished he'd use his calming hum for her right now.

There were darker, scarier gods in attendance that she didn't know, and her gaze roved over them quickly. If she hadn't met them, there must've been a reason. Many of their faces she didn't even recognize from the days of festivities.

Melinoe and Hermes were missing. She hadn't seen either one since the descent—the Day of Deviance.

Cyane reached Cerberus and knelt beside him, lowering her face to the gleaming obsidian floor.

She feared, more than anything now, that Hades would split her and Cerberus apart. She couldn't bear the thought, couldn't swallow the lump in her throat, or inhale enough air for a sure breath. She wanted to reach out and take Cerberus's hand but didn't dare.

Hades spoke. "You have defied my wants and wishes, schemed to upend my plans, and coerced loyal subjects of my court to aid you in your betrayal."

Was Hades speaking to her, to Cerberus, or to both of them? Her heart thundered.

"You, Cyane, danced with Melinoe a day too soon. You conspired not only with her, but with Hermes and Cerberus to leave without my knowledge. Not only did your choice go against my wishes, but you came back to us in an unnatural way. You are not a god, and do not have a contract in place to come and go as you please."

Hades sighed audibly. It took a fair bit of willpower for Cyane to keep her eyes down. She knew of some of her transgressions, but dancing with Melinoe came as a surprise.

"Cerberus"—Hades's voice darkened—"you ignored my commands on several occasions during the festivities. You conspired with Hermes, Melinoe, and Cyane against me and my wishes, knowing full well I granted no being allowance to leave my realm for the duration of the celebration. You assumed to know my thoughts and questioned me in front of the court. You lied to me on numerous occasions. And above all," the tension in the ballroom built, "When I told you to enjoy yourself, I didn't mean for you to enjoy yourself that much!" A few of the courtiers dared to giggle, but more of Hades's long-winded sighing followed.

"Cyane, raise your eyes," Hades ordered.

She jerked. The God of the Underworld glared down at her with annoyed solemnity. She glanced at Persephone who smiled. Cyane's muscles eased, if only a little, knowing that her friend would not let harm come her way.

But would it shield Cerberus?

"Queen Persephone has spoken on your behalf, but that doesn't mean you'll not go unpunished," Hades said. "Starting today, this hour, this very minute, you will begin your servitude to the queen. You will be her handmaid, her protector, and if need be, her shield. You will guard her with your life and your soul. And like all punishments from the gods, it is eternal." Hades stood and languidly stepped down from the dais to stand in front of Cyane.

Hecate joined him and moved to Cyane's side. They placed their hands upon Cyane's head.

Power fused through Cyane, first prickling her scalp from which it shot through every nerve in her body. Her mouth parted.

Hades continued speaking as her skin began to burn, "We bestow immortality upon you and restore the gifts of your former life. If you should fail, all will be stripped away, and death will follow swiftly."

Hecate chanted.

Cyane's eyes brightened, and her vision wavered. She pulled her hands from the floor and brought them to her mouth as her body filled with power. She worried she'd be burned alive, without the chance to be immortal, much less serve, when the gods' hands lifted from her head, and the pain went with them.

She lowered to the floor with a gasp. Hades and Hecate moved back to their places. She rested her brow on the cold stone.

I'm undying... The words were weak and filled with awe in her head. Strength surged through her veins. Her body cleansed itself of all the impurities of mortality.

"As for you Cerberus... Queen Persephone and I spoke at great length about your punishment," Hades mused.

Cyane stiffened and lifted her head to peer worriedly at Cerberus.

"My beautiful queen is benevolent and kind," Hades said. "She is far more merciful than I am. If it were up to me, I'd restore your primordial form and chain you to the gates for the next ten thousand years. I would deny you speech, deny you souls, deny you companionship. For you knew...how much I cherished you.

Hades slumped back into his throne with a flourish. "But perhaps I can't fault your reasons for doing did what you did."

Cyane curled her fingers and held her breath. She wanted to pray for Cerberus, but didn't know who to pray to.

"For your punishment. You will suffer as I have had to suffer. Cyane will join Persephone above for six months of the year where she can fulfill her duties. And you, Cerberus, will remain with me in the dark, waiting for Cyane's return. You will never have more than I, in this or anything. Look at me," Hades ordered.

Cerberus raised his head, his shoulders were stiff, his eyes a ruby glow that shined outward. Cyane knew his eyes glowed when he was overcome with emotion. She traced the sleek and sharp curves of his Grecian warrior helmet, swallowing the lump of dread in her throat.

Six months? Six months apart for every year of all eternity?

"You will never know if she is safe without your protection. You will worry by my side and know what true longing is like. Do you accept?" Hades asked.

"Yes, my lord," Cerberus said.

Cyane glanced up at Hades. A cup had magically appeared in his hand. He grumbled and stood again, offering his free hand to Persephone, who took it. Her adoring smile had not left her face. Cyane's chest filled with love, even though her heart was heavy.

She didn't want to be apart from Cerberus, but she didn't want to be apart from Persephone either. Her punishment wasn't really a punishment, but it still hurt.

"My queen and I have a bed to return to." Persephone rose and slid under Hades's arm. "The court is dismissed."

One by one the gods vanished into thin air, swirls of shadows and darkness slipping around them, only to immediately dissipate. Hades and Persephone remained.

When the four of them were alone, Cerberus rose and helped Cyane to her feet. Persephone rushed forward and enveloped Cyane into an embrace made of flowers and sunshine. Cyane hugged her back, having missed her goddess greatly.

Hades joined them, his eyes as ruinous as ever. "Eternity is a long time," he said.

Persephone and Cyane released each other. Cyane bowed her head. "Thank you for the gift, my lord." She truly meant it, astonishing herself.

"We will have so much fun!" Persephone giggled a little too mischievously.

Hades sighed and gulped back his drink. When he was done, he pulled Persephone back into his arms. "Come."

They vanished.

Cyane smiled, relieved. "What now, my god?"

Cerberus reached up and slowly pulled off his helmet. His dark curls fell out to tousle around his sharp and darkly enchanting face. A very familiar, although a little more grave, a little more constrained, wicked gleam sparked his eyes.

Eternity.

Abysmal, devouring, scorchingly wonderful eternity.

Her stomach danced with butterflies, and an entirely different rush of power shuddered through her. She licked her lips, hungry.

"Now," his voice darkened with sinfulness, making Cyane's skin prickle. He curled a finger under her chin and lifted her face. "I get to teach you how to serve."

EPILOGUE

ELEVEN MONTHS and one week later...

HE HUNGERED. His pants chafed his erection.

The Day of Deviance had come and gone in a rather boring fashion. After the events of the previous year, nothing out of the ordinary had happened. Not a soul tried to flee or a rain of flowers try to drown the guests.

Except, perhaps, the return of Melinoe and Hermes.

The winged god was no longer winged, nor was he golden and gleaming. His once sun-kissed skin was pale and taut, and his hair a dirty blonde—as if it had soaked up the Underworld's endless pitch—and the once muscled curves of his body were now lean and sharp. There was a crazed, possessive darkness in his eyes that hadn't been there. And now his hatred for Hades was palpable and no longer hidden behind fake smiles.

Hermes kept his grasp tight on Melinoe's wrist, as if she'd vanish if he didn't keep his hold on her, as if he owned *her*, instead of the other way around.

The once God of Crossings had been wrecked by his lady love's problematic daughter. Cerberus couldn't have been more pleased.

Hermes and Melinoe had taken the celebration by storm, offering the only entertainment to be had. It was all the better, because the blighted princess of Tartarus soaked up the attention, leaving Cerberus and Hades alone.

Hades rose from his throne and paced, glancing to the ballroom doors again and again. Watching his lord in such impatient distress helped Cerberus give the pretence of calm, even though he was anything but.

More than anything, Cerberus wanted to leave the ball-room and wait at the Gates of the Underworld, where Hecate, Persephone, and his Cyane would sail through once the shores spread out and the river became the beginning of an ocean. But the descent was ritualized, and even Hades was a stickler for tradition.

There was power in tradition and in the stories that the mortals told each other. No one—not even a god as powerful as Hades—turned his face away from what mortals believed.

Cerberus could care less about the beliefs of mortals.

He was ravenous, and his hunger was and would remain, far from being quenched. Sinful souls no longer sustained him, not now that he knew what he was missing. Cyane's submission fed him, warmed him.

He longed for her just as Hades told him he would. That longing had him pacing the shores of Styx for weeks on end, xiphos drawn out, lashing at the rocks that stood between him and where Cyane dwelled.

Whenever his mind grew black with fear for her safety— the gods of Olympus were no better than those that lived in Tartarus—he found himself stretching his mouth open, breaking his human jaw, and tearing his skin, just to listen to the screams of souls within.

It reminded him that he was not alone in his torment. That he was just as trapped as they were.

For the first time in his long existence, Cerberus welcomed the start of the Celebration of Descent, and he finally realized why Hades threw the weeks-long party every year. The waiting grew worse with each day, and the distraction of the event helped.

A little.

He was rubbing at his thumb, where her hair lay hidden under his glove when he heard it. The soft sound of footsteps. He, his hounds, and Hades all pivoted to the foyer at once. Three women appeared, as glorious and as beautiful as dawn.

Hades stilled as Cerberus stepped off the dais.

Queen Persephone, in her chiton gown of pale yellow, bringing with her the fresh scent of life, of flowers new and old, stopped when she saw her king. She was heavily pregnant, and exuded the aura of fresh godly power soon to enter the world.

Hades strode to her, bringing all the shadows of Erebos with him, eclipsing Persephone in the full force of his protection.

Cerberus's eyes fell on Cyane who appeared behind his queen.

Their eyes met. He inhaled sharply. His heart quickened.

A soft smile brightened her face. She bowed her head slightly, demurely, pulling her gaze down to the floor at his feet.

Cerberus smiled behind his helmet.

The wait was over at last.

The End.

AUTHOR'S NOTE

Cyane, Kyane, or Ciane, is in fact a real mythological naiad. She is known for her blue-green waters. Her story takes place during the Abduction of Persephone by Hades, where she (Ciane) was the only one who saw and tried to stop the God of the Underworld from stealing Persephone.

She grabbed Persephone's belt, but the belt tore, and Ciane lost the Goddess of Spring. In her grief, she cried herself into a spring, dissolving away. When Demeter and Hermes searched the world for Persephone, it was because of Ciane that they were able to find her. Ciane gave them Persephone's belt.

Ciane is honored to this day in Syracuse, Sicily. Fonte Ciane is the only place left in the world where papyrus still grows wild.

Thank you for reading *Six Months with Cerberus*. If you liked the story or have a comment, please leave a review!

What's next on my plate, you ask? The seventh book in Cyborg Shifters (Cypher!!), the third book for the Bestial Tribe (Thyrius!!), and a collab project with some friends.

If you love cyborgs, aliens, anti-heroes, and adventure, follow me on facebook or through my blog online for information on new releases and updates.

Join my newsletter for the same information.

Naomi Lucas

ALSO BY NAOMI LUCAS

Naga Brides

Viper

King Cobra

Blue Coral

Death Adder

Boomslang (Coming Soon!)

Cyborg Shifters

Wild Blood

Storm Surge

Shark Bite

Mutt

Ashes and Metal

Chaos Croc

Ursa Major

Dark Hysteria

Wings and Teeth

The Bestial Tribe

Minotaur: Blooded

Minotaur: Prayer

-

Stranded in the Stars

Last Call

<u>Collector of Souls</u>

<u>Star Navigator</u>

-

<u>Venys Needs Men</u>

<u>To Touch a Dragon</u>

<u>To Mate a Dragon</u>

<u>To Wake a Dragon</u>

<u>Naga (Haime and Iskursu)</u>

<u>Valos of Sonhadra</u>

<u>Radiant</u>

<u>Standalones</u>

<u>Submitting to Cerberus</u>

<u>Cyber Pool Boy</u>